The Redemption of

Anna Dupree

The Redemption of

Anna Dupree

Jim Christy

Ekstasis  Editions

National Library of Canada Cataloguing in Publication

Christy, Jim
    The redemption of Anna Dupree / Jim Christy.

ISBN 1-894800-48-6

    I. Title.

PS8555.H74R43 2005   C813'.54   C2005-901509-5

Published in 2005 by:
Ekstasis Editions Canada Ltd.   Ekstasis Editions
Box 8474, Main Postal Outlet   Box 571
Victoria, B.C. V8W 3S1   Banff, Alberta ToL oCo

THE CANADA COUNCIL | LE CONSEIL DES ARTS
FOR THE ARTS | DU CANADA
SINCE 1957 | DEPUIS 1957

BRITISH
COLUMBIA
ARTS COUNCIL
Supported by the Province of British Columbia

The Redemption of Anna Dupree has been published with the assistance of grants
from the Canada Council for the Arts and the British Columbia Arts Board administered by the Cultural Services Branch of British Columbia.

This book is for Brad Benson.
Ahora, dos se quedan.

PROLOGUE

"Okay, folks. This will be it. Last shot of the day. Nightclub patrons, you've all had a chance to study the videos, so remember your positions. As well, my assistant, Juan Escalero, has given you Polaroids of your own photogenic selves. We know how much of your drinks have been drunk and how far down you've smoked your cigarettes and cigars, but you have to help us by making sure your hands and elbows are where they were the last time we were together.

"Juan has tipped me the wink that the band is ready and we're all in place. Even Ms. Dupree…"

"Oh, stuff it, Maestro. Excuse me — Senor Maestro. I'm always ready, always reliable and dependable. Not to mention available."

"You're a dear," said the director, El Maestro, Rodrigo Luzardo Amundez. "That is precisely why you got this part in the first place."

"No, it is not. It is because I'm the ugliest woebegone seventy-some-thing year old gringa you could find who speaks halfway passable Spanish."

"Well, there's that too."

"I'm glad you admit it. We must put a stop to these rumours about the casting couch."

Luzardo laughed, which for him amounted to a snuffling sound near the middle of his thin nose. He was tall and very dark-skinned, very much a mestizo. It was said he'd had his wide Aztec nose romanized when still a street urchin in his native Mexico City, the Federal District; a gamino who dreamed of improving his lot — perhaps he'd go to dive off the cliffs at La Quebrada or, better yet, be a gigolo. But he spent too much time at the cinema.

Juan took his place at one of the tables — they were in a disco in modern Zihuatanejo made over to look like a nightclub in Acapulco,

7

1952. At the centre of a stage skirted with green, white and red crepe paper, the Mexican colours, was "The Emcee," Little Cesar — a four-foot three dwarf, standing on a wooden crate before a microphone. In back of him were Los Abajos, a sextet of trumpet, drums, bass, guitar, accordion and mandolin. In the wings, stage left, was "Helen Burns," Anna Dupree, gaudily made up in a red sheath dress with padded shoulders.

Julieta Rivera leaned close to Juan and spoke in back of her hand. "The old biddy never ceases to amaze me, Gato. I'm so glad you spotted her."

Julieta herself had been discovered by Luzardo and his producer Jaime Munoz at a circus in Salina Cruz. Julieta had been walking the tightrope ten feet above a drunken crowd of longshoremen and dock workers. Munoz right away had offered to pay for an operation to fix her harelip, saying that when the operation was finished, she would be the most beautiful woman in Mexico, more beautiful even than Dolores Del Rio. Julieta refused.

"Yes, she's a real piece of work."

"All right!" Luzardo called. "Quiet on the set. Background action. Action!…"

"Senors and senoras, the last set of the evening. Our star needs no introduction…"

Fake diamonds glittered on Little Cesar's stubby fingers as he waited for the smattering of applause to die down.

"Yes, senors and senoras, how, after all, does one introduce a legend? Nearly fifty years ago, she tried to start the Mexican Revolution, and it was several years before certain gentlemen, now famous heroes with boulevards named for them, caught up to her. After all this time her soul is still on fire. She sings songs of love and revolution, of the struggles and laughter of the streets. For her last set, she will interpret part of Los Cantares Mexicanos."

The crowd began to applaud.

"Helen Burns!"

Trumpet fanfare.

Anna Dupree walks slowly to the microphone. Luzardo has done nothing to hide her years. The make-up people had told her they'd been instructed to take her to the very edge of grotesque, and Anna had laughed, saying she was already there.

When she is at the microphone, she reaches for Little Cesar, pulls

him to her, bends down and kisses him full on the lips.
The audience goes crazy.
Little Cesar jumps down, grabs the wooden crate and scurries off stage.
Anna raises a hand for quiet, the drummer begins beating three-quarter time with his brushes, there are four bars from the trumpet:

Tocotico, tocotico, tocotico
I am the woman of the earth and the woman of the sea
I am the old woman whose soul burns and burns
I am an old woman who had a young man
Who burned for me. You may laugh but it is true
How much happier he is now where he has gone
And I am a little bit happy, but mostly sad
With my old woman's memory

How he wanted me, my sweetheart. My Axayacatl
Somebody made me a whore and so you found me
On account of what I had been you were pleased.
You had twice the pleasure and twice the kingdom.
My sweet, does your heart burn for me where you are?
Do you burn for me down there?
If so, somehow, let me know, and I will do you slowly,
Sweetly, wholeheartedly.
Take this whore into your spirit house

From where I spin and nowhere else I utter you!
From where I weave my tales and nowhere else
I shall recall you, my sweetheart darling boy.
O heart of mine! I am a whore and I was your mother
Your grandmother too. I was everything, oh babe.
Just an old whore pretending to be something else.
I live on to pleasure you in my dreams, my dolly.
My darling, my sweetheart, with your arms
Catch me, hold me, rock me tonight. Enjoy us.

Then slumber gently darling sweetheart babe of mine.

ACT ONE

he first time Colin Childs laid eyes on Anna Dupree, she was talking to Dr. Drushka outside the Discussion Centre where the latter had just given a talk entitled "Aging and Desire: Getting Reacquainted with your Sexuality."

Colin's attention had been on his own stomach and, thus, he heard Anna Dupree before he ever saw her. He had a vague, dull pain in his stomach but was hungry, nevertheless.

"Oh, yes. I prefer bottles," is what he heard, and looked up.

The speaker had long thick hair, unexpected with an elderly woman, he thought to himself. More typical was the other old woman beside her, whom he discovered was named Dorothy Detweiler. This one had the tight perm and it was obvious immediately that she was batty, with that unmistakable wide-eyed and open mouth gaga stare.

Ludmilla Drushka's expression was fixed somewhere between embarrassment and fascination. Ludmilla acknowledged his presence with only the quickest glance before looking back at the lady with the wavy hair.

"I've tried all the dildos, big or small, smooth or knobbly, with or without batteries. When I was a girl in England, in the orphanage, the Home, this was in the Depression, don't you know, there was a dildo, they were wooden then, that we passed around from girl to girl, bed to bed. Maybe that's why I've never been too keen on them since."

The other lady giggled, and giggled so hard that she began ever so slightly to drool.

"What I did fancy later — wipe your mouth, Dotty — when I was full grown, not every day, mind, but for variety, was turning on the water full-force in the bath and as hot as I could, as it were, bear it. I'd position myself just right and let it hit me. Fat lot of good that would do me now. Even if I could get my bones in the right spot, I might never be able to get up. Imagine! Perhaps after I'd missed a few meals, inquiries would be made and a search party sent out. You must admit it would be a rather undignified position in which to be discovered. But, of course, continual delight would be some compensation, I should think.

"But to be serious, if we must, nothing beats the reliable Coke bottle. The old-fashioned model. The new ones do not suffice because they lack that ever so important rounded rim, or lip. Now they have a couple of sharp ridges. Luckily, I've kept one of the old breed for years. It has seen me through many a dry spell."

"Where'd you get it?" asked the other old lady.

"Why, Dotty. Remember Saint Nicholas in his easy chair with his cap off and his beard all white? The jolly fat chap gave it to me after he came down my chimney one Christmas Eve."

Dotty Detweiler broke into another fit of giggles and, turning away with one veiny hand to her mouth, noticed Colin, flushed deep pink, sputtered and seemed about to hyperventilate. He took a step forward to offer assistance before stopping short. Ludmilla patted the old woman on the back and gave her shoulders a firm squeeze. Colin had remembered that male employees were not allowed to touch residents unless it was to shake hands or to offer emergency aid. He wondered whether the disciplinary board would have considered this an 'emergency.'

He proceeded to shake hands with both women while being introduced by Ludmilla. Anna Dupree was small and slender, neatly dressed with big dark blue, or indigo, eyes. Took good care of herself, he noted, even if she did use too much make-up.

He was reminded of those computer projections of aging, then of black-and-white studio photographs of glamorous female movie stars with luxurious hair and sultry looks. It was as if one of those photographs had been updated by thirty or forty years. No, fifty. This woman, Colin was thinking, could be the living computer projection. It was eerie, it even made him uncomfortable so that when he heard her name — Anna Dupree — Colin stammered, tried to cover up by consulting his clipboard. "Oh, yes. I thought your name was familiar. I was hoping, in fact, to meet with you this afternoon."

"Why?"

"Well, we could…I mean, if there's anything…"

She was wearing a wry smile that disconcerted him.

"You must be my counsellor?"

"I hope he's going to be my counsellor, too," put in Mrs. Detweiler.

"Mr. Childs is new," said Ludmilla. "He's only been here at Valley View since Monday."

"Anyone under sixty seems new to me," said Anna Dupree. "This one looks positively freshly minted."

"He hasn't met everyone yet."

"Well," said Anna, drawling out the word, and looking Colin over, from foot to head. "He can come up to my room anytime."

"Uh, how about, instead, I mean, if we could meet in the day-room or the coffee shop, at three-thirty?"

Anna smirked. "The stuff about the bathtub and the bottle scared you, eh? Don't worry, I believe those kinds of things should go on strictly in private. But, certainly, the coffee shop at three-thirty, then."

With that she turned on her heel, took hold of Dorothy Detweiler's hand, and off they went. The other lady in a dull yellow jogging suit. Twenty years ago, Dorothy probably would have been four inches taller than Anna but now was shrunk to her size. She was saying, "Anna, my daughter just got out of the hospital. The operation went fine. She's coming to see me in a couple of weeks. No more kids for her. Will you give thanks to God with me?"

"No," said Anna Dupree.

*V*alley View sat among dry hills alongside a three-lane road to a ski resort. The place looked like a contemporary 'old-fashioned' ski resort. At first the hills that rose from the plain reminded Colin, a prairie boy, of camel humps. But then he realized that wasn't right at all. The plain was exactly the colour of a grill in an old diner and the hills looked exactly like hash brown potatoes. In the daytime, from the grounds and from many of the rooms at Valley View, one could see the medium-sized city down there sprawling for several kilometres. Sprawling, because it seemed to enlarge itself even as one watched. In the distance were the lake and a big, new ostentatious hotel with a casino to attract the wealthy orchardists in white shoes.

Just a few years ago, it had been a small-sized city. Then retired people from the prairies began to arrive, seeking warmer weather, and people from Vancouver began to arrive, fleeing crime and seeking what they believed would be a more relaxed life style.

Kelowna was better by night, or at least didn't look as bad. The pollution trapped between the hills was not as evident, nor were the housing developments so obviously eating away at the mountainsides. No, at night it was like looking at fireflies or down at the stars; even the traffic was beguiling then, a glittering Aztec snake.

All of it — the outside world — was just over there, down the hill. But for the old people in Valley View, it might just as well be Samarkand.

Colin Childs and Ludmilla Drushka were not old people. They were in their late-twenties, extremely intelligent, already earning substantial salaries, and the wonders of the future that stretched before them was not illusory. From them, daylight did not steal the nighttime's promise.

They had met just three days earlier, Monday, when Colin started at Valley View. The youngest and brightest of the staff, and both single and unattached, it was as if they had no alternative but to get together. Colin was shy, however, and it took him all three days to suggest that they might have lunch together.

Here they were sitting with their plastic trays at a table on the terrace outside the staff cafeteria at the rear of the main building. The tables were round, made of cement, and had umbrellas. There were Yuccas in clay pots on top of a low stone and mortar wall. Colin felt almost as if on holidays — the South of France, perhaps, — and said as much to Ludmilla. He had never been there, but she had.

Colin had to move his head from one side of the white aluminum umbrella pole to the other for an unobstructed view of Ludmilla's face. It was broad and pale and absolutely smooth, eyes small and dark and far apart, and Colin was intrigued by the way they appeared to be slanted. He stared at her eyes, trying to determine if the outside corners of her eyes actually did turn up. Her lips formed a small bow of faded maroon. Ludmilla's hair was dark brown, almost black, and it flared out from a widow's peak, like a shadow on the moon, her moon face.

As a child she had gone with her parents to Odessa. Later, a teenager but still with her parents, there had been Nice.

"It sounds very romantic," Colin said.

"Romantic? It was horrid. Me, awkward, gangly, self-conscious. And even more self-conscious about my parents. So Eastern European. My father with his skinny white legs and little hairy pot belly. And, of course, to make matters worse, all around us were bronzed bodies in skimpy bathing suits. Gorgeous young women with perfect figures. Handsome young men, preening, coconut oil glistening on their chests. Everyone with sunglasses, everyone smoking Gaulouises."

She laughed wryly. Ludmilla had big white teeth.

"Beigne au pomme! Pomme pomme pomme pomme!" Ludmilla chanted in a sing-song.voice.

"What's that?"

"Really, Colin! You have no French?"

"Well, not really."

"'Not really?' What does that mean?"

"I can read some."

She pressed her lips together; it didn't warrant a full grimace.

"There was this solidly built, middle-aged man who walked up and down the beach wearing nothing but a leopard skin bikini and toting a box filled with doughnuts. 'Beigne au pomme,' he called. 'Pomme pomme pomme pomme.' Then, what was it that came next? Reve? Yes, 'Live the dream of your life, eat my fritters.' Oh, my God! I thought it was so chic and continental."

"Sounds as if it must have been quite interesting."

"Interesting? It would make me sick now."

Colin said he admired her cosmopolitan background whereupon Ludmilla changed the subject. He concluded that she was reacting to him getting personal. They talked about the big morning at Valley View.

That morning, the Privacy Room had been inaugurated. There was a small ceremony in the Auditorium. A young reporter from the Daily Courier was there as well as a cameraman from the cable station. The Director emphasized that this was the first such room in any facility for the aged in the entire country. When the director was done with that, he introduced Colin. "Another innovation," he smiled, adding that residents were not permitted to request time in the Privacy Room with Mr. Childs. It got a hearty laugh. From some. Others, Colin noticed, just stared. They didn't seem offended by the Director's remark. In fact, they didn't seem to register anything at all — as if, only their bodies were present and accounted for. Colin wondered if the cable guy would turn his camera on them.

Colin did as the Director had recommended before the ribbon was cut and things got underway, saying he was glad to be at Valley View and was looking forward to meeting everyone, to being part of the family. He summed up his qualifications and experience in a few sentences and took just a few more to remark upon the need for privacy and intimate time.

"Keep it general," the Director had told him. "Euphemisms will do for now. Drushka and myself will get into specifics — you know, the graphic stuff — later."

And they did, evidently. Dr. Corrington with the men; Ludmilla, the women. It was when Ludmilla's discussion group had broken up, that Colin came upon the scene to take her to lunch.

Over coffee, he referred to the woman, Anna Dupree. "She's

quite the character. I couldn't believe what she was saying."

"Yes, you did look taken aback. But there is surely no reason, no biological reason, why the elderly should not be concerned with sex. It is proven that while the male sex drive decreases with age, for seventy percent of women, it stays the same their entire life. Seventeen or seventy."

"That's not what surprised me." He was vaguely annoyed, her lecturing tone. "She was just so outspoken."

"But it is perfectly okay for the elderly to be outspoken. If a young person was outspoken, it wouldn't take us aback."

Colin supposed it might indeed take him aback — where did that word 'aback' come from anyway, he wondered — to hear a teenaged girl frankly relating her masturbatory aids and techniques.

"Sexual expression can take various forms. For many of our residents, a gentle touch can have sexual connotations."

She went on stating the obvious, as if he were in teacher's college. Colin nodded every few seconds, while considering what form her own sexual expression took. He tried to picture it, tried to picture her doing it, one way or another. Before lunch it might have been easy to picture, and he surely would have enjoyed trying to picture it, but now, listening to her, it was another matter entirely. Her schoolmarm tone was not exactly conducive to such thoughts.

Ludmilla was tall and would never be thin, not with those bones, but she'd probably never grow fat either — stout, perhaps, in late middle age. For now, though, at twenty-eight, Ludmilla had a sort of statuesque, Amazonian presence. He was attracted to the body but feared the personality might get in the way. Feared? He hadn't had sex for many months. It seemed a possibility with Ludmilla, but he worried he'd be put off by her lecturing and hectoring. Or there would be a clash of egos and hers would surely prevail. She had four degrees to his two — had earned them at places like Strasbourg, Edinburgh and Toronto. He'd gone to the University of Saskatchewan and to Simon Fraser, on a hill in exotic Burnaby, British Columbia. His salary was large; her's was larger.

Colin had to go back to work and so took his leave of Ludmilla, not altogether reluctantly. His stomach bothered him and he wondered whether it was the beef stroganoff or the thought of getting involved with her.

He went to call on Mr. Murray in his room. Mr. Murray was seventy-nine, but looked at least fifteen years younger because he was so fat, his face entirely unwrinkled. The rules permitted Colin to visit male residents in their rooms as long as the door was kept open a minimum of one foot. Under no circumstances was the door to be shut.

Mr. Murray sat in the standard issue plastic chair and smiled when Colin entered. Every room came with the same basic furniture, but residents could bring their own things. The facility would store the standard issue stuff. Most, however, arrived with nothing but their clothing and, perhaps, a cardboard box of mementos. Mr. Murray had photos on the wall over his dresser and, to get things going, Colin expressed interest in them. Mr. Murray didn't move from his chair but supplied commentary like a tour bus driver. "On the left is my brother Saul...that one's me and a friend, fishing. I'm the fat one with the skinny fish...That there's my wife and me in Cuba, long time before Castro. I had hair, imagine that..."

Colin, of course, had a file on Mr. Murray and had studied the contents, prepped himself, but didn't like the idea of carrying the file with him. He knew Ludmilla did that when she made her rounds. To Colin, however, it seemed too impersonal. Evidently, Mr. Murray harboured bitterness toward his one son who lived in Kelowna.

Colin noted that there were no pictures on the wall of Mr. Murray's son, or his daughter-in-law or their kids.

Colin wanted to hear the story but couldn't ask directly so he remarked on Mr. Murray's accent.

"You're from the States? Where, New York?"

"Hah, all you Canucks, you say New York. None of you can tell the difference between Boston, New York, Philadelphia accents. And why should you? I never even heard of British Columbia, I don't think, unless I'd heard something about the great salmon fishing, and now I'm living here. Can you beat that? I'm from Connecticut."

"You're a long way from Connecticut."

"Tell me about it. I was in business. Had my own small insurance company in Hartford. Did well because I was an alternative to the big guy, the giant company they got there. I provided a good life for my family, but I had this kid who don't like his life. He becomes a rabble-rouser, what we called then, a peacenik. This was back in the Nineteen-Sixties. Long hair, granny glasses, the whole bit. He goes around the country in a beat-up school bus with some other pinkos and barefoot girls — but whenever the bus breaks down, there's the phone call back to his capitalist daddy in Hartford — collect — 'Wire me money, dad. Oh, yeah, I'll come home and get my degree. Yeah, sure, I'll get a haircut too. Uh huh.'

"He thinks I believed him, that he'd actually do this. To this day, he figures he had me fooled. Anyway, he doesn't come home but disgraces his mother and father by running away from the Armed Forces and going to Toronto, Canada."

Colin nodded, smiled sympathetically every once in awhile. Mr. Murray required nothing more of him. Let me talk, kid; just listen.

"Me and his mother, God rest her soul, we move to Delray Beach after I retire. My son and his barefoot woman go west to, hey, British Columbia. Someplace on the ocean starts with a 'U.' I couldn't never pronounce it, but it sounds kind of like 'ukulele.' So they live in a commune. He starts making furniture out of branches he picks up in the forest. They have a kid, and another kid. He sent me Polaroids of the furniture one time. I didn't believe him, but he claimed people were buying it."

Here was the opportunity to do more than nod and smile.

"It seems," Colin said "as if your son was trying to, at least, establish communication with you. I mean, if he mailed you photographs. Maybe he wanted to establish or reestablish some sort of bond by letting you know he was making a living."

"Right. Sure. I forgot to mention that along with the Polaroids was him asking me to lend him money to buy a power saw of some kind. This way he could do the furniture work better or easier and make more money. Well, I sent the money to him and held back from mentioning that this sounded like capitalism to me. Didn't want to make him go backwards to spite his old-fashioned papa. So, okay, he's supporting his own family; his common-law wife and born out of wedlock children. My own wife died in '94. Laura. We were married forty-seven years. My son comes down to Delray Beach for the funeral and I didn't know who he was at first. My own son, I swear to you, I didn't recognize. Short hair, a suit, contact lenses. He didn't make furniture no more; he sold furniture. And not furniture out of sticks and branches, but uncomfortable looking chairs from Finland and places like that. So he only stays two nights. He's anxious to get back to Vancouver because of business. You think he talked to me much? No, sir. Most of the time he was on the phone, calling suppliers. Could hardly get a sentence out of him. I says, putting the needle in, I couldn't help it, 'Those leather chairs, you sell? How can you do it? Living creatures had to give up their lives to make those chairs.' But he just gave me a look.

"So he goes back to Canada. I couldn't live in that house nice as it was without Laura, so I get a little apartment but I can't look after myself so good. I was old and fat. I am still, thank God — old and fat. Going down the steps to the street and walking three blocks to the store was like an expedition. And what if I needed something else and it was at another store somewheres? So I went into a home. It was no big deal. All I had to do was shuffle a few yards down the hall to the cafeteria. A few yards more to the mailboxes. But it was depressing, not having your freedom. I lived for the mail. All my life I kept in contact with people I met in business, guys I went fishing with. So I wrote letters every night. People don't do that much anymore. They don't have the time. What do they do with their time? I'd write a real letter, put it in an envelope, lick a stamp, send it off. It's old-fashioned, but what the hell. Christmas time, you get a letter comes out of the computer, the same letter that goes to seventy-five other people. There's not the human touch, know what I mean? I wrote my letters with a fountain pen. You maybe never even seen a fountain pen..."

"Uh, yes. Yes, I have."

"Yeah, so anyway, I still write the letters. But when I wasn't writing the letters or reading 'Field and Stream' magazine or whatever, I was down in the dumps. The place. The Home. Run for profit, you know, down there. Sure, I was in business for profit, too but I didn't make money by hurting people. I helped people. Those places down there — save a buck here, save a buck there. No regulations. The

accountant makes this great discovery that if they hold back a few carrot chunks from the soup they might save twenty-seven dollars over a
year. You had janitors, orderlies, making minimum wage; why should
they give a shit, if you'll excuse the language?

"Anyway, kid, I just kept getting more and more blue; nothing to
live for but the goddamned mail. The body goes but, what's worse, the
mind longs to follow it. You feel yourself dying bit by bit, giving up,
losing your hold on life or, rather, you stop trying to keep a grip on it
because what's the point?

"Then, out of the blue, comes a letter from my son, the hippie
turned capitalist. 'Come to Canada,' he says. 'Whaa?' I say to myself.
I'm thrown for a loop to think my son has humane feelings. 'This is a
pleasant town,' he writes me. 'Come here and be close to your family.'
He used the word: family. He's still not married, though, and, techni-
cally, those two girls aren't my grandchildren, but these days, well, I
mean, you got men trying to getting married to men and women to
women, and them kind also adopting children — in comparison to
that, yeah, what my son was involved in was family. Me, I'm looking
for the catch. He says the right things, but I don't feel the warmth
behind the words or, and I hesitate to use the word, the love. But, hell,
beggars can't be choosers. That's what you are when you're old, a beg-
gar. Alright, so I may not have to worry about money, but that's still
what I am. My son says, 'You've got a pension, money in the bank,
you can get into Canada easy.' At first, what I think is, 'Hey, I'm an
American.' But next I think, 'And what the hell has *that* got me?' I'm
a guy that played by the rules, fought in the war, Second World War.
Well, I didn't fight overseas, but I served — warrant officer, Camp
Borden. Worked hard all my life, all the rest of it. And I wind up in a
crummy old age home.

"So, I emigrated. Hah! Guy at the airport in Toronto makes a
joke, says 'You a draft dodger?' 'No, a deserter,' I tell him. 'Yeah?' he
laughs. 'What war?' 'Boer War,' I says. Anyway, I'm at my son's home
three weeks. I might have been on Mars, that's how strange it was. The
wife, so to speak, talks a language I don't understand. Tries to get me
to drink soya milk, tells me about aromatherapy. She goes to a different course every night, always yapping about being centred and never
shuts up about being a woman. As if no one else has ever been a
woman. Meanwhile, some other woman looks after her kids and

another woman comes to clean the house. And those kids, a couple of girls, thirteen and fifteen — brats, quite frankly. I can tell you this because I know you got your professional ethics."

"Don't, I mean, don't worry," Colin was taken off guard. "Anything you tell me is strictly confidential."

"Yeah, you're a good kid. So, where was I? Oh, yeah, it's not the loud music or the way the kids talk, though a day of that could drive you crazy. Everything that should be a statement becomes a question. The sentence starts out like it's going to be some information then, on the last word, it turns into a question and sort of a challenge at the same time. 'I'm going to the *store?*' But it is not even that, even. It's the way they look at me, little snarls at the corners of their mouths. 'Gross' is how they referred to me when they thought I couldn't hear. And my son, he basically ignored me. There's a phone in every room of the house including in the two johns — but, still, he walks around the place with one of those cell phones glued to his ear.

"Then one day, he says, 'Well, dad, I've been looking around for the right home and I found just the thing.' I didn't know what he was getting at, so I said, 'What, you're moving? What's wrong with the place you got?' So he gives me a fake laugh. 'No. Ha, ha. For you. A home for you.' The way he said it was *a home*. In case I thought he was buying me a house. And here I am.

"The catch I was looking for? He hadn't said, 'Live with your family.' He said, 'Be closer to you family.' He manouvered me here for the insurance. I was in the business, remember? Insurance that the will turns out the right way. No surprises. Like I might have met a dame at the place in Florida or left my money to one of those orange-haired evangelists they got on television down there. And he never had to pay a premium on his insurance. I paid my own airline ticket. I pay for this place."

"And I imagine this all makes you feel rejected," Colin said it quickly, eager to appear to be doing his job.

"Hell, no. Disappointed in him, yeah — but, let's face it, I couldn't have stayed in their house anyway. I felt like an alien. But it's strange being in a different country and you've never seen any of it. From one old folks' home to another, it was. The room here is fine. I got a better view out the window than in Florida; the people are nicer, the staff is friendlier; there are more activities for us and all that."

"So, in general, Mr. Murray, you feel your situation has improved, eh? You, at least, prefer Valley View to where you were."

"I can't say that. Not really."

"But you mentioned all the advantages."

"The mail."

"I don't understand."

"Remember I said that I live for the mail?"

"Yes."

"In the States you got mail delivery six days a week."

*B*ack at his office, Colin set to work organizing social and cultural events. He'd earned a Master's Degree in sociology, spent a year on fellowship analysing the findings of a government white paper on verbal abuse of the elderly, another year developing an online course for sociology students who wished to work with the elderly, had attended seminars and delivered papers on the non-medical aspects of gerontological care — and here he was, in what seemed like a dream position for one of his studies and ambition. And what was he doing for nearly an hour-and-a-half every day? Acting as a combination social director and talent scout; his biggest worry being to find enough people to fill the thrice weekly, after-dinner activity hour. They phoned and they faxed, they emailed and they pounded on his door. This had shocked him, but only that first day. The paying elderly had to be entertained, after all. They were not going to sit around knitting or playing gin rummy. And so, the previous afternoon, Colin had held his first audition. There was a woman who called herself a storyteller and a fellow in dreadlocks with a guitar who played songs that Colin's own parents used to listen to, and who sounded like his father's moldy old favourites, Neil Young and Bob Dylan. He couldn't tell them apart. Colin was now faced with the agonizing prospect of having to reject people. Sure, he needed to fill the spots, but didn't believe the seniors wanted to hear something called 'Lovesick Subterranean Blues.' He almost told the young man to come back in a few years when there'd be a new era of old folks.

Fortunately, Colin had a secretary or, at least, shared a secretary with Dr. Corrington, and it was with relief and just a hint of guilt that he gave Ms. Dickson the job of breaking the bad news.

The woman turned out to be better than the Bob Dylan or Neil Young imitator. She just wanted to tell stories, showed Colin a certificate from a community college attesting to the fact that she had taken a course called 'Story Telling.' She told him one about an enchantress who visits a little girl. Later, it turns out she isn't really an enchantress, but the girl's subconscious. Colin didn't understand it, but the young woman was sincere and she wouldn't upset any of the residents and, furthermore, he was worried about filling his slots. He'd have Ms. Dickson telephone the young woman and schedule an Activity Hour for her.

There was a long list of others, and he would have to see them — unless he could find someone else to take on part of the chore, though Corrington preferred him to do it all. "We want your input at Valley View, Colin. You are our young blood. You and Dr. Drushka. We want you to circulate, let your fresh faces be seen by the residents. Yes, indeed. Young blood."

That had made Colin slightly embarrassed, self-conscious, knowing he had never felt like young blood or a fresh face. Hadn't his Aunt Eleanor in Wetaskiwin called him, at age five, an old soul? Colin's youth was notable less for his studious behaviour than for the absence of mischief. He'd played no pranks in high school; abhorred rock and roll music — had never drunk to excess, even in college. He sucked on a marijuana cigarette one time and had coughed so much he thought he was going to choke to death.

He scanned the list of hopefuls that had been prepared by Ms. Dickson. "Harold Trobo: sings barbershop quartet favorites; Jenny XX: performance artist; Nicola Burden: dramatic monologues..."

There were a dozen or so others: a magician, a juggler, a clown, an interpretive dancer, several musicians including a man who played the bandura, and one lady who offered to do an environmental pantomime while accompanied by her partner on an Andean flute. Colin sighed and looked at his watch. He had to visit the Dupree woman. He'd suggest to Ms. Dickson that she tell them all they were hired; all except for Jenny XX and the environmentalist.

Sunlight flooded the dayroom and softened everybody and everything so that the residents playing gin rummy or walking about, gesticulating as they talked, all seemed suspended in time — and the couches seemed about to levitate and playing cards to take to the air like doves.

For a moment Colin felt dizzy and as if he were losing his balance. He tilted his head back and rotated it, squeezed his eyes shut and opened them again.

"Dr. Childs? Yoo hoo! Over here."

Anna Dupree was seated at one of the square, formica-topped tables with Dotty Detweiler who, upon seeing him, buried her head in her arms and giggled. Colin thought he might have a club soda to settle his stomach. He should ask if they wanted anything.

"I'm not a doctor, Ms. Dupree. Hello Ms. Detweiler. I only have a Master's Degree."

"So, then, you're our master, eh?" Anna came out with that just as her companion was lifting her head, but Dotty lowered it again to giggle some more into her forearm. He smiled indulgently.

"Can I get you ladies anything from the cafeteria?"

"Black coffee, no sugar," Anna said.

Dottie said something that sounded like "Rye and Seven," but it was muffled in the sleeve of her sweatshirt.

"Now, now. You have plenty of that in your room," Anna teased.

"I'm going to report you two for drinking!" This from an overweight woman at the next table.

"Piss off, Rennie." Anna tossed it off without looking at her.

Colin left them to squabble if they would, but upon returning from the cafeteria line, saw the heavy woman moving away, fat feet in flipflops, throwing a parting shot over her shoulder, "Dried up old cunt!"

"Maybe so, you cow, but at least I got some use out of mine."

Ms. Rennie plodded away with fierce looks backward.

Colin was glad she wasn't one of his.

Anna's expression changed instantly from sheer malevolence to graciousness. "Please sit down, Master Childs. Ah, and thank you for the coffee. You look a mite disturbed or, rather, dismayed. Did that little bit of business bother you?"

It had bothered him. Had it occurred between men, his reaction would have been entirely different. It wouldn't have seemed so ugly.

"When we girls mix it up, we mean it."

She might have been reading his thoughts.

Dottie fixed her rheumy eyes on Colin. "You know I was born the last day of driving on the left-hand side of the road."

"Pardon?"

"That's right. That's what my Momma always said. The very next day you had to drive on the right-hand side in British Columbia."

Colin hadn't even known people used to drive on the left.

Dottie was saying something more about Momma when Anna interrupted her gently. "Dottie, dear. This nice young man must do his job. He and I will pretend to have a friendly chat while all the time he will be making all sorts of assessments. You have to run along now, whilst we carry out our little charade. Bye-bye."

Mrs. Detweiler sprang to her feet, nodded, giggled, waved jerkily and hurried off — bent over, but rapidly.

"She reminds me of Groucho, poor thing."

Colin looked at her blankly.

"You know, the Marx Brothers. 'Animal Crackers,' 'Duck Soup,' 'A Day at the Races.' You see any of those?"

He shook his head. "Not really."

"Not really? What the hell does that mean? One has or one hasn't. I assume you haven't or you'd remember."

"There was a campus pub where old movies were shown. I didn't go there much. The movies were in the background."

"Okay, I suppose I'll let you get away with that 'not really,' but I don't imagine you're the person to ask who the fourth brother was, much less the fifth. Most people don't know there was a fourth brother, let alone a fifth. That Harpo though, he was a true primitive and a devil with the ladies. Zeppo was the fourth but you have to be a genuine fanatic or really old to remember Gummo."

"Were you in any of those movies?"

"Yes, love. I played Margaret Dumont. No, just kidding. But I see you come prepared, young man. You have studied the intelligence file. Hah!"

He blushed.

She'd caused him to do that twice already.

"Ah, I see I was right. They think they're so bloody smart. God knows what they say about me. Not that I care."

They said, thought Colin, that you tell exaggerated stories out of a need to impress which, of course, is rooted in a deep insecurity. It says the name you were born with is Durkin. That many of your fellow residents resent you for tying to appear more important than they are; for telling tales or making up wild stories about contacts with the famous, experiences in show business and various other unlikely escapades.

"No, I wasn't."

"Excuse me?"

"I was never was in a Marx Brothers movie."

"Were you in movies?"

"My, yes. Movies. 'Pictures,' we used to call them. On stage too. Radio. Travelling shows. Toured the provinces, I did. Some tely, in the early days, when it was live and an adventure — we made it up as we went along. I'll tell you, young man, it bore no relation to the rubbish these fools stare at in here. They sit mesmerized by the nonsense. Sit *Calms*, indeed. It is truly disheartening. Enough to make one sick forever, if one thinks about it too much. Not that there is much 'forever' left to me. Women on talk shows, going on about being abused, being victims — complaining; blaming, blaming. I am heartily fed up with all that rubbish. They won't get any sympathy from me, I can tell you that. When I hear them nattering about 'taking charge' of their lives, being 'empowered,' I want to pull their bloody hair out. Sisterhood be damned. They're no sisters of mine, that's for sure. Blaming everything on men — their fathers, their brothers, the minister, the school principle, their husbands and boyfriends and the lout on the corner who gives them the once over. Some of them, they go out on a date, a fellow puts his hand on their leg in the movie and they're yelling about being sexually abused. Not that this stuff doesn't go on. And how. There is certainly more of it than there used to be. And the reason may have plenty to do with the fact that there are no real men anymore. Sorry. I beg your pardon. No offense intended. But how can there be real men when they are all watching television or sitting behind computers all day and night. Grown men playing these computer games where superheroes are killing half of Hong Kong with their feet. They get frustrated and have to take it out on someone. A woman meets one of these abusers — kick him in the nuts, if you're able. If not, stick a knife in him when he's asleep. I'm serious. Problem solved. When the time in your life comes to kill, kill, to paraphrase the preamble to a great play I appeared in once. But one can't kick them all in the nuts, stick them all with a kitchen knife.

"You know, I feel sorry for a man on a date. How does he initiate the romantic scene? He has to start somewhere, somehow. But how does he know she is not liable to let out a scream. Soon, one will have to sign a statement of intent. 'I, the undersigned, hereby make known my intention, whilst sipping wine at dinner and peering into your limpid eyes between the candles, to stroke the back of your hand lightly with my fingertips. This pursuant to attempting to nuzzle the back of your neck when we get into the automobile.' Some folderol like that. Think of it, Master Childs."

"You can call me Mr. Childs or even Colin."

"Think of it, Mr. Childs — I'm not ready for 'even Colin' yet. Even Colin. Is that sort of like Honest Abe or Doubting Thomas? Think of it. You and Dr. Drushka, you are on a date...Oh, oh. Blushing again. You think I didn't see the look you gave her when you came upon us? Me talking about my, well, you know what."

He was uncomfortable thinking that his feelings might be so obviously on display. Ludmilla would no doubt be aware of his intentions, if this elderly woman could see through him.

"I'm sure you think I'm an arrogant, foul-mouthed old biddy, and I am. I am also angry and bitter. A bitter biddy, indeed. I resent being in this joint, as comfortable as it may be, and I'm raging against the dying of the you-know-what whilst bemoaning the thought of my decrepitude. These women complaining about being regarded as sex objects. Oh, Lord above! To be so regarded once again. At least by someone under sixty-five. Ah! What am I saying? Under Seventy. But none of these doddering old farts in here. One of them was coming down the hall after me last week, step by step, inch by inch...Niagara Falls...You don't get the reference, I suppose? No? Anyway, he's making these sad little exhalations. Huh...huh...huh. A cataract over one eye, a cobweb of saliva between his lips. What the hell did he think he'd do if he caught me? I went into my room, read a magazine, peered out the door, and he's still on his way."

"What happened?"

"Dinner. He started out right after lunch. Poor old sod was almost there when an attendant came, put him in a cart, took him to the dining room.

"Yes, I went through the men in my time. Don't think for a moment that I didn't. I feel sorry for you young people today what with all your worries, precautions, and the like. We didn't have that frustration in my day. But just wait until they come up with a cure for this sex plague, if they ever do. Then the world will see an explosion of pent-up tension unlike anything in history. Instead of the liberation of desire, it will prove devastating, the consummation of another disease, this one catastrophic. Mark my words. I have spoken.

"But, no, wait, I'm not finished. Now it does occur to me that I do talk about sex a great deal. At least when you're around. Just kidding. Although you'd probably be quite smashing if you lost a few pounds. Let your facial bones emerge. Fellow your age shouldn't have that extra weight around his middle. Oh, I don't mean to hurt your feelings. What must you be thinking? What kind of report are you going to prepare? Well, stop me from going on and on. But you won't because you want to see where I go when given the reins. Oh, you're all so clever."

She stopped. Looked away. Smirked. And Colin was taken by surprise when she didn't start up again. Right away Ms. Dupree seemed to deflate in front of him.

He fumbled. "Well, um, for a woman with, I mean, you're quite vivacious, you impress with your energy, it must be extremely difficult being…"

"You're not kidding. Being in here…"

She was back, all pumped up again. Colin thought of being a kid, taking his bicycle to the air pump at the service station, one hit of air and the tire almost burst.

"Some days I want to scream, beat on the wall with my bony little fists. Who can I talk with? My fellow inmates? The dullest group of humans I have ever seen assembled in one place. Old Dotty Detweiler excepted. She is so looney she makes for delightful company. She is free, totally free, thanks to her craziness. It could be 1939 for all she knows, and the boys marching off to war. Dotty gets a notion to make wee wee in a corner of the dayroom, she simply drops her drawers and squats. Of course, when Dotty becomes a little more erratic, they'll have to take her out of here. But, then again, perhaps, it won't make any difference to her in a nursing home.

"Me, I'm far too sane."

That's not, Colin thought to himself, what the reports say. Used to escape from her daughter's house and head for Highway 97, the Strip, her destination usually the same franchise restaurant.

"Although, when one gets old and one lives in a conservative community, and does anything the slightest bit different from the neighbours, one is liable to be called crazy."

"Unfortunately, Ms. Dupree, every community has its standards, its norms; a person deviating from these is often, in more rigid societies, considered mentally ill."

"Yes, yes," she snapped, brusquely. "Of course."

Her impatience annoyed Colin. Why should it? If he were a true professional, it wouldn't. He went on, "There is no precise definition, no clear-cut parameters, for this thing we casually label 'crazy.'"

"No, kidding, kid?"

But Colin was sure one could recognize true craziness when one was in its presence. He should, perhaps, amend that to, "could recognize its presence when it manifested itself." Was this woman crazy? Mentally ill? Insane? Those words didn't seem to apply. Perhaps it was waiting for the right moment to creep out from its hiding place. He was aware that, despite her talkativeness, something was held back. An underlying tension was almost palpable. He'd have to consult the master files and retrieve the reports of her original counsellor.

"Oh, we're not done so soon, are we? Yes? Well, we each have our allotted time. Next! Don't you get tired of listening to our tales of petty woe? We are all hard done by, of course. I don't get along with the others as I have indicated and as you know if your file is halfway adequate. But I'll tell you one thing we all have in common — we're all in here for 'our own good.'"

She laughed, genuine, unabashed laughter. Others stared. He tried to take a professionally polite leave, but she waved him off, not interrupting her laughter to say goodbye.

olin Childs was so busy over the next couple of weeks that he hardly thought of Anna Dupree, until the eve of their next meeting. Certainly, in the minutes after their dayroom talk, she'd been on his mind, categorized as a bit of an eccentric. But there were his others — what else should he call them? They weren't patients; they weren't exactly his charges; they were his — others. The others on his caseload. In addition to them, there was a daily staff meeting, the social events to organize, an occasional get-together with local media, innumerable problems such as might arise in any institution, and those peculiar to Valley View. Predominant among the latter were ones relating to the Privacy Room. "A place to share tenderness, to have one's own space, a place for touch," is the way Ludmilla described it.

Dr. Corrington, tall, patrician, white-haired, tanned and sixty, taking Colin aside in the hallway, put it differently. "The randy old goats want to go in there and screw. Or try to. Mr. Bednarick booked the room with Gertrude Solty. You know her, eh? The little one with the orange hair and gigantic bosom? No sooner was Bednarick out of there than he had to ring for the medical team. Nearly had a seizure. There are legal implications to think of."

"But the provincial charter of rights of the aged has been amended to provide for privacy rooms and…"

"Yes, my boy. Certainly. But don't be so naïve. The threat of a lawsuit and the ensuing bad publicity is something we do not want. No way. Imagine the editorials. *The Courier* would have a field day. 'Sodom and Gomorrah on the Hill,' 'Septugenarian Satyrs,' sort of thing. You know, just between you and me, a few woman are going in there together."

"You don't…?"

"That's just what I mean. Shocks you, eh? You'd be surprised, young man. Lesbos lurks in these halls. Indeed, yes. As Mrs. Gratton explained it to Dr. Drushka, 'The old *men* can't do anything.'"

Colin made no response. He was thinking about the elderly having sex. He'd had courses that touched on the subject, but it was always theoretical; he'd never thought of them actually doing it, especially two old women together.

He was trying to imagine it when Dr. Corrington said, "Yes, it's not a pretty picture, is it? Another thing, just between you and me, and I tell you these particulars only because I wish you to monitor the situation. I don't mean eye to the keyhole stuff. I mean, in a general sense. Yes, it is strictly between you and me, what I'm about to tell you."

Colin waited. Dr. Corrington looked him in the eyes. "It is about Mr. Weatherill and Mr. Clough."

"You mean...?"

"Again, I'm afraid that's exactly what I mean. Two days from today."

"Oh, my."

That match-up was even more difficult to picture than the two old women.

"My, boy, remember: what I've told you is not to be bandied about by the staff. They, the residents, seem to know everything. How they know, I have not as yet determined. Bookings are strictly confidential. The Privacy Room is tucked away way over there in the East Wing. No loitering is permitted in the area. Still everyone knows everything. Maybe there's a mole."

"A mole?"

"Indeed. A mole. Anyway, I leave it with you, my boy."

"Leave what with me, precisely, sir?"

"The situation. The situation. Look into the situation. Circulate. Protect Valley View. Circumvent negative potential."

So, to his list of duties, Colin added, 'Circulate and Circumvent.' He didn't know how to go about that, really; so, while making his rounds, he made half-hearted attempts at eavesdropping which amounted to standing still at odd moments and listening. Listening for what? It occurred to him once, standing stock still in the middle of the dayroom, that he must look damn foolish. He couldn't tell from the expressions of the residents, many of whom were staring at him, because he knew they could be thinking of their wedding day or that he was on television. "Am I eavesdropping yet?" he asked himself.

When, after a few days, Colin hadn't heard anything — heard what? — he put it out of his mind.

His mind was increasingly on Ludmilla. There was no camaraderie of youth between them. They were unrelentingly mature, no matter what Corrington said or their birth certificates might indicate. Intellectually, Colin could, of course, grasp "old age and its problems." But not as something that awaited him. It was a concept. Really, with Colin, it wasn't so much old age as gerontology. He was twenty-eight years old, a few pounds overweight — well, perhaps, twenty, maybe even twenty-five pounds overweight — but they were easy enough to lose. His stomach was giving him trouble lately and that was probably due to the stress of a new job. Actually, it had started before he came to Valley View. He'd get over it. He had no other health complaints; didn't suffer from headaches, depression, blurred vision. He really was only twenty-eight!

Still Colin told himself, when I do reach my senior years, I could do a lot worse than to end my days in a place as pleasant and progressive as Valley View. The staff cares and the physical surroundings leave little to be desired. There is plenty to keep the seniors occupied.

He thought about the arrival of the ambulance.

The swirling light pulsated, the ambulance crew burst through the wide double doors and pushed a gurney down the hallways. The residents assembled near the entrance in a sort of mass trance. They were quiet; and orderly, careful not to disturrb operations — after all, it might be them next time. Who is it this time?

They stared with grim fascination at the body on the gurney, its eyes — his, her — eyes shut or, worse, open and rolling about. Intravenous bottle jiggling on its post, oxygen mask in place. The eerie colour of the ambulance light as it tracked across the drapes in the night. "Oh, it's poor Charlie Bennett. And weren't we playing canasta just the day before yesterday. Of course, he was getting feeble."

Colin was astounded the first time he witnessed the coming and going of the ambulance. It was the day after he arrived. Astounded to realize that the residents weren't left depressed or morose in its wake. Quite the contrary. They were in high spirits. The dayroom was suddenly filled with good cheer and conviviality: "It wasn't me! I'm still here! I'm alive, alive-oh!" You half expected them to start doing the Funky Chicken, he told himself, whatever that was.

Colin made a mental note, the next time the ambulance took someone away, to check for a rise in bookings of the Privacy Room. Might be a paper in that.

And so the days passed at Valley View. He conducted his interviews, or chats, as he preferred to call them — two or three each day. The residents were nice enough, save for the odd, ornery old man or bitter old woman. Nice enough they might be, but not one, he had to admit, engaged more than his half-hearted interest. No one, that is, save for the Dupree woman. He didn't know what he had expected. Perhaps several people who would provide anecdotal information on which he could develop the themes of papers for the journals. Yes, it was raw material he had hoped for.

"*A*h, doctor. So nice to see you. The past fortnight has simply dragged by. Please forgive me if I don't get up."

Anna Dupree was on the mauve couch in the dayroom by the picture window. She was seated at the exact middle of it, and patted the cushion beside her. Colin pretended not to notice the gesture as he drew up a chair.

"You needn't be afraid," she said.

"What? Oh." Colin smiled, unbuttoned his jacket, glanced out the window where, beyond a line of hills, on a plateau above the valley, he could see an orchard, trees in blossom in June.

"Now then. What do you want to know, Mr. Childs? Into what corner of my life do you wish to pry?"

"Oh, Ms. Dupree. Don't think of it like that. Let's just talk. Anything you wish."

"Anything?"

"Yes, of course. You were married, I believe."

"I was married, you know. Must we ruin the mood of a beautiful day by talking of my ill-starred marriage?"

"Not if you don't wish. We might…"

"The bastard. I gave up my career for him. No. Let me be fair. He was a bastard, at least figuratively, but I didn't give up my career for him. That was vanishing on its own. I was in England. It was the late-Sixties and I was already into middle age. The youth culture had society in its stranglehold. Work was difficult to find. I could dance a little bit, sing a little bit, and the little bit could be overcome when I was a kid because of my looks. Hard for you to believe, eh?"

"Uh, no. No. Not at all."

"I looked all right for my years, mind. But no one over thirty was working, unless it was on the BBC. And then it was only older people, older than me even, as foils for the swinging young. I used to get work there in the kitchen sink days. But now it was all plays about the sons and daughters of upper middle class twits running off to Soho. I didn't have the plumy tones to play their mothers. I was slaving nights at a casino, a cocktail waitress. And that is where I met Andy. And I married the creep. Andy Anderson. Oh sure, he was nice enough at first when he was courting me. And he was wealthy. My big butter and egg man from Canada. I was honest with him when he proposed. I told him I didn't love him. He answered on cue, 'I only hope you'll come to love me in time.' Never got anywhere close. When he popped the question, I took stock, as they say, of my life. My career? What a laugh. In the previous year, I had been in a play that ran for twelve nights, posed for one magazine advert — for shoes, sensible shoes. Look."

Anna's legs were crossed and she raised the top foot, rotated it. She was wearing a pair of rope-soled wedge heels with canvas uppers.

"I have slim feet and nice ankles. Or, at least, I did then. Try to imagine them with fewer obvious veins."

Colin caught himself doing just that. He looked up, cleared his throat.

"And I did an educational film. You know, like they show in schools — with simple little dramas to wrap the message around. This one was about the dangers of drugs and motoring. I mean simultaneously. I was a nurse at the information desk when the distraught parents rushed into the hospital, frantic for news of their son who'd been driving under the influence of hallucinogens and thought it a capital idea to get ahead of a pokey lorry by steering his mini up its middle, between the wheels, you see. 'Take a seat, please,' sez I, all businesslike. They don't naturally.

"'But our son! We must see him this instant!'

"'Have a seat, please, and I will page the attending physician. Doctor Bulwer-Lytton! Doctor Bulwer-Lytton. To the emergency desk, please!'

"Big time, eh? What a come down. Me, the girl Robert Rainer really loves in 'Eaton Place.' The girl he should have married, but instead he gave in to family pressures and got hitched with Claire Rutledge, that ninny. We said goodbye on the dark street; naturally there was thick fog. I walked away into the night, high heels clicking on the wet cobblestones. Came the war, the bombs, he realized he'd made a mistake when he saw the horror up close — realized what was truly important in life. Yes, a terrible mistake. And, on leave, he returned for me. But I was gone. I was no more. The Blitz, you see. He found my street — nothing but rubble. Oh, God. I'm afraid I'm beginning to cry…"

And she was.

"Ms. Dupree, forgive me. My questions have disturbed you. Perhaps I should leave now."

She sniffed, dabbed at her eyes with a crumpled little ball of Kleenex. "Typical man. Wants to flee at the first sight of tears. No. No, I need to talk. Really, you don't know what it is like for me to have no one to talk with except poor Dotty D., and mainly I just talk at her. Poor thing."

"But amongst the others, surely…"

"Dullards!"

With one word and a frown, she dismissed the lot of them.

"'Eaton Place.' Perhaps you might find it in a video store. The one he really loved. Yes. But that was in 1950 when I was twenty-one. So suddenly it is 1966, and Andy Anderson is proposing. 'Let's face it, girl,' says I to the myself I see in the mirror, who has wrinkles that seemed to spread even as I watched — some girl. 'You're a has-been. Think about your future, your declining years. Be sensible for once. When do you ever expect to get another opportunity like this one?' So, then, the one and only time in my life that I have pulled myself up by my bootstraps, mounted, as it were, and rode resolutely into reasonableness, it got me nothing but the misery.

"We were married in a small chapel in Herefordshire, very picturesque. Ran off to the Mediterranean for a two-week honeymoon. Nice, Cannes, St. Tropez. He thought everything was hunky-dory, and that he was the Count de Seingalt and Porfiro Rubirosa, both in one. I remember so vividly the first night of our *luna de miel.* That is the first time I let him have even a little bit, by the way. When he was finished, when he had gotten his breath back, he said, 'Well?' There was an obnoxious twist to his lips. 'Well?' Can you believe it? 'Oh, yes,' I replied. 'It was absolutely divine. You were simply wonderful, dearest.' For me the train never left the station. And it never did get very far down the track whenever he was at the throttle. I considered taking up smoking so I might have something to look forward to when he was finished. It got so that I simply dreaded it. Andy Anderson would get this look in his eyes and commence to swagger. Often this was when he'd gotten off work and had completed some business that had him feeling particularly manly. He'd come home for another bit of business, want to bend me over the arm of the sofa or like that. Fortunately being twelve years my elder, he wasn't after me all that much. And, frequently, he was out of town. Did I dread the day of his return! I can still see him emerging from the shower, thinning hair plastered down, silk robe stretched tight across his belly. He would douse himself with cologne. What was it he used — horrid, perfumey stuff? Thought that would get me so wildly excited, don't you know. He would stare at me with half-closed eyes prior to pouncing. In and out, in and out, once around clockwise, around once counter clockwise to impress me with technique, and that was about it. One time he said, dared to say to me, 'You've never had it like that!' Can you imagine? 'No,' says I. 'You're right about that.'

"He was jealous of my former life, my show business associates. He was especially insecure about men I'd slept with, or that he suspected I'd slept with years before we ever met. Not that I told him the half of it, nor even the quarter. He wanted me to assure him it was better with him than with someone like Conrad Morgan, for instance. 'It is, isn't it, sweetheart?' 'Oh, yes, darling. Yes, yes.'"

When she paused for a moment, Colin rushed to get a word in; after all, he told himself, I have to do my job, ask questions — better come right out with it, there's a reference in the file, "Did he ever hit you?"

Before Colin could consider that he might have been too direct, Anna answered. "Yes, but only twice. The first time was not too long after we were married. I had gone with him back to Toronto. It was while we were having sex, or he was having sex; I don't know the proper word for what it was I was having. Anyway, this particular time, he was slogging away, grunting and groaning above me, turning beet red, huffing and puffing and right before finishing, he grabs my shoulders, shakes me a few times like a rag doll, then: biff! bam!—twice, hard across the face. I shrieked. He finished — I was stunned. I was too stunned to be angry. After a few moments, I said, 'Darling, you may paddle my bum a bit if that gets you excited, but this other stops right here. I'm warning you.'

"He was contrite, I'll say that much for him. So apologetic; claimed he was so passionate about me that'd he'd simply been carried away, transported by mad desire, or some such tommy-rot. You, Mr. Childs, are probably thinking, 'Oh, come now, be serious. How could anyone ever have gotten carried away with desire for this old bird?' But they were, alas. I had it, if I may boast. And who's to stop me? Yes, I did have 'It,' whatever 'It' is. Or, I should say, was. Whatever 'It' was.' I must have had a score of movie bits, one liners, as sluts, tramps, nasty little vixens. That's what my daughter called me, 'a tramp.' I was never the girl one took home to show Mums. That's my daughter's role."

In his mind, Colin underlined these first mentions of the daughter.

"I read for the female lead in 'The Man in the White Suit' — the daughter of the textile mill owner. It was a fine part and I was a decent actress. It was well within my range. There is a scene where they have Alec Guinness locked in a room for fear he'll talk to the press about his invention: a suit that never needs cleaning and will, therefore, last forever. The tycoons want to suppress the invention and so does Labour. In order to persuade Alec to keep his mouth shut, they send in the daughter to make advances, an inducement with a plunging neckline. He rejects her, being a paragon of integrity. That one scene lost me the role, the best part I ever had or ever would be considered for. The powers-that-be concluded that the audience would never believe Sir Alec would pass up the opportunity to roger the likes of me. With Joan Greenwood, they would believe such a thing. Oh, well. But just to show you I am not the type to stand on pride. We are the same size and structure, Greenwood and myself. So when they offered me the job as her double, I took it. Beggars can't be choosers, and all that. It is me comes running toward Alec after he's knocked down by the sports car that the girl's driving.

"It was Alexander Korda who one day explained to me, quite succinctly, the nature of my appeal. He said — you do know who Alexander Korda was?"

"No, I don't think I do. Sorry."

Anna shook her head in dismay before continuing. "I hope this doesn't shock you. That's not what he said. What he said was, 'Anna...' With his Hungarian accent, it was 'Ah Nah...It is as if you are wearing a sign that says, 'Magst Du Meine Muschel Maschen.' And he certainly wanted to know first hand. Didn't he just...Ah, there. You understand German. It did shock you."

"Oh, no. No, it didn't."

"Excuse me, then. I beg your pardon. Your youth makes me forget sometimes that you are a thorough professional. But, getting back to Andy, Andy Anderson and my new life. It was years later, the second time that he hit me. Before I tell you about that, however, I must set the scene. Toronto was not the most exciting place to be in those years. I had some notion of getting back into show business in whatever shape or form. There was not exactly a cornucopia of opportunity in that dour burg. Spring Thaw was about the best of it. Still, I'd have settled for neighbourhood amateur theatre. Gets in your blood, you know. But he, the lord and ruler of the household, as well as of my entire life, would not permit it. At first, that didn't bother me. I was in a new country where I didn't have to wait on tables, tote a drinks tray while men copped feels. He had a large apartment that I immediately busied myself remodelling. I kept the place looking swell, I must say — and just did. Entertained his business associates and their wives. I never decided who were more boring: the men with their white-collar chatter or the women and their domestic nattering. I prepared elaborate dinners. I'd never cooked before, really; just odds and sods and a tin of beans on a backstage hotplate. But it was something to do so I approached it with enthusiasm, and learned to be a decent cook. I added a bit of flair to Andy's social life, helped his business along. Except for one occasion. I thought all this was fair exchange and that I should be entitled to a little freedom once I'd seen to my obligations, so called. At least, I might take my picture and resume around? But he'd have none of it. What if I got a job and he had scheduled a dinner party? My goodness!"

"Would you mind telling me about that one occasion?"

"What, love?"

"You mentioned helping his business along except on one occasion."

"Sometimes, as I said, I'd prepare dinner; other times we'd dine out with his business associates. The restaurant evenings were far worse. At home, I could play at hostess and keep myself under control. But in public there'd be nothing to do. I had no interest in the pitiful conversation. A couple of gin and tonics and the reins slipped.

"And there we were of an evening in Salem's which was considered a big deal in Toronto. One might see a cabinet minister! Oh, be still my beating heart. That sort of thing wowed an Andy Anderson. Well, this one evening Andy is trying to make a sale to this particular gentleman, an overweight captain of industry dressed in expensive dull taste. A George Groscz caricature. He's brought along his wife, a little prude who resembled a sort of suburban Jacqueline Kennedy. My job: to lend these affairs an air of European worldliness, thereby enhancing Andy's status. As in: You know, she gave up quite a decent career in show business for him — You don't say — Why yes. They say at one time she was involved with Robert Rainer. They met on a film and started a scandalous affair — which was complete rubbish since Robby was a flaming poufter. And I had to keep the wives occupied while the men conducted important business.

"Andy had been working on the deal for weeks — and comes the big night when the fish is sure to take the bait, and Andy'd reel him in. But it seems Mr. Tycoon thought I was the bait and he'd get away with a little nibble at the very least. He starts pressing his leg against mine under the table. We're at a banquette booth. I inch away discreetly. He inches after me to continue his little game. Somehow the man manages to slip his foot out of his shoe and he runs the foot halfway up my leg. Again I slide away. I am, by now, on the edge of the bloody seat. I give him a look meant to wither, but he is only encouraged. He pays no attention to my husband other than to offer condescending little nods as Andy rattles on, oblivious; this way he's letting me know he can do that sort of thing because he is oh-so-very important and powerful and, therefore, a good fellow to hop into the sack with. By now I've run out of booth. I am not enjoying his fat foot on my leg, much less the hand he's suddenly clamped on my thigh, so I pick the swizzle stick out of my third gin and tonic — only the third — hold it three inches from the tip of his nose, and say, 'My good man, if you do not get your hand and your smelly foot off my leg, I shall thrust this stick up your nostril and into your tiny brain.'

"I must not have said this *sotto voce* because it got the attention of everyone in the surrounding area. My husband and the tycoon's wife came immediately to the man's defense. 'Anna!' spurts Andy, aghast. 'Why, she must be drunk!' spits the wife, contemptuously. But I manage to kick the shoe out from under the table. I shall never forget the scene — all four of us, as well as the couple at the booth across the way, staring at this size twelve, black wingtip on the pearl gray carpet. Circumstantial evidence, perhaps, but it did cast the shadow of a doubt, at least, in the mind of his wife. The tycoon meanwhile fumes and my stalwart knight in shining armour makes excuses for me, 'High strung…too much gin…You know how they get sometimes.' Mr. Childs, I sure know how to ruin a sale."

"Then you went home and had an argument and that's when he hit you?"

"Oh, no. That was later. A few years later. I had a baby first. I've not said much about her. What a surprise. Pregnant at forty. Things did not improve. They were horrible, indeed. I was in despair."

"Ms. Dupree, I thought," Colin glanced at his watch, "that you were setting the stage, as you put it, I mean, for the next time he hit you."

"But, darling, I am setting the stage."

"Well, I'm afraid I have to leave now. I'm awfully sorry. I'm late already."

"Yes, I understand. So many old biddies you have to listen to, and I'm but one of them."

"So then. In two weeks?"

No sooner had he said it than two weeks seemed like a very long time. He liked listening to Anna Dupree, so unlike the rest of the residents. So unlike anyone he'd ever met, really. How much of the movie stuff was true?

"Could we possibly meet sooner?" Anna asked. "I realize you have your rules and regulations, your obligations. But, as I said, I have no one to talk with. I feel a bit alive with you."

"I, uh, it is…"

"Highly irregular? Yes, I know it must be."

She seemed to grow smaller before his eyes. Just skin and bones beneath that wavy and strangely luxurious, iron-gray hair — her eyes disconcerting because so youthful and fixed on him now like those of a sad young girl. Was she acting?

"I'll see what I can arrange. Perhaps we can meet earlier. I'll send you a message."

"Oh, good!" A young girl, happy now.

She flashed a huge smile. Is it sincere? He wondered.

*C*olin found himself thinking of Anna at odd moments. He was surprised that her small but big-eyed and finely-etched face appeared to him more frequently than the large and smooth, heart-shaped one of Ludmilla. The way Colin construed this was that the old woman posed an intellectual problem; she represented a type for which he had not been prepared by his schooling.

Colin had taken his studies seriously, even in the earliest grades. He was thinking of his bookish youth as he walked in the garden at Valley View, a shady, half-acre refuge from the relentless Okanagan summer sun. Back then, when he opened his textbooks, he had not just been looking for good grades but seeking explanations, feeding his curiosity. Looking up from the pea gravel path, he saw a hummingbird and, looking back down to continue his line of thought, recalled how as a child he wondered why birds flew in a V pattern; why, for that matter, birds sing. How many times a minute did a hummingbird's heart beat? The acquisition of the answer was of more interest, much more interest to him, than the birds themselves. If he were to be perfectly honest, he wasn't at all interested in living birds, just in birds as problems that required explanations. It had disturbed him, after his father told him that the hummingbird stuck its long needle-like beak into the flower to get the precious nectar, to discover this was only incidental, that the hummingbird was usually after the insects that it lived upon. But discovering that his father wasn't the fount of all knowledge didn't disturb him as much as not finding the answer to the question of why birds fly in a V pattern. He acquainted himself with all the opinions, but when it got right down to it, no one knew for sure. Colin believed it had to do with magnetics; fish migration, the same thing,

When barely a teenager, Colin had studied the origins of twentieth century conflicts in Europe, the origins taking him far back into history. And it was just a few years later that Colin chose as his field of study, the wants and needs of the elderly, and the wants and needs of those who provide them care. The subject, he reasoned while still in high school, was inexhaustible and given the reality of population projections for the next several decades, there would be, literally as well as proportionately, more elderly than ever before. Hence, more people would be needed to care for them, administer to them, and Colin, by the time he graduated high school, saw himself rather like a modern pioneer in this field.

In all his specialized schooling, including graduate school at Simon Fraser University on its beautiful suburban hill outside Vancouver, Colin could recall only a few minutes that were devoted to dealing with that rare senior citizen who had energy to burn and faculties intact and who actively resented being institutionalized. Of course, he had realized from the very beginning that the majority of those with faculties intact resented being institutionalized and that a few of these must be healthy and energetic. But he'd read nothing, heard nothing, that dealt with an excoriating resentment. What Colin had gleaned from those few minutes in the middle of a lecture, was the professor's recommendation that the resentful senior's energy and mental acuity must be channelled. Perhaps the senior could be encouraged to assist others. One might say to him or her, "You have invaluable resources gained over a very full lifetime, it would be a pity not to share them with others. Your love of life will prove infectious."

He could not imagine this tough old bird, Anna Dupree, sharing her invaluable resources with the others, enthusiastically organizing yet another shuffleboard tournament or low impact aerobic program.

The Dupree woman seemed old only in years and, sometimes, maybe just for a moment, didn't even look that old, particularly from the rear or when her head was turned or tilted a certain way, the movement stretching the skin along her jaw line. And behind those big dark eyes burned that will to live. How does the institution deal with someone like her without smothering that fire?

There must be a way. He'd have to find the answer. Colin decided he would first check the abstracts and go to the literature indicated. Maybe there are colleagues working on the same problem.

Retracing his steps on the pea gravel path, Colin noticed again the hummingbird and this time, he stopped. He'd never more than glanced at a hummingbird. He wondered about the relative density of cartilage connecting wings to body. But what does it matter? Yes, why in the world did that matter? Or whether it lived primarily on nectar or insects. Look at it: so tiny, wanting to live, living to its capacity there right before one's eyes. A miracle that would cease to be if it was removed from its true life, put in a cage. And then he felt rather embarrassed for thinking like that, sounding to himself like a senti-mentalist or a daffy romantic.

Later that day, Colin made up his mind to look for some of that zest for life within himself. To get his nose out of books, and take part. He was seized by this novel idea right in the middle of Sarah Levitch's audition, her one-world performance. She was waving her arms and bending at the waist while a fellow sitting cross-legged on the audito-rium floor, blew into a wooden flute. "So you appreciate our piece, eh?"

"Uh? Oh, excuse me. Yes." Colin had been roused from his thoughts. The woman was finished, staring at him.

She smelled of curry and garlic and as if her hair needed a good shampooing. Her gaunt partner had hair like a bird's nest. Colin won-dered how he could stand it in the Okanagan in the summer.

"I think, well, Ms. Dickson will call you. Yes, thank you very much."

Back at his office, he was surprised to see Ms. Dickson tidying papers on her desk, dusting off her terminal. She grabbed her hand-bag.

"Do you have an appointment, Ms. Dickson?"

She was no more than five feet tall, always smiling, hair cut short in bangs, dyed a dark red, almost maroon coulour. Ms. Dickson was nearly sixty, looked twenty years younger. He knew little about her personal life beyond that she was divorced and religious about exer-cise. That must explain her figure; Ludmilla had said it only explained her figure partly — tummy tucks and liposuction made up the rest of the explanation.

"Why, Mr. Childs. It's ten after five, time to go home. The week is over, da dum! You're thinking too much about your job. Enjoy yourself. There's a concert at Lakeside Park tonight."

"Ten after five. It's that late? I had no idea. Thank you. Have a nice weekend."

Colin had a brief feeling of panic. What if Ludmilla had gone? No, she never left Valley View before six. If he was going to participate in life, he mustn't put it off any longer.

Colin was aware of feeling resolute as he left the office and strode along the hall. But a few steps after he'd turned left, and was fifty feet or so from Ludmilla's office door, Colin encountered doubts, like bullies coming the other way. What if she turns me down? What if she turns me down coldly? Worse, what if she thinks I've acted improperly? Or laughs? She might laugh. She's so worldly.

He made it to her door, which was open a couple of feet. It wouldn't be so bad, really, staying at home by himself. He stepped back. Perhaps there was something worthwhile on television.

"Colin! What are you doing out there? Come in, come in so you don't seem to be lurking."

"What? Lurking." He made an attempt at laughing but only managed to sound like he was grunting. "I just stopped there wondering whether I'd locked my files. Yes. Was about to go back to check. I guess I should do that."

"Wait. Just a second, please."

"Yes, Ludmilla."

"It is okay to call me Ludmilla now because there is no one else around. But when residents or non-professional staff are near, remember, please, to call me Dr. Drushka. Okay? The other day you said 'Ludmilla.' We have to maintain some sense of formality when around them or they will lose respect for us."

"Of course. Sorry. Well, I'll be off now. Have a good…"

"Wait, Colin. That's not what I wanted to say. See here, do you have an active social life in Kelowna?"

"Social life? No, no I don't as a matter of fact."

Maybe he shouldn't have told her that.

"Nor do I."

She looked at him directly. He glanced away, muttered, "Uh."

"Is there a woman you live with?"

"Oh, no. No, not at all."

"You're not…You know?"

"Huh? Oh, no, not in the least. No."

"I've not met anyone whom I really want to go out with since I've been in this town. I've hardly met anyone at all. Men, I mean. Have you met any women?"

"No, I haven't."

"So here it is, the weekend, and neither of us...you know."

Colin found himself unable to speak. He wanted to speak but couldn't. He felt paralyzed.

"Colin!"

"Yes?"

"My God. He says 'Yes?' Colin must I do all the work? Well, I suppose I must. Would you take me to dinner tonight? Or, rather, will you go to dinner with me?"

"Why, I. That is...Sure. I mean, I'd love to."

For a horrible, split-second, he had a picture of himself telling her no. His apartment suddenly seeming cozy, all dark except for the light from the television; no worries there. Safely ensconced.

He was pleased when Ludmilla suggested they go directly to have a pre-dinner drink rather than to their respective homes to change, make preparations, and the like. This way, Colin thought, he could be taken along with the flow of the thing rather than be at his apartment and susceptible to making excuses for backing out.

Ludmilla suggested a place by the lake called El Dorado. There were the cars to deal with so she gave him directions, how to avoid the strip traffic by taking a series of roads across the southern limits of town, coming out directly across from the El Dorado. Alone in the car, his relief vanished temporarily, knowing he again had the opportunity to get out of the thing. Tell her later that the car broke down. Geez, that was pretty lame. He just let the car take him. There were new homes being built in former orchard land. An entire subdivision going up. Giant homes on tiny lots against the dun-coloured land. He was nervous. Ludmilla seemed so strong, overpowering.

She was waiting in a lounge adjacent to the dining room. There were also tables for dining on a verandah that extended out over the water. "I thought later, when we're ready for dinner, we could go out there," Ludmilla said. "They don't permit you to merely sit and drink outside. All these silly North American rules."

He said that was fine, suited him perfectly.

She ordered a Campari and soda. Colin had never heard of Campari, was surprised when it arrived, surprised by its colour. He hadn't known what to order, thinking that a beer wouldn't be right.

Too common. He couldn't decide but then remembered something Anna had said, and heard himself asking for a gin and tonic. Ludmilla said she hadn't pictured him as the gin and tonic type. He'd never had one before but certainly didn't tell her that. Let her have the idea he was unpredictable.

Ludmilla right away said that she had no desire to get involved with anyone, to have a "serious commitment" or, God forbid, to marry. But she did feel the need, now and again, for male companionship.

"Oh, sure. I know what you mean. Me too. I mean, the need for female companionship. It is very difficult here in Kelowna. Where do you meet anyone? In university that wasn't a problem, of course."

"In the city, it wouldn't be either," Ludmilla said. "But this is such a conservative, family-oriented area. You know, I told you I hadn't met anyone I'd consider dating but I actually went so far as to answer a personal ad in the newspaper."

"You did?"

"Well you needn't seem so astonished. He said he was fifty, financially independent well-travelled, adventurous, and interested in culture. He turned out be closer to sixty, his travels consisted of numerous vacations in Hawaii and Mexico where he had time-shares; all his adventures were, evidently, in the stock market and, as for his notion of culture, I didn't discover what that was unless eating in a Vietnamese restaurant qualifies. That's where he took me. He did have some money, I suppose. After dinner, he suggested going to Sergeant Flaherty's. You know the place? Across from the city buildings? It was filled with jocks and loud rock and roll. He'd made it seem like a spontaneous idea but all his friends were there, and they were expecting him and the 'young babe' he was out with. He bragged about playing hockey when he was a young man, boasted of his prowess on the market and, by inference, with women, and complained about his ex-wives."

"What happened, Ludmilla?"

"You mean did I sleep with him?"

"Oh, no. I wasn't prying. I meant..."

"I told him I had to leave. He asked if I wanted to go someplace quiet. I said, Yes. Home. Alone. He suggested I invite him in for a nightcap. When I declined, he tried to paw me there in the car. I struggled free and he told me I must be frigid or a 'lessy.' That's the word he used. I'm neither, by the way."

It would be engraved on his mind, the way she looked at him when she said that, her lips about to meet the rim of the tall glass filled with red liquid and ice. Her expression neither coy nor suggestive, rather like an animal who expected her prey to put up no resistance. Colin was confused by the implications of that look.

At dusk, they moved outside to dine. They talked about their schooling. Ludmilla referred to her romantic history. There had been one boy in particular. This was at Strasbourg. He was a philosophy student. They'd run off to Paris and sit at cafes; there were croissant flakes in the bed in a small left bank hotel. Colin, while at the University of Saskatchewan, had gone steady with Laurel who wanted to be a nurse.

They talked about music. Rather, Ludmilla talked about music. When she said she abhorred — the word she used — rock and roll, Colin said he agreed with her. Then he saw himself, should she come to his place, rushing ahead of her to make sure his Bare Naked Ladies album and his Bruce Springsteen album were out of sight. He hoped she wouldn't come to his place. It was so messy. And how would he explain to her that he had a Springsteen album — albums not CDs or even tapes — but didn't like Springsteen; that back at school, way back in freshman year, his friends had said he had to have 'Born to Run,' a classic of the times, they'd called it. Adding that Colin ought to loosen up. Nearly ten years later, returning home to Saskatoon before starting his job at Valley View, his seventeen year old cousin, Ian gave him a going away present, a CD by someone called Kylie Minogue, "A real hottie," he'd called her. "She ought to warm you up."

Ludmilla was going on about contemporary English composers. Colin didn't know anything about the subject. To be honest, music was not very important to him.

She talked. He listened, nodded, added a word, now and again, mostly in agreement. In the moonlight, they could see fish jumping. In place of candles, lighted wicks floated in oil in rounded glasses, the flames illuminating their faces from below, the affect somewhere between ghastly and funny. Ludmilla reminded him of an Eastern European comic book witch. He thought of her as the proprietress of a dank castle in the Carpathians, having any lovers that failed her thrown into the dungeon, and he began to giggle.

"You're laughing. So you've heard that relentless piece, eh? I know some people think Gavin Bryars is funny but…"

"No, no. I wasn't laughing at that."

"Is it the alcohol?"

"No. I'm perfectly sober. I've only had three drinks."

She studied him, said, "Good, then let's order a bottle of wine. Shall we?"

And without waiting for an answer, she summoned the server, a blonde girl who was probably a windsurfer by day. She had perfect white teeth, a deep tan and a nameplate that read: "Hi, I'm Megan."

At ten-thirty, having finished their meal and split the bill, at the bottom of which Megan had drawn a happy face, Ludmilla suggested that, since they'd had a fair amount to drink, enough anyway to fail the breathalyzer, that they take a cab to her place which was only a couple of kilometres away. Colin felt quite the man of the world, telephoning and giving the dispatcher the strange number and street name.

The feeling could not be sustained during the short cab ride as he sat close to Ludmilla in the backseat, the slight but uncontrollable trembling in his legs. He moved them away from hers. He considered the aptness of the old expression about butterflies in the stomach.

She lived in Tillinghast Mews, a compact, mock Tudor arrangement of duplex apartments. Hers was an upstairs two-bedroom, and strangely impersonal. The extra bedroom was converted to an office. The desk was an arborite top on stainless steel legs holding the computer and printer. There was a scanner on a smaller table, also of arborite and stainless steel. Ikea bookshelves. A drawing of a whale in an aluminum frame. Did she care about whales? The noncommital carpet extended throughout the entire apartment. In the living room were two sling back chairs and a gray two-seater sofa as if she anticipated three visitors some evening. There was a television, DVD player and compact sound system. Colin noted all this while Ludmilla was in the washroom. She came out wearing a robe, her legs and feet bare. Her toes were thick but shapely. She'd put on fresh lipstick, a dark maroon colour.

Ludmilla went into the kitchen and turned on the harsh overhead light. There were no dishes in the sink, not even a cup with traces of the morning coffee. Nothing on the counters except a coffee bean grinder and a toaster. She poured them each a healthy portion of brandy and handed Colin a snifter. He recalled the rounded glasses holding the floating candles back at El Dorado. She turned off the light and walked away, through the livingroom and into another room. Colin thought it had to be her bedroom. Not sure what to do, he was waiting by the living room window, looking at the stuccoed side of the next building, when she called to him, "Col-lin!"

Ludmilla had the bed covers turned down and was lying on her side on dark green sheets in her bathrobe that had separated enough for him to see more of her legs, how white and strong they were. Large but not thick. "Don't be shy, Colin. Get undressed and join me."

She said it so matter-of-factly, she might just as well be telling him there were three new seniors on his caseload. There were no longer butterflies in his stomach; instead he felt like he was going to be sick, and he definitely needed to pee. "I'll be right back."

"Colin, do you have condoms?"

"Uh, no." He'd never thought about it. "No, I don't."

So this is how the evening ends, he said to himself, in a frustrating stalemate.

"Look on the right hand side in the medicine cabinet, bottom shelf."

He peed, careful to hit the sides above the waterline; wanted to vomit but didn't because Ludmilla would hear him. There was an unopened package of condoms. He took two out, thought about putting one on now but decided it would look foolish, him walking out like that.

Ludmilla had turned off the bedside lamp, for which he was grateful. When he had removed his clothes, he took the condom out and started rolling it on. He'd read that forty-five seconds was the average time it took a man to put on a condom. How did they figure that? It took him longer because he began it the wrong way. Now he had the lubricant on the head of his penis and on his fingers. He wiped his fingers across his hip and got into bed Ludmilla had removed her robe. She was so tall and solid, white like a flash of magnesium in the dark room.

She reached out a hand, her fingers, long, maroon nail polish. "Ah, you're ready. No, Colin. Please. Don't kiss me on the lips. Thank you. Yes, touch me there if you wish but eventually you'll have to, I need you to, well, the only way I can obtain satisfaction is orally. Yes. And please wait for me to finish before entering me."

He did as he was told. Followed her instructions.

"No, not directly on it, it's too sensitive that way. Uh. Around the edge. Yes. But not too far away from it." Colin, his head down there, thought he might be listening to an instructional tape. "That's it. Yes, that's it. Uh huh. Around and around the edge. Good."

Ludmilla was not possessed of the kind of legs that could easily be manoeuvred for his convenience — couldn't just fling them around any which way. She had put them where she wanted them and that is where they were going to stay. Her thighs became scratchy, halfway up. Probably had to shave them every day. Ludmilla had a sort of neutral smell. Neither pleasant nor unpleasant. Antiseptic. Sort of like her kitchen. The words 'sui generis' came into his mind and he wanted to laugh and, in stifling it, his lips made a sound like a discreet raspberry.

Ludmilla offered no endearments; there were no passionate exclamations, no growls, helpless murmurs. Except for the occasional "uh" she was quiet until the end when "uh"s came more rapidly, ending in a longer one, "uuuhhhhh."

When the note died away, she reached for his shoulders, indicating that it was time for him to do as he wished. Colin got in position, knew it wouldn't last long. The condom was slippery on him, the lubricant having gotten inside. Ludmilla didn't make any movement with her hips, just lay motionless until he finished. And when he had, she was still for only a few seconds before rising onto her elbows and twisting her hips, signaling him to get off.

Ludmilla took a sip from her snifter and went into the bathroom. He heard the water running, the toilet flushing. Five minutes later, it was his turn. He wrapped the condom in toilet paper but didn't know what to do next. If he dropped it in the waste paper basket, she might see it later, maybe tomorrow, and be disgusted. It might stop up the plumbing if he tried flushing it down the toilet. So he brought it out of the bathroom with him and bent to put it into the pocket of his slacks on the floor.

They stretched out on the bed and Ludmilla talked about work. He thought of the people at Valley View. He thought of some of them doing it, having sex. What was their sex life like? Or what had it been like? Here he was, just having had sex with a woman who'd be desired by most men, and he was not elated — relieved, but certainly not elated. Is that the way it was for most people? What sex life did Dr. Corrington have? Ms. Dickson? Did everyone just talk about it so much, make a big thing about wanting it and about doing it, in order to make up for the disappointment no one dared admit? Mr. Murray'd had a sex life. Even Dotty Detweiler. And old Anna Dupree who seemed obsessed by memories of it. All those men she'd talked about. Probably had sex with dashing movie stars. Did they lay back afterwards with a snifter of brandy, feeling melancholy?

And Ludmilla wanted to do it again. Or, more accurately, wanted it done to her once more. And Colin was obligated to oblige. This time, down there, there wasn't even novelty. It was work. When it was Colin's turn, he had barely finished when Ludmilla began to snore. Not loudly. What he thought of as small, female snores. She was out, and never moved the whole time Colin lay there wide-awake.

He lay there until dawn had its first peek in the window, then dressed, left Ludmilla a note saying he couldn't sleep. He walked back to the restaurant parking lot — exhausted by the time he got there — admonishing himself all the way. You've just spent the night with a beautiful woman — well, a very attractive woman. You had sex with her twice. You're only twenty-eight years old, you're salary is nearly double your age. Lighten up, for god's sake.

*T*he events of that weekend would remain indistinct in his memory. Colin was aware at the time of everything seeming somehow remote, as if he wasn't connected to anything — life moving at a regular pace while he was in slow motion.

Colin worried about how he would get along with Ludmilla at work. But, come Monday, she gave no indication, other than a single smile of particular recognition, that anything had occurred between them. He was amazed that she could remain so self-contained, even for the few minutes during that week when they found themselves alone.

On Thursday, however, Ludmilla said, "Colin, I must tell you, I'm pleased that you haven't exaggerated what happened between us. I feared that you might be constantly hovering about, touching, whispering, leaving me notes. Acting foolish. But you're not a silly boy, I'm glad to find. We're both adults with needs. If you like, we could meet again. Say, next weekend? The one after this one. I'm off now to consult. Do think about it."

At first he was offended by her audacity, her thinking he might be sentimental or inclined to leave her sappy love notes. What conceit. For a moment, he imagined telling her the lovemaking had been boring. But she might have responded by chiding him for being romantic about a simple biological need.

An hour later he reverted to being detached, even flattering himself, if only for a moment, that such is the way an experienced man of the world feels in such circumstances.

Another week. The same people to consult with. Feeble or falsely active, holed up in their rooms or relentlessly pacing the corridors, sitting alone and staring out windows, waiting by the locked cafeteria doors half an hour before meal time, forming groups by the mailboxes half an hour before the absolute earliest time the postman had ever arrived; boasting of petty achievements in the past, excoriating the past, lamenting the past, crying over dead spouses, dead children, dead pets; the past, the past, the past; at ten a.m. dressed up and seated in the lobby for a one p.m. visitor.

The job soon became routine for Colin who'd had hopes of daily insights into the condition of aging, of care for the elderly, insights that would surely lead him to revolutionary theories expressed in papers commanding the attention of the care-giving community. He'd be quoted wherever gerontology was discussed, academic journals would solicit his writings, he'd be invited to seminars and conferences at home and abroad.

But it had turned out to be routine, save for the visits with Anna who increasingly seemed to him a kind of freak of nature. She'd gone to sleep young and beautiful, awakened a withered old woman. No, no, there must be some mistake; mirror, mirror, let me just go back to sleep for I must find the way out of this bad, bad dream. Only from her was Colin learning anything about aging or, rather, about living. What precisely that was, he had no idea — but if anyone could supplement his book knowledge, it was Anna Dupree.

Already he realized the particular drawback of his job, the constant reminder of decay. Fortunate to survive accidents and disease, one's reward is to wind up with the spoon trembling between the oatmeal bowl and the quivering lips. In school, there had been all that nonsense about the dignity of aging or, rather, of reaching the golden years where one could reflect on life's bounty. Bullshit. Old age is...

"Old age is a desert of time," Anna Dupree was saying from her seat on the residents' terrace, while looking toward the brown hills that descended to the town and the highway. "That's exactly how I thought of it when I was living down there, an unwanted guest in my daughter's home. You have a barren, dried-up landscape to traverse before falling off the edge of the world into bleak nothingness. There are no oases in the desert of time, just thorns and scorpions. And an unquenchable thirst. For *me* there is an unquenchable thirst; I don't know about the rest of them. Do they long for anything but the past? That would be the true hell, not to thirst. It is what keeps me going. I want a drink, but I want it out there. I want out of this place. I'm going to make my break, Doc — Don't say it; I know you're not a doctor — like Paul Muni in a prison picture, dragging my chains through the desert, the swamp — what's the difference? — pursued by baying hounds. I'm Marlene Dietrich at the end of Morocco, carrying her high heels as she sets off across the dunes, going after Gary Cooper, her man. Mark my words, young man, this joint won't hold me."

She had said that last sentence in a jocular, teasing manner that only emphasized her frustration. Colin made no comment. There was no getting out of Valley View unless a relative appeared to assume control. They couldn't just call a taxi. If a resident managed to get past the front desk staff and circumvent the secret access code that controlled the unbreakable glass doors to the outside — the access code was changed three times a day at the beginning of each shift — yes, if a resident managed to do this and get past the outside security guards and not be noticed on video screens monitered 24 hours a day in Security Headquarters, he or she still would not, could not, get very far. It was four kilometres to the nearest house, ten kilometres to the Strip. You could count on the fingers of one hand, the number of residents capable of walking four kilometres under the best of conditions, let alone ten kilometres, and certainly not in the summer when the temperature was above thirty degrees every day, occassionally over forty; certainly not in winter when it was always below freezing, often ten or twenty below.

But Colin did not remind her of any of this. Let her have her illusions, if she genuinely entertained them; maybe they were all that kept her going.

"Toward the end of my sentence at my daughter's home, they tried to confine me to the house in order to keep me out of what they called 'trouble.' I'd dress up, something chic, don't you know. I had an old moth-eaten cape from some picture, a black beret, the cheapest of jewelry — I long ago sold all the good stuff — maybe a satin blouse, or a silk one with the fewest stains. I had silk stockings with runs. Always have abhorred pantyhose. So, dressed to the nines for my big walk downtown, I strode right along Bernard Avenue through the tee-shirt slobs and the cows in polyester. I'd raised my hems an inch or two just to irk them. '*At her age, skirts above her knees. She should be ashamed of herself.*' Hell's bells, I *always* had good legs, great

Mistinguett legs — still do, as long as they're veiled by stockings. So, past the old men loitering by the newsstand, past the mini mall, the restaurants, the bingo place on the corner filled with harridans whiling away the time until the next charter bus to Reno, and across the supermarket parking lot to the library.

"The old bags who worked there fervently noted my entrance, eager for me to turn my back so they could snigger and whisper. 'Old bag,' I said — the eldest bag was fifteen years my junior. But old is a state of mind. 'Oh, lord; here's the nutty old fruitcake. What'll it be now, how waste our time today? Oriental rugs or famous dogs in history? Why isn't she down on Bernard playing bingo with others her age? Or taking a computer course designed for the brittle finger set?'

"So I told them what I was after. 'Oh, it is deserts now, is it dear?' I hated that 'dear.' One bitch was particularly condescending. 'Thinking of going to live in the desert, are you dear?' — 'I'm already living in a desert, madam,' I told her. 'A desert of the spirit, a desert of the soul.'

"And so I studied deserts, and discovered a lot goes on out there. The desert is its own complex world. There is a gallimaufry of living things. Besides the rattlers and other snakes, you have kangaroo rats, scorpions, of course; all manner of birds and, at night, the coyotes make their music. And the marvellous plant life. Do you know desert plants have wide, shallow roots in order to suck up as much moisture as possible? As well, they have glossy leaves to retain moisture and toxic roots to keep other plants at a distance. Ah, yes, I learned that the desert is actually very rich."

"That must have helped you."

"The hell it did. It was just a dull metaphor, the desert. Old age is not a metaphor, it is a pain in the goddamned ass, and a pain everywhere else, too."

"Ms. Dupree, I wonder if you would mind telling me how you came to be living with your daughter. She…"

"Did she tell you about my trips to Tamale Town?"

"Well, no. I mean there's nothing in the files…"

"You make for a poor dissembler, Mr. Childs. It does not become you. Stay as honest and naïve as you genuinely are."

"I'm not…I'm interested in…"

"You're interested in knowing about how I came to be picked up by the police at Tamale Town. At least, you want to hear my side of it. There is no mystery. The bitch — that's my daughter — called the police one time when I went 'missing,' as she called it. And later told you folks at Valley View that I had gotten lost. I was missing from nothing but the stultifying life at her and her husband's ranch house. I wasn't lost. I knew exactly where I was. My private booth at Tamale Town. I had been originally attracted to the place because of the big neon green cactus out front. Do you know it? Out on 97? Somewhere in the vicinity of Lumberland and Reptile World, or is it closer to Door World and Garden City? What it really is is Inanityville. That big, green tin-and-neon saguaro cactus sticking up there appealed to me, given my desert penchant. I used to go there, read my books, try to start conversations, and spin a yarn at the slightest hint of encouragement. And that makes me daft? Well, if one is of malicious temperament, one could make it sound that way, and the bitch did just that. 'My crazy mother went to Tamale Town and thinks she ran away to Arizona. She sat there reading about scorpions and bored the staff to tears with tales of movies she was probably never in anyway. She needs to be put away in a Home. For her own good.'"

As recounted in Colin's file, the incident did not much resemble Anna's version. It showed a foul-mouthed senior citizen causing a scene, hollering at anyone in earshot and being belligerent with the police. But, to be fair, who could the information have come from but the daughter? The police report, a copy of which Colin had in the file, merely stated that they located an elderly woman, who had been reported missing, at Tamale Town where she was engaged in conversation with an El Salvadorean bus boy, and, that upon being taken into custody, said elderly woman insisted vigorously that she had done nothing wrong, had caused no harm, was bothering no one.

"Ms. Dupree, last week you were going to tell me about the second time your husband hit you."

Anna leaned forward in her chair, smiled coyly, ducked her head and raised her shoulders, glanced left and glanced right, and in a stage whisper, said, "There's no one around. You can call me Anna."

"Oh, Ms. Dupree, I couldn't; I shouldn't do that. As I have told you. You see, there has to be the same policy for all. Some residents would resent being put on a first name basis. There needs to be a consistent policy. A whole host of complications might…"

"That's quite all right. Do not worry your handsome head about it."

Anna settled back in the chair. It had a hard, straight back as did all the chairs on the terrace. They looked incongruous, formal; but had there been deck chairs most of the residents would never have been able to get out of them, assuming they could have gotten into them.

"You probably know all about why my husband hit me. Or, at least, your reports contain my daughter's side of it, though she was eight at the time it happened. What she related to you was, therefore, my husband's side of it.

"You know, I have no hesitation in admitting that I never loved my own daughter. I don't even believe I have ever liked her much. Perhaps as an infant, maybe as a toddler. But from the very beginning, almost from the moment they brought her to me at Toronto Western, I thought she wasn't mine. Not like there was a mix up in the maternity ward, like they used to say there had been with Clark Gable. No, it is as if a malicious trickster-spirit used my womb to convey her into the world. Laura. My husband chose the name. Not that she is some horribly evil person. She is merely mean-spirited, spiteful and narrow-minded in a thoroughly banal way. I must say, though, she found her Mr. Right. Indeed. They are meant for each other, two peas in the proverbial or, rather, provincial pod. They do things together which is increasingly rare in a marriage. One thing they did together is form a neighborhood Vigilante Committee. The good citizens take turns driving through the streets of insipid tract houses with their cellular phones, vigilantly on guard against anything out of the ordinary, probably praying to God — their God: some white fellow, the world's greatest salesman, don't you know, in an off-the-rack suit behind a celestial desk — praying, as I say, that they find some native person or other dusky type lurking about so they can shoot him or her."

"Really, Ms. Dupree. Aren't you being a little harsh?"

"Not by half. They still believe in communist bogey men, and they are convinced the people of Quebec have no other goal in life than to force their kids to learn French in concentration camps. The kids. Kyle and Morgan. I feel sorry for the little twerps. Unless someone or something rescues them, one will grow up like the mother, the other like the father. Either is as unfortunate as it probably is, alas, inevitable."

"About your husband hitting you…"

"Yes, I know I don't sound very nice going on like that. No doubt, I am lowering myself in your opinion but I made my mind up a long time ago to be honest. What is there to lose at my age? He hit me because I was fooling around on him. He thought it was with just a couple of men in the previous couple of years. Little did he know and little of it did I tell him. There were several, a dozen or more, over several years. My daughter when she reached her teenage years began to call me, and never tired of calling me, a tramp. Well, there it is. But it was my only release, the only way I had of proving to myself that I was indeed alive. I had, much to my surprise, gotten pregnant, with Laura. And there went my vague hopes of doing anything in the show biz line. There went my hopes for a few years, anyway. Then, when Laura was four years old, my ambitions were rekindled. What the hell was there for me to do all day? The kid began nursery school. We lived in an apartment that I could have cleaned top to bottom in a couple of hours even if we didn't have a maid who spent an entire day there every week. But it was not as if I ran right out the door the moment my daughter left for preschool and into the arms of the first thing with something dangling between his legs. I told Andy I wanted to get back into the theatre but he put his foot down, like he had done before. Went absolutely bonkers this time. No wife of his was going to tread the boards. I tried to reason with him. What did it matter? His reputation might be hurt? What? He would not even let me take a regular job. I married him to get away from being a cocktail waitress and there I was, six years later, wishing I could be one again.

"And what did you do to occupy yourself?"

"I'd get my daughter off to school. I'd mope around the apartment. I'd go shopping. Andy said, 'How can you be bored, go shopping.' I told him I hated shopping. He laughed, 'All women love shopping.' What the hell did he know about women? So I walked around. I looked in windows. I stopped for coffee. I noticed young men give me the eye occasionally. I did nothing about those looks for at least a year. I shopped, read, took care of the little girl, made fancy dinners even when we didn't have guests. Not that my captain of industry, my big butter and egg man, appreciated them. But I didn't do it for him.

"The first one was not much past his twentieth birthday. I was walking along, feeling desolate, crossing the square out front of City Hall. There was this young man, tall, broad-shouldered, broken-nosed but bohemian looking. He was hawking newspapers, of all things. He and some friends had published what they called an underground newspaper. I took one look at him and thought, 'Well enough of this misery.' Went up to him, and said, 'I'll take one of those.'

"Just laid the big eyes on him and that was all it took. I must say I was proud of myself, that I could still do that. He was less than half my age, as I indicated. We talked for all of five minutes. I must have been giving off the scent pretty strongly because he'd picked right up on it. Me, I could feel the sexual tension so thick in the air, it would take a machete to cut it. 'Let's go, honey,' I said. And off we went. Back to his room, his pad.

"It had been seven years, at least, since before I was married, that I'd had a decent roll in the hay. The first time with the young man, it didn't take me more than a minute and a half to reach my climax. I'm sorry, if you feel I'm being offensive, please tell me."

"No, no. Keep on."

Colin wondered how things would be if Ludmilla was like this.

"We began, that young man and me, to meet every couple of days. I told him, 'Honey, I got a lot of time to make up for.' And didn't we just. I couldn't get enough and neither could he. I must have run him ragged, poor thing. He had a little sweetheart somewhere. I hope he had something left for her. I used to tease him. How is it with her? 'Nothing like with you,' he'd say. I had to be discreet and so did he. So it was our big secret. We couldn't show each other off. I'll never forget one time we did it outdoors in broad daylight in the middle of summer on that strip of land between the Royal Ontario Museum and the Conservatory. Did I say something about being discreet? A pleasant spot, it was; grassy banks, some trees. We were behind a bank, under a tree, right below a conservatory window but shielded from view by an ivy-covered trellis."

Colin was uncomfortable hearing this. Uncomfortable in a way he could not explain to himself. So, to cover up, he asked her how long it went on.

"That time? Oh, about four and a half minutes."

"No, I mean…"

"I know what you meant. Six weeks. Then he went off to the west coast with some others in an old jalopy. The last time we were together, we both knew it was the last time, I put everything I had into it, threw every trick in the book at him, and when we were done and set to go our separate ways, I said to him, 'Tell me the truth. Was I a good fuck?' He said, 'Gee, Anna. You're the best and second isn't even close.' — 'Honey there is something you should know,' says I, solemnly. 'What's that?' he asked with a trace of trepidation, wondering maybe if I had a disease. Was my husband in the mafia. I said, 'I'm the best you are *ever* going to have.'

"Oh, it was the devil in me made me tell him that! And tell you that too, Mr. Childs. I wonder where he is now. His age has doubled and more. I like to think he's bragged about me in some bar somewhere. 'That's nothing, boyo, the best I ever had was…'"

In an instant, Anna's expression changed. Gone was the smirk of self-indulgence and haughty pride. Colin saw her deflate before his eyes. A corner of her mouth twisted in bitter, self-mockery. 'Yeah, the best I ever had must be seventy years old, at least; she's in an old age home in Kelowna.'"

Her face collapsed again and she stared before her at the low concrete wall. Anna didn't move. Not a muscle. She didn't blink. Colin had been carried along by her stories, had for a moment, here and there, glimpsed her as a much younger woman. Not even as she might have been when she met the young man but even earlier, seeing her as a beautiful woman in her thirties. Now he stared in horrible fascination at the funny-haired little woman with the big dark eyes before him. Oh, my God. Is she dead? Catatonic? But, no, Anna returned briefly from where she'd gone, to say, "That's enough for now."

She took no notice of Colin getting up and walking away.

*C*olin spent the weekend studying, and left the apartment only to drive to the shopping centre. At the video store, he tried to recall the name of the movie Anna had talked about appearing in. He walked up and down the Classics row, and stopped before one called 'East of Eden.' He picked up the box and read the synopsis but that wasn't the one. Anna's had been set in Britain. Colin was almost glad he couldn't remember the title because if the movie was available, he might discover that she wasn't in the thing at all or that she was some extra in a crowd scene, and would not only feel disappointed in her, he'd be embarrassed when they met again.

The next week, Colin was so busy he hardly had time to think of her. There were only two distinct occasions when she crossed his mind for more than a moment. One was on Monday while he was lecturing to a second-year sociology class at Okanagan College. He spoke about the importance of trying to imagine how the elderly actually felt, their every movement impeded. He asked for volunteers, a male and a female. He taped the young man's wrists to the desk; gave the woman ten pound packs for each arm, secured there by velcro straps, and ten pound packs for each ankle, asked her to walk about the classroom, write on the blackboard, close the blinds. One of Colin's professors had done all this, and Colin thought it was a good way to instill empathy. Colin heard himself mouthing Professor Lindsay's homily, "Empathy is a great gift, and one that each of us should strive to develop."

As if that was all it took to stop from being impatient when some old fogey was inching down the hallway, blocking one's way, or was taking an interminable amount of time to extract, with crooked trembling fingers, thirty-seven cents from her change purse while you waited behind her in the checkout line.

Colin felt like a phony. He knew others in the class would want to have their wrists taped and move around with weights. It was sort of like a party trick. What if you were old yet light as a feather, moved like a dancer but had nowhere to dance? What if you burned to live but were trapped, the fire consuming you?

The thought distracted him, but Colin snapped back to attention as the host teacher congratulated him "for giving us all something to think about," and invited questions from the students. The thought returned while he was crossing the parking lot but didn't survive the drive to Valley View.

There was plenty to do up on the hill. Two new residents had been added to his caseload. Mr. Hartley and Ms. Orloff. But by Thursday Mr. Hartley was gone from Valley View; by Friday morning he was dead.

Mr. Hartley had been one of those nondescript, standard issue old men you never really notice. At least not individually. Medium height, thickening through the middle but you couldn't call them fat; not much hair but you wouldn't say they were bald. They never wore dark colours or bright colours, just whites, creams, tans, pastels. When he first showed up at the man's room, Colin methodically began searching for some individual characteristic of Mr. Hartley's. He had trained himself to do this. Concentrate and observe. He had file cards, 3 by 5's, on the backs, the unlined sides, of which he wrote two or three word reminders to himself. Touchstones. He'd come across the technique in an old textbook on institutional administration, and found it to be quite helpful. He also liked the low-tech aspect of it. Colin was shy about sticking them to his terminal or pinning them on his office bulletin board, so he kept the cards scotch-taped to the inside walls of his desk drawers. This way he was constantly surprised and, thus, reminded anew upon seeing them. Concentrate...Focus...Always Appear Interested.

He concentrated. Hartley was pink. Colin focused. Hartley's face was actually pink and there were freckles on his forehead. His fingers were also freckled and long or, at least, seemed long because the bones on the backs of his hands, from wrists to knuckles, were so prominent. He drummed those fingers constantly.

Hartley flicked the tip of his tongue repeatedly across his bottom lip. He wore brand new white running shoes with velco fasteners, which made Colin think of his experiment at the college the day before. When Hartley paused in his finger-drumming long enough to emphasize a point, by shaking his fist, Colin saw his hand tremble and realized why he didn't have lace-ups.

"I see you looking at my shoes. Nice, eh? My son bought them for me on Saturday, my last day at my own place. He told me I needed a new pair of shoes for my new home."

Colin, trying to appear interested, said that, yes, they were very nice; asked Mr. Hartley how he felt about leaving his own place.

"I'm a realist. That was always my guiding principle during my working life. Look at things realistically. The final straw was the cheque book. I wrote all the cheques. Forty-seven years I was married, and my wife, she's been gone since '98, never had to write a cheque. Never. I never let her. A couple of weeks ago, the lady from Meals on Wheels was there. I had to give her the monthly cheque, and she looked at it, looked at me, said, 'I'm really sorry, George but we could never get this cashed. It's, well, it is really illegible.'

"I tell you I blew my stack at the poor woman. Nothing wrong with the cheque, signature perfectly legible, maybe you need glasses — that kind of thing. She took it and left but they called my son who came over. Had the cheque with him. He held it up before me. So I looked at it realistically. It was just crooked lines and scratches. That was it. See, I had Meals on Wheels and someone to clean house for me, and a nice young lady stopped by to see if I was okay and did I need anything. The only thing I was doing for myself, or thought I could do for myself, was write the cheques. It was my anchor. Now that's gone. Let somebody else write the cheques. I wrote enough of them in my life."

Mr. Hartley died three days later, on Activity Night. The skinny man with the big Adam's apple in the striped shirt and boater was singing barbershop quartet favourites. Colin had auditioned him. He was right in the middle of 'A Surrey With the Fringe on Top' when Mr. Hartley stood as if to do a little soft shoe shuffle. He lifted one arm and fell right across fat Mrs. Lorimer's lap. She shrieked, pushed at his head in horror, tried to stand, and shrieked louder when she couldn't. Mr. Hartley fell to the floor.

The emergency squad got him out of the performance room within seconds and administered to him in the lobby until the ambulance arrived. All the commotion put an end to the show but the residents didn't complain about that. What they did complain about was that they were made to stay in the Performance Room. It was quite a job, keeping control of them, Ludmilla at one door holding them back, Colin at the other, and Corrington at the microphone speaking in soothing, old-money tones. The residents did not like missing the arrival of the paramedics and the departure of Mr. Hartley. They wanted the dramatic, visual testament that they were still alive and keeping on.

In the midst of the confusion, the lead crooner of old barbership quartet favourites approached Colin who was at that moment trying to reason with a knot of ladies while, simultaneously, Mrs. Lorimer recounted her ghastly experience to him yet another time, and the man firmly demanded assurance that he and his pals would receive the full fee even though they had only gotten to do two and a half numbers.

Hartley died in Kelowna General early Friday morning.

Colin heard the news from Ms. Dickson when he got in at nine. By ten, when he left the office, he was able to discern an obvious buoyancy among the residents, people he'd never seen talk with one another were chatting away like old friends. There was even light in the eyes of the most sullen of chair sitters; well, in the eyes of many of them anyway. Before going to visit his other new resident, Ms. Orloff, he remarked to Ludmilla, "They're in particularly good spirits today. Is there anything special slated? There're no bus trips or visitors that I can recall."

"Come on, Mr. Childs."

"What?"

"You can be slow at times. They're celebrating, in their way. We should issue skull masks every time it happens. Have our own Dia de las Muertas. Day of the dead."

It was a long moment before he understood, "Oh, yes. I see. Of course."

"By the way, Mr. Childs. How about tonight? You might just come directly to my apartment. There really is no point in going through any preliminary charade."

"Yes, of course."

Colin pictured the residents dancing around the dayroom in skull masks, maybe brandishing scythes. Then he pictured him and

Ludmilla with scythes and skull masks in the bedroom.

It wasn't like him to think like that, in those sort of unusual images. His stomach was queasy.

"Are you all right, Mr. Childs?"

"Yes, certainly. I'm fine, Dr. Drushka."

"Eight o'clock, then?"

"Eight o'clock."

Colin was distracted the entire time he was with Ms. Orloff. They met at the end of her hall, at the juncture where the hall continued on to the left. The juncture was rounded and just wide enough for three chairs and a coffee table. Colin was put in mind of the wooden construction set he had as a kid, putting dowels into the holes around the circumference of a round disc. These areas were supposedly for the convenience of residents who had difficulty getting around, and Ms. Orloff was one of them. Most officials, Colin included, wondered why they were rarely used. He'd see these old people surrounded by their aluminum walkers struggling along the corridors.

Here came Ms. Orloff in her walker, a little lady with short, tightly curled, smoke-coloured hair, wearing a purple sweat suit. On her feet were a pair of flat-soled Chinese slippers.

Ms. Orloff told him how she came to be at Valley View but he only half-listened, aware all the time that he should Focus... Concentrate...Observe; yet he wasn't doing much of any one.

She was saying something about housework. Her daughter coming in, doing the cleaning and dusting when she, Ms. Orloff, was no longer capable. Colin's stomach bothered him. He thought of these people dying off one by one. Ms. Orloff saying how angry she'd get because her daughter didn't do a good job. Ms. Orloff sitting at the kitchen table frowning while the daughter rushed around, also frowning. Ms. Orloff noticing the crumbs her daughter didn't get up off the table though they should have been obvious, she must have seen them. The water left standing on the countertop by the sink. Once a week, the daughter ran a vacuum through the living room and the former dining room that had been converted to Ms. Orloff's bedroom so she wouldn't have to battle the stairs. The daughter never moving even the lightest chair or end table. Week after week, Ms. Orloff watched dust accumulate and expand like ink blots.

"I always kept a spotless home," Ms. Orloff told Colin. "I was proud of that, no one could ever find fault with my housework."

So there she'd been, not able to clean house for herself and getting furious with her daughter for not doing it properly. "By the time she left, I'd be nearly sick with rage. Of course, I knew she didn't want to be there doing it; she has her own work to do and her kids to raise. So it made us both angry. Finally, I couldn't take it anymore and made my own arrangements to come here."

Colin told her, aware of his effort to sound sincere, that he hoped she would enjoy her stay at Valley View, enjoy being relieved of those anxiety-ridden situations; said we're all a community here, don't hesitate to contact me, and he bade Ms. Orloff goodbye. Left her sitting there beside her walker.

He went directly to the cafeteria and got a glass of milk and a big chocolate chip cookie, wondering why he had hunger pangs only two hours after eating a substantial lunch. Chewing his cookie, swigging milk, he made a few notes about Ms. Orloff. Questioned whether he had been as cursory with her as the daughter had been with the housework. Answered himself that the daughter had put in more effort. Enjoy her stay here? Had he really put it like that? It is not something one looked back on and determined if it had been enjoyable or not. In all but the rarest cases — so rare he hadn't yet learned of an example — one did not get the chance for any hindsight assessment. After Valley View there was intensive care or death. One did not improve one's situation. Colin hadn't even heard gossip concerning white knights or generous relatives appearing from out of nowhere to get the ancient out of there.

Colin reached his apartment at six and was at Ludmilla's by eight. They talked and had a drink and were in bed by eight-twenty. Things weren't much different than the first time except that he wasn't nervous, and he'd brought his own condoms. Ludmilla was not one for variety and, in between times, was not given to intimate pillow talk. There was one moment when he was down near the foot of the bed that he thought she might have been sculpted by some genius in the Renaissance. There was another moment when it was his turn that he realized what he was doing was 'labouring' over her and not getting any help. She was indeed like a statue, Colin concluded, and showed just about the same amount of movement.

When he got dressed to leave at ten-thirty, Ludmilla said good-bye as if they'd been having a business meeting. Driving home, Colin felt it might as well have been business.

Monday morning, Colin had to stop at a travel agency to make arrangements for an outing, and didn't get to Valley View until nearly eleven. Ms. Dickson greeted him with a cup of coffee and his messages. He thought again about how she certainly didn't look sixty, or act it. Short, vivacious, hair obviously coloured but cut in bangs across her forehead. He wasn't good at guessing ages but Ms. Dickson, now and again mentioned a son and a daughter, and one of them was over thirty. She was divorced. Went on dates. Men phoned her at work. Yes, Colin said to himself, as she sat at her desk and crossed her legs, a fine figure. He remembered mentioning her to Ludmilla, who'd grunted, said, "It is amazing what can be achieved with a nip, a tuck and a little liposuction."

He wondered.

He was still staring at Ms. Dickson when she turned in her swivel chair, smiled when she saw him looking as if she expected him to be, and said, "I almost forgot, Ms. Dupree called this morning; said to tell you her feelings are hurt you haven't been in touch."

Colin muttered awkwardly, and Ms. Dickson winked, "You're becoming mighty popular with the ladies around here."

He took that to mean his relationship with Ludmilla was not a secret.

"You're blushing."

The phone rang and Ms. Dickson answered it before Colin could defend himself.

*C*olin made his excuses, feeling guilty for not having seen her, aware that this giving of explanations was not professional. Aware that he wouldn't have explained himself to any of the others. Telling her that besides his caseload and routine chores and obligations, there had been a talk to the Okanagan College class, as well as a bus trip to arrange. Added to all that was the disruption caused by poor Mr. Hartley dying. He was uncomfortable mentioning Mr. Hartley, didn't think it was right to allude to death.

"Death is the big topic in here," she said. Colin thinking she was reading his mind again. "Among us it is, anyway. The residents. Not on your side of the fence, of course. It is not real to someone your age. And don't give me any nonsense to the contrary. I know it wasn't real to me when I was your age."

"It is a fact of life. For everyone."

She fixed those big eyes on him.

"Oh, *really*? I'll just pretend you didn't say that. Anyway, it certainly wasn't real to me until I was about sixty. Always, in the back of my mind, I kind of had the notion they might make an exception in my case."

"From your stories, I certainly get the idea you've lead a full life."

"Uh huh. I've travelled each and every highway. The byways, side roads and every goddamned cul de sac, too."

"I mean, you've lived more than most in here."

"Than *most*? Honey, I have known the high life and the low life. Sure I have acted in movies and on the stage, I've sung and danced, but I never thought of it as my art. At the risk of sounding utterly pretentious, I believe my life was my art. Sorry, but it really is true. Unfortunately, I was born a hundred years too late so I never got a big enough stage upon which to strut my stuff. With any luck I would have been born in 1829 instead of 1929. I would have been Lola Montez. 1729 would have been even better; I could then have slept with Casanova. But Anna Dupree has had her hour. Or her fifty-four minutes. I regret the way it seems the last six will be spent."

"You should feel satisfied to have done as much as you've done." To himself revising it: Or say you've done.

"Not in the least, young man. It is no consolation. No matter how extravagantly one has lived, no matter how gaudy the life has been, when you're approaching the end of it, when you're at the fifty-fourth minute, so it speak, it all seems so pathetic and flimsy.

"But I don't wish to go down that road on a beautiful day such as this is."

"Then perhaps, you might continue where we left off. Your, uh, affair with the young man, your husband hitting you the second time."

"It was not because he found out about that affair, the first affair, that he hit me. That came later. But, don't worry, I'm not going to give you a day to day, week by week, account of those couple of years. To be succinct — not my strong suit, succinctness — there were other men."

She jumped right into it, telling him about the other affairs. She started at precisely the point where she'd left off at the last session. Having studied the file, Colin was not prepared for this mental sharpness. He had been lead to believe that her mind wandered, that she had troubled with continuity, was terribly forgetful. Maybe his predecessor hadn't understood anything about her, Anna's perspective or her rhythm. Maybe the compiler of the file had never met anyone remotely like her and, having no precedent, inferred she was beset with an early stage of Alzheimer's Disease. Of course, he himself had never met anyone like her but he had empathy; or so he told himself.

Anna's husband apparently hit her when he found a man's phone number on a matchbook in her handbag.

"Pretty banal, eh? He'd become suspicious, you see. Had been for quite some time. Andy marched into the bedroom, seven o'clock of an evening in May, just home from the office, holding before him, between pudgy thumb and forefinger, and up by his manly chin, a matchbook from the Pilot Tavern. 'What's this!' shouteth Andy Anderson, and wouldn't stop shouting long enough for me to answer.

He grabbed me by the shoulders and shook, shook, shook. 'I will answer you,' I said — it came out all tremulous, 'when you stop acting like a Corgi with a rag doll!'

"'It is, it is a man's name and telephone number,' says he, a veritable Sherlock Holmes. 'Are you seeing him, sleeping with him? Have you been sneaking around behind my back, you whore?'

"'No to the first two and yes to the third,' I told him.

"This took him aback, as one might say. And he demanded a 'straight answer.' 'I haven't been seeing that man nor have I been sleeping with him,' I said. 'I intend, however, to sleep with him, as, I admit, I have slept with others.'

"Well, biff! bam! And boom! I got the old Andy Anderson one-two-three. The first punch backed me against the wall, the second set me on the floor and the third, a back hander, was evidently, for good measure. There he was standing above me raving, red-faced, fists clenched. Blood is pouring from my mouth, my nose is broken, but not directly from his punch; my rapid plummet floorwards was interrupted by the brass cross piece at the foot of the bed. My nose made its acquaintance. It is true what they say about seeing stars. When I stopped seeing them, everything was blurry. It was like looking through a shower curtain. I was determined to stand up. I was not going to let this captain of industry defeat me. I was prepared for him to hit me as much as he wished, but I would not be vanquished. I let him rant while I collected myself, as it were. Then he stopped screaming and started taking in great gulps of air. Thinking his anger had subsided, I rose to my feet using the brass rail to help me. Alas, seeing me upright set him off again. 'Slut. Whore. Tramp. No good bitch!' The usual. He then grabbed me by the throat — the throat, mind — and began to strangle me. I gasped, thinking: I have only two or three seconds. I'll black out then and I'll die. So I brought my knee up as hard as I could and got him between the legs. You may recall I have advocated this technique; well, I would preach only what I have practiced. No sooner was he bellowing than I reached for the lamp on the dresser, swung it like an axe and got him across the back of the head with the base of it. Unfortunately, this is when our daughter chose to walk in. In my peripheral vision — and emblazoned on my memory — she is there in the doorway, open-mouthed as I am bringing the lamp down on his head. So precious little Laura sees her frenzied, wild woman mother clubbing her dear father, the poor victim, who is already crouched in fear and obvious pain.

"Out he went. Me, I was nearly there, down on hands and knees. But I did manage to tell Laura to phone for an ambulance, spitting teeth and blood as I gave her the number. It turned out, Andy was unconscious for only a few minutes. Laura was a self-assured little girl though only eight at the time. I can still hear her at the phone in the hallway, dialing the number, requesting an ambulance, giving street address, apartment number, family name. Then there was a pause, obviously she was listening to the dispatcher's question. 'Daddy's been hurt,' she said, finally. 'He's on the floor...No...No, he's not moving...My mother beat him up...Goodbye.'

"So they arrived, prepared to deal with a fellow on the verge of dying only to find a man sitting on a dining room chair with his hands caressing his privates. Were it not for the police who showed up at the same time to investigate a possible homicide, I would have had to call a taxi to get to the hospital. I was in the kitchen with an icepack to my face. While waiting for the ambulance, I'd had the presence of mind to take Polaroids of my face. One never knows.

"I was a week in the hospital. Beside the broken nose, for the first two days, my eyes were swollen shut. They made a deft inch and a half slit in my throat to get a peek at my trachea."

"Did you press charges?"

"Press charges? Are you kidding? It was still the 1970's. The only time the subject came up was when one of the inspectors told me he supposed I didn't want to press charges; very messy situation, family dispute, what would be the benefit: — all that. Well, I didn't. I just wanted out."

"Out of the hospital?"

"Out of the situation, the marriage."

"Did you separate, divorce?"

"I was married to the poor man until the day he died. Except for one stop to pack my suitcase, I never was in that apartment again. A divorce would, indeed, have been messy. But he did try to get those photographs from me, even as I lay in the hospital.

"He actually said that he would forgive me and we could try and make another go of it. But I despised him, despised myself even more for selling out my life. As shoddy as it may have been, it wasn't as shoddy as what I had got in exchange. I settled cheap, too. To get it all over with. I didn't want to see him even one more time, see his lawyers, watch him put on his pathetic, important businessman show, having me to an office where I would, presumably, be intimidated by the solemnity of the petty power he was capable of wielding. So, he got the little girl; I got a measly three hundred dollars per month, deposited directly to a bank account. For life. His life. He lived another five years. Died of a heart attack in the back seat of a taxi while on his way to a retirement party for the vice-president of a forestry corporation. My daughter was raised by Andy's niece, his sister's daughter. I didn't see Laura for twenty years."

"What was it like being out on your own again? You were no longer…"

"Young? Hell, I was holding on to late-middle age as tightly as I could. I may have been too old for the job market but I was also too old to get pregnant. I had my three hundred per which meant I wasn't able to live high off the hog but it paid the rent when I had rent to pay. Also, speaking of practical matters, the entire nine years we were together, I managed to pinch five or so bucks a week from the grocery money, and put it aside. Yes, Andy Anderson used to keep an eye on it, balance those grocery books. When at first I chided him, he replied it was such things that made him such a success. Anyway, five or so, call it six, bucks a week times 52 times nine."

"And what did you do?"

"I did, my dear, what any self-respecting, newly freed woman nearly fifty years old should do."

"What's that?"

"I went to Paris."

"Oh."

"But that's another story."

"For next time?"

"If you're a good boy." She winked at him. "But, before you go, tell me. This bus tour you've arranged?"

"Yes. It is to Yuallum. You know the Indian Reserve, or Reservation, as they call it over the line. For bingo."

"Over the line? You mean the border? Washington State?"

"Yes. An all-day trip. If there is enough interest, it will become a monthly thing."

"Well sign me up."

"You? You mean, you want to go with the others to play bingo?"

Colin knew she had no friends in Valley View except for Dottie Detweiler. Anna kept to herself, didn't take part in activities.

"Colin — oh, excuse me — Mr. Childs. The truth is, I've been thinking, I should socialize more and I just *love* bingo."

It was a few minutes before noon when Colin left Anna and went directly to the employee's cafeteria. He didn't usually have lunch until 12:30 but today he was incredibly hungry. Actually, Colin realized, he seemed to be incredibly hungry quite a bit lately. He had hamburger steak with fries, coleslaw, a glass of milk, a cinnamon bun for dessert and two cops of coffee with cream. He read the Globe and Mail. He tried to picture Anna Dupree playing bingo in Yuallum. He made a few notes for his next lecture at the college. He glanced at his appointment book.

Only an hour later, while listening to Mr. Shellenbarger tell, yet another time, the story of his son putting him in Valley View against his will, Colin was distracted by images of food. Mr. Shellenbarger's son, who was a "spineless jellyfish with no backbone of his own," had been provoked into his drastic action by that "conniving bitch he married." Colin felt a sharp pain in the vicinity of his navel. They'd told Shellenbarger, he'd be better off in the Home, someone to care for him, someone always there if he needed anything, good meals in "a caring environment." And, oh, yes, by the way, might as well sign these papers, his son had said then. They give me power of attorney, this way I won't have to come running to you when the house sells or Valley View requires a cheque. And this one here makes me executor of the estate should the worst happen. Shellenbarger could picture the wife at his son's side, giving him the elbow, whispering, telling her husband: don't forget to make him blah, blah, blah…Colin felt he could eat lunch all over again.

What he did was eat another cinnamon bun and drink a glass of milk, the cafeteria lady saying, "You back again?"

The pain retreated.

The next morning, after his first consultation, back in the office, leafing through his messages, standing there in front of his desk, suit jacket opened, Ms. Dickson handed him a report she'd just put through the printer and patted him lightly on the stomach. "Is that a bit of a belly, I see?"

Colin blushed and instinctively sucked in his stomach.

"That won't help," Ms. Dickson said. "You ever think of jogging?"

"Never."

But that night Colin did think about taking a walk. The night after that he did take one. Dressed in old khakis, long sleeve shirt and runners, he went out at dusk. After a couple of blocks he noticed people in cars staring at him. Later, two Mounties slowed and passed and did a U turn for another look. Colin realized he must indeed be a curious sight, a walker. Nobody walked in Kelowna. There were joggers in some neighbourhoods but no walkers. He imagined the people in those cars discussing him. 'What's he doing? He doesn't look like a B & E artist. Well, then, why is he walking if he's not some kind of criminal? Ah, maybe he's a nut. Yeah, must be some kind of nut.'

Colin started to jog. After ten strides he stopped, he was sweating under his collar, had a pain in his side.

When Colin got back home, he was starving. There were a few slices of whole wheat bread in the cupboard — he knew the white stuff was no good for you — and he spread peanut butter on them.

He woke in the middle of the night with pains in his stomach, tried telling himself it had something to do with the jogging but he knew he was just fooling himself.

Colin thought of consulting with Dr. Corrington, who was a medical doctor, but if something was wrong with him, he didn't want it to get around Valley View. So the next morning, he went through the yellow pages, picked a Dr. Joel Hickey.

The office was on the third floor of a building on the highway, separated by two parking lots from the library where Anna had gone to read about deserts and — what else? Famous dogs in history. There *were* famous dogs in history? On the table in the waiting room was a Time magazine, a Maclean's, a real estate brochure and a pamphlet, titled: 'Common Sense and Family Values.' On the cover were eight people from three generations: a little girl, a little boy, parents and both sets of grandparents; they were all tanned and had perfect white teeth and their clothes looked sanitized; they were standing on a perfect green lawn.

Colin was glancing at the real estate flyer when Dr. Joel Hickey opened the door and smiled, bidding him rise and enter the office. Dr. Hickey was a young guy, mid-thirties, who could have been the husband on the cover of the pamphlet.

Dr. Hickey patted the top of the examining table, "Hop up here."

What Colin did was not so much hop, as lift his right leg, get his rear end on the table and pull the rest of himself up by pressing down on the leather mat with the palms of his hands. He needed a couple of deep breaths when he was finished. The doctor consulted the screen on his computer, then came to stand in front of Colin. Starched white lab coat, dry-cleaned, button-down pinstriped shirt. Colin felt childish, his legs dangling.

Colin told him the problem. Dr. Hickey inquired into his medical history, Colin thinking he had just read it on the screen. Kind of like him talking to his people at the Home.

Dr. Hickey took his blood pressure, asked him about his diet, exercise habits, job stresses.

Dr. Hickey nodded, then went into an adjoining room. Colin heard what sounded like a spoon hitting the sides of a cup or glass. Maybe Dr. Joel Hickey was making them each a cup of coffee or a glass of iced tea. But, no; he came out holding a beaker of cloudy liquid, handed it to Colin. "Just drink this down."

When Colin had done so, Dr. Hickey told him to open his mouth. He stepped closer and put his nose practically in Colin's mouth. Colin hearing him sniffing.

"Ah, I smell the unmistakable smell of H. pylori.

"See, these things aren't caused by stress and bad diet like we used to think, though they don't help those who've got them."

"Got what?"

"Duodenal ulcers. Usually they occur in middle-aged men but it is not really such a rare thing in men your age. We could do a barium, if you want. A barium ex-ray. But I'm certain it is a duodenal ulcer you have. I assume you know what that is, eh?"

Dr. Hickey didn't wait for an answer. Told Colin how the stomach was like a cauldron, all those peptins and acids, hydrocholoric acid, for heaven's sake, an orgy of seething enzymes and fiery gastric juices. "In a sense the stomach wants to digest itself. And when the balances aren't maintained that is exactly what occurs. And this is what is called — da dum — an ulcer."

Colin pictured a witch standing over a big black iron pot. He had a hard time with the part about the stomach digesting itself.

"Any blood in your stool? Mixed in with it? Dark tarry blood? Stool comes out looking, the blood mixed with it, sort of in a barber pole effect?"

"No. None of that."

The idea was horrifying.

"Good. Of course, it would have been better if you had come to see me earlier. Much earlier. But at least you didn't wait until you were in severe pain. You'll have to watch your diet, start getting some exercise. You could stand to lose thirty, even forty pounds. You'd never miss it. But don't go overboard. Lose it gradually; don't want to shock your system. I'll prescribe something to cut down the gastric secretions. Also, I recommend a full physical. Your blood pressure's higher than I'd like it to be. I'll put you down for next week if that's all right. But, really, I think you need a break from the stress of your job. A long break. Not just a two week vacation."

"But I've only been at Valley View a few months."

"You have to make your own decision. This kind of ulcer can be managed. As long as we've caught it in time and you adhere to the rules, that is. And take your medicine. If not — bad trouble. I just hope we did get it early enough."

Dr. Hickey wrote out a prescription and walked Colin to the waiting room. "This is for an H2-blocker called famotidine."

After shaking hands and patting him on the back, Dr. Hickey picked a real estate brochure from the table, "Please take this. I saw you were interested."

"I was just looking at it before."

"I've put this development together with another doctor. Orchard Estates, we call it. Fifty townhouses, each with an orchard view. Good clean air up there on the ridge. Nine-hole golf course practically at your doorstep. Just the kind of lifestyle for you, Colin. Shoot a round, sit on your patio and watch the cherries blossom. Look at the lake, try to spot Ogopogo. Give you a good pre-construction price. Think about it."

That evening, Colin drove to the athletic field at Okanagan College and took a walk around the track. He did that three nights in a row, missed one, came back another night and then had to leave for a conference in Vancouver. He took his medicine and watched his diet, and lost four pounds that first week, and that made him feel good. Good enough that in Vancouver when he went out for dinner with a few colleagues, he figured it was all right to loosen the reins. They went to a Vietnamese place near the hotel on Denman Street. Later, he wasn't sure what set him off, the weird shrimp and noodles dish or the incredibly spicy soup. Talk about a bubbling cauldron. When he started feeling nauseous, Colin asked the waiter for milk or ice cream and the guy said, "No, have. No have this kind thing."

His companions asked him, teasingly, if he'd ever been to a Vietnamese restaurant before, or what? Colin made an effort to grin, hoping they'd think he was just eccentric. But when they walked up Robson Street and came upon the ice cream place, with a five-foot high, black and white cow out front on the sidewalk, Colin went in there and came out with a double-dip cone.

The next day, with the conference concluded, and with a couple hours free before heading to the airport, he made up for his indiscretion by walking to English Bay and along to Sunset Beach. It was late September but there were still people lying on blankets on the sand. One fellow in a skimpy pair of trunks with a towel around his neck, stepped off the sand and onto the walkway in front of Colin. The man, in his forties, gave him a big friendly smile. Colin was surprised and smiled back, awkwardly.

"May I buy you a drink?" the man asked.

Colin couldn't believe what he'd heard. He just stared at the man.

"Well, what do you say? I'm clean."

"Uh, no. No. Of course not."

Colin hurried on. To his back the man said, his voice mildly taunting, "Oh, come on. You hesitated. Admit it. You were thinking about it. Who'll ever know back home. Live a little, why don't you?"

Colin was irritated at the man's presumption. He almost made a reply but thought better of it. He returned to the hotel by another route.

Back at Valley View on Monday morning, Dr. Corrington was filling him in on the big bingo trip to Yuallum across the line. "Quite a success. There were no medical incidents and a good time was had by all."

"Anna Dupree told me she was going. Did she really? She doesn't seem the type."

"She was fairly subdued until we got to the border crossing. Below Osoyoos, eh? Sitting in the back with Ms. Detweiler. I was a bit worried about Ms. Detweiler. At the bingo palace, she kept shouting out every couple of minutes or so, Detweiler did, 'Bingo!' My lord. We had to take her gently out of there. 'Bingo!' At lunch, she didn't eat, just stuffed her handbag and pockets with packets of sugar and vinegar. But she, and we, came through the ordeal relatively unscathed, as they say."

"And Ms. Dupree?"

"Came alive at the border. Chatted up the officials there. Made them laugh. But, back on the bus, she stayed quiet, Kept to herself. Didn't appear too enthusiastic about the bingo aspect of the trip. She played but in a rather desultory manner. Walked around quite a bit, looking at this and that. She became a bit testy later on when I wouldn't allow her to buy a drink. On the return trip she was a bit lippy. She and the Detweiler woman laughing in the back. I think they gave the other people a difficult time whenever one of them went back to use the can. I was up front though so I didn't hear what was said."

*O*ctober came around, an Okanagan Valley golden autumn when hills glow under lapis lazuli skies. Despite the burnished warmth of the season, people were melancholy knowing it wouldn't last and raw November was just around the corner.

Colin didn't notice the beauty of it and was never melancholy, being too busy, busier even than usual. There were, he learned, always a spate of new residents admitted each Autumn. There'd be no shuffleboard or terrace sitting for months and that meant more indoor activity, more people to audition for performances. He never even noticed.

But Anna did, sitting outside for hours, wrapped in a shawl or sitting by the picture windows, enveloped in the mood of it. Colin had only seen her once, briefly, in the entire month since his conference in Vancouver. Now there she was over by the window that faced in the direction of town, legs crossed, hem at her knee, wearing a beret, no less. He couldn't avoid her; indeed, he wanted to speak with her, even though he had a consultation scheduled.

"Like your beret."

She smiled at him and turned back to the window. "It's in honour of the bittersweet memories I have been entertaining these last couple of days. October is my favourite month."

"But what does October have to do with a beret?"

"Everything. Don't you remember I told you that I left Andy Anderson and went to Paris? It was in October, you silly goose."

"Well, pardon me."

"You dear, dear boy."

"What did you do there?"

"I sang on the streets."

"You sang on the streets? In English?"

"Yes, and of course not. I was walking down rue Bernardins of a Sunday morning, having just been to the street market, on rue Mouffetard, and there in the little park at rue des Ecoles, where they have a statue of Francois Villon — can you imagine such a thing happening in North America? Erecting a statue of poet who was a thief and a murderer? You've read 'Ballad of the Hanged Men'? Do you know Francois Villon?"

"No."

"Then, of course, you saw the movie 'Petrified Forest,' Bette Davis. Her dad owns the petrol station-diner in the middle of nowhere, and she's all dreamy, reading Francois Villon. Meanwhile the football lout is sniffing around her. Then — Allo! — comes Leslie Howard, that archetype of a certain kind of young English aesthete. Never mind that he was Hungarian. On shank's mare. He notices the book. Bette calls the poet Frankus Vi-lun. Which he was, and, ironically, that's how his last name would have been pronounced in his own day. Next, gangster Humphrey Bogart and his gang show up. Duke Mantee — Francois Villon."

"I'm sorry."

"Sorry they showed up?"

"No, that I don't know the movie, either."

"You should be. Anyway, right outside the iron fence near the statue, three kids were playing music. Accordion, guitar and the girl on the mandolin. It was early October and they were doing 'La Vie en Rose.' A real song. Not like something that young fellow with the bird's nest hair sang at Activity Night, last week. Tell me, what does it mean? 'Been in the desert on a horse with no name'?'"

"I, uh, I don't know."

"Nor should you. It doesn't mean anything. It is vacuous nonsense trying to pass as mysterious. Now, 'Been in the desert on a horse with no mane' that would be interesting, or, even better, 'Been in the desert on a Norse with no name.' Or, better still, 'Been in the desert *under* a Norse with no name.'

"Anyway, dried little leaves like crabs scuttled across the ancient pavement. I stood rooted to the spot watching them and, assuming I was a tourist, the guitar player nudged the upturned hat forward with one scuffed winkle-picker. I noticed there were three pathetic coins in there. So I stepped forward but didn't put anything in the hat. Instead,

I began to sing.

"And didn't those kids look at me with wonder. And wouldn't you know, while I was singing — I just couldn't stop — a lady walking her dachshund, a wire-haired one, by the way, dropped a five franc note into the hat.

"The song over, I thanked them and was about to leave when the accordion player, Paul, the leader too, it turned out, asked me how I came to know that song. I told him I had a million of em. He says, 'Oh, yeah? How about 'Fais-Moi Valser?' And he smirked, the first time I saw that look which was to become so familiar. I says, 'Just give me my key, mec.'"

"Do you actually mean to tell me that at, at your age, you began singing on the streets? Singing on the streets of Paris?"

Colin was going to be late for his appointment but he had to ask, adding, "That took, it took real courage."

"And at least a soupcon of talent, as well. We busked for a year. Parisian street songs, music hall stuff. Aznavour, Trenet. I memorized the entire Mistinguett song book; might as well have since I already had her legs. Left Bank, Right Bank, the Metro. In the winter we went down to Nice. It was a good year."

"After which you returned to Canada? To England?"

"I eventually did return to Canada, of course; as you can see. But I delayed it for fifteen years."

"Fifteen years?"

"I was working."

"Working?"

"Yes, working in the theatre, my darling little echo. There were good parts for old or aging ladies in Europe, continental Europe. At first, they had to make me look older. Later, well…A few movies. Even a couple of spaghetti westerns. They had a fake wild west town on the plains outside of Madrid. In one I was the madam of a brothel in Deadwood. Smoked a stogie, had a gun in my garter. Of course, all my lines were dubbed…"

Colin glanced at his watch as responsibility tussled with curiosity inside him, and responsibility won out. "I'd really like to hear all about it and about your bingo trip but I have to go. Oh, yes, what was the title of the movie you told me about, the one set in London during the Second World War? You and the hero were in love…"

"'Eaton Place.' Now be off with you. People will begin to talk."

She laughed and Colin replied with a polite chuckle and, by way of farewell, said, "You know I never would have figured you for a bingo player."

Anna smiled, "I'm not."

*L*ate Friday afternoon, work done, Colin drove to the shopping centre, bought his groceries for the week, and would have forgotten the video store if he hadn't noticed the new sign in the window. A big orange '3' is what caught his eye. Weekend Special. Any 3 movies — new releases not included — for just fifty cents more than the price of one movie. He went in there, to the Classic section, and found 'Eaton Place.' He was surprised that it actually existed. Thinking he would see Anna Dupree as a young woman gave him a curious feeling, a little thrill of anticipation. But her name wasn't on the box. The cover displayed a photograph of the original lobby card, a drawing of a handsome man with an RAF moustache, his profile and that of a beautiful young woman — in the background, sketches of fighter planes, bombed-out buildings, a stately old mansion. On the back, it gave the name of the director, Darwin Read, and the names of the stars: Robert Rainer and Heather Rutledge, and somebody called D. Austen Smythe. Well, thought Colin, they can't list everyone's name and Anna never claimed to be one of the leads.

He grabbed two more movies, modern ones, knowing he wouldn't get a chance to watch all of them but it was only fifty cents more. Not that he'd be seeing any of them tonight. He had his twice-monthly date with Ludmilla.

Back at the apartment, Colin fixed dinner, debated with himself about going for his walk. There was time, — four and a half minutes to drive to the track, four and a half back. Twenty minutes for walking, plus a few minutes for a shower. He'd easily be able to get to Ludmilla's by eight. On the other hand, why be anxious about it? Dr. Joel Hickey had said that being free of stress was as important as taking his medicine.

Colin sat on the couch, turned on the tv news and looked through the newspaper.

He had the first twinge of pain when he was in Ludmilla's wash-room rolling the condom on. It wasn't bad though and he told him-self it was just gas. When he was on the bed, down where he usually was, it hit again, not sharp at first but later it was as if someone stuck a pin in through his navel. He was going around clockwise with the tip of his tongue, the ways she wanted it, when the pain got bigger, like a knife now, and it stayed there in his abdomen. The pain caused him to stop what he was doing, Ludmilla saying, "Don't stop now, Colin. I'm not finished."

He was on his stomach, lower legs off the bed, body flat out but he wanted to curl up into a ball. Even as the pain tore through him, Colin was aware of the heat from the inside of Ludmilla's thighs, her impersonal smell. There was less time between "uh's" now. The knife was hot, splitting him apart. Colin thinking, "Get it over with, for god's sake."

She did. Colin hurried to the washroom and went down on his knees, arms around the toilet bowl. But he couldn't be sick, just hugged the cool porcelain and gasped for breath, suddenly scared. He didn't know what was going to happen, didn't know if the pain would ever stop. Ludmilla called him but he couldn't answer.

In a few minutes, the pain vanished. The intensity didn't slacken or fade gradually, it was just gone. Still, Colin waited, afraid that mov-ing would start it all again. Finally, he loosened his grip on the toilet bowl and got to his feet. He was cold. The condom hanging down off his penis. Ludmilla rapped on the door, "Are you ill?"

He opened the door.

' "What's the trouble, Colin?"

"Don't feel good. Sorry. Stomach pain."

"Were you sick?" Ludmilla looked past him. "Did you clean up?"

"I wasn't sick."

"Are you coming back to bed?"

"No, I don't feel so great."

"Then you should go home."

"Yes, I'll go home."

Ludmilla lay on the bed, back propped up by pillows, looking through some reports while Colin put on his clothes. She was com-pletely naked, the bottom edge of the papers bisecting her thick, black pubic hair.

Driving home, there was no pain. Colin went over the last scene, Ludmilla telling him goodbye. Not, Goodbye, hope you feel better soon. But, Goodbye. He was thinking of himself down there when the pain had really begun. Her legs. Saw the pubic hair, the white paper. The nausea rushed at him. All at once so sick he had to jam on the brakes, throw it into 'P,'open the door. Barely got the seatbelt unfastened and lunged a few feet away from the car before vomiting right there on the asphalt in the middle of Johnson Street. When he was done, he looked around — nobody about, just little houses in a double line, lights on in living rooms.

Back at his apartment, Colin didn't want to get into bed; it was still early and he was almost afraid of falling asleep. He got partly undressed, down to his underwear and socks and dragged the comforter into the living room. After inserting a video into the machine, Colin lay back on the sofa, feet on the coffee table, comforter around him. He didn't put in Anna's film but, instead, one about a man and woman his age who spend a lot of money on a big house, start fixing it up and rent out the first floor to help with the mortgage. But they chose the wrong tenant. Colin gave up on it after forty-five minutes, the main characters were too privileged to elicit his sympathy and, in fact, he found himself rooting for the mad tenant, hoping he'd chase them off and secure title to their stodgy gingerbread monstrosity.

He got a dish of vanilla ice cream and turned off the lights, curled up again on the sofa, started Anna's movie.

There were Robert Rainer and Heather Rutledge riding across fields on big beautiful horses. They get off alongside a hedgerow and she removes her riding cap, shakes her hair free and she's very beautiful in a wholesome way. Rainer looks at her with adoration.

In the manor on another evening, a fire blazing, their bootheels on the hearth, and there's D. Austen Smythe who's about six and a half feet tall and has thick eyebrows. Heather's father. He offers a toast to victory in the war which will interrupt the wedding plans but there is nothing to be done about it.

Robert goes off to war. He's a flyer, his mates all like and respect him. He's ready to take any dangerous mission. But soon come the maddening bureaucratic manoeuvres that wreck havoc and lead to the death of his best buddy, played by David Bleven. Robert himself is wounded. There are terrible days and, especially, nights in the hospital. But, finally, he is well enough to go on convalescent leave. All this time, Colin has been watching closely for Anna, paying attention to the extras, thinking, all right, she exaggerated her part, never suspected he would actually seek out the film. Colin expected her to be, at most, one of the nurses in the hospital, but, no, twenty minutes into the film, and no Anna.

Rainer gets off the train at Victoria Station, goes into a pub, orders a whiskey. He's raising the glass to his lips, and there she is. There is Anna Dupree. Colin recognizes her despite everything, despite the medium shot and the five intervening decades. It is unmistakably her. Rainer stops the glass at his lips and looks stunned. Quickly knocks back the whiskey to cover up his reaction. There's her face, the screen full of it now, big dark eyes, cheekbones like they'd been stuck on as an afterthought, the lips insinuating, and exactly the same hairdo as she affected now.

Was she beautiful? Colin asked himself. Not what is generally considered beautiful, not like Heather Rutledge. But, then, what did the word signify anyway? Beautiful. What was it Anna had told him she once possessed? An indefinable something. No name or word for it yet it made itself felt to him from out of a twenty-four inch screen across half a century.

Rainer is hooked. They proceed to have an affair, the intimate details merely hinted at in those old movies, and it was better that way, everything left to the imagination. You know they're having their tryst at his town house on Eaton Place but you're spared the camera inching over their bodies, spared the groans and gasps. Anna may not have been classically beautiful but she was just the type for whom a man would throw away everything. Everything except what could not be thrown away, the realities of class. Or, so, at least, Rainer is made to believe by the presence of his family, and by Heather Rutledge and her father.

And here's the scene Anna had told him about: the misty pavement in London, the street lamps extinguished because of the threat of an air raid, but still the night-time street is in chiaroscuro when Rainer tells Anna what must be. "You're just going to end it?" she replies. "You are never going to see me again?" Her face full screen again, in soft focus as to herself she acknowledges the truth of it; lips glistening, eyes glistening and starting to fill with tears as she turns abruptly and walks away, her heels clicking on the wet pavement. Colin sees her trim legs. Earlier there was the great, sexy scene when Anna showed Rainer how the girls drew an eyeliner pencil from the heel to the back of the knee, to make it appear they were wearing real seamed stockings.

So she's walking away from him, the skirt tight — she's heart-broken but making the heroic effort to be gone with dignity. Step by step; you know she's trying to make it to the corner, half a block a way, around the corner before breaking down. Rainer watches after her, eyes filled with longing and uncertainty.

Soon enough, the further devastation of the war and subsequent upheaval of values, causes Rainer to rethink everything. After all he's gone through, he wonders if he can be happy in the life that is laid out before him. Married to Heather, servants at Eaton Place, weekends at the country house where there are more servants, children, ponies, lawn parties, riding to hounds. No, it won't do. Rainer sees the terrible mistake and goes to Anna's part of London, finds her street, finds her doorway, but the doorway stands there amid rubble — the house and the houses on either side, gone. The old rag picker lady tells him everyone was killed. Yes, the pretty young woman, too.

The movie ends with Robert returning to Eaton Place after a day tending to business in the City. The butler takes his coat, and three little kids rush to greet him in the foyer, calling, "Daddy! Daddy!" Heather Rutledge is in the drawing room, smiling; she's chic and radiant. She hands him a whiskey. He stands by the fireplace and stares into the flames.

The tears in Colin's eyes had begun when Robert Rainer told her it was finished, and he saw Anna's face full screen, the way her expression registered the hurt. The sob just came out of him before there was time to think about stifling it. And his eyes filled again when Rainer went to look for her. Rainer standing in the rubble from the bombs. Colin unsure whether he was crying because of Anna's character being killed or because he was thinking of her own devastating looks killed off by the years. Consumed by flames of time was the way he thought of it. Rainer staring into the fire. Everything reduced to ashes. Hadn't Anna talked about the fire of life still burning? Burning despite her circumstances, a little flame alight in the most unlikely of places.

And it made him sad seeing her name on the cast list. There were film scholars who no doubt knew all about the rest of them. Rainer and Rutledge, of course, and probably even a couple of the others. But who knew what had become of Anna Dupree?

Colin rewound to the parting scene, played her walk again, her hips, her rear end moving in the tight skirt. Was she rolling her hips just a bit, perhaps to indicate what could possibly become of her? He replayed the part where she runs her finger up the back of her leg, showing Rainer how she drew a seam; she's sitting, her weight on her left hip, the other turned toward him. She stops her finger just above the back of the knee. There's a fadeout.

In those two bits, Anna was far sexier, Colin realized, than Ludmilla was in real life lying on her back with her legs open. But, as the movie rewound to the beginning and he pressed the eject button, Colin chided himself for being naïve. It was the movies. Makeup. Lighting. Magic. Nevertheless, he couldn't deny that the image of Anna had moved him; hell, had stirred him sexually. But, hey. It was from out of the past.

he scare that Dr. Joel Hickey threw into Colin the next afternoon left him more shaken than had the pain. "You want to live to be thirty, you have to make a drastic lifestyle decision. Remove yourself from stress and overwork. Or else. I'm serious. Your body is pleading with you. I told you about how that ulcer is eating through the wall of your stomach. It is working its way as we speak and you're not doing anything to stop it. If it completes its work, you've had it, buddy. Maybe you can get a leave of absence from your job. Take three months off, minimum. If not — quit. I tell you what, I have a condo down in Ixtapa. I'll let you stay there, cheap. You go down there, lie in the sun, take walks on the beach. Look at it this way, it's like, Ixtapa or peritonitis."

By Tuesday, Colin's life had turned completely around. He went to see Dr. Corrington, explained his situation, gave him a letter from Dr. Hickey — feeling like a kid with a note for the principal from his mother (some other kid, not himself, because his father *was* the principal). He expected Corrington to be distantly polite, offer sincere-sounding expressions of sympathy, before explaining that, regrettably, a leave of absence was out of the question; there was the difficulty of finding a qualified replacement willing to work on a temporary basis, the expense of training, etc, etc. Sorry but, ahem, alas... But, no, Corrington told him his leave of absence was effective immediately, and take the two weeks pay. Be off with you, lay in the sun, find a pretty senorita, get well, and come back to us. The doctor winked at him. Colin wondered if Corrington drank. He could have been in the movie the other night, save for the accent. Maybe Rainer's father, presumed dead, or the old air force major that kept a flask of single malt in his greatcoat.

There remained papers to sign and good-byes to make. Ludmilla didn't seem exactly overwrought that he was in poor health and leaving Valley View. She shook his hand, wished him well, and left for a consultation. Colin felt himself dismissed and slotted away; maybe there was a file in her hard drive to which he'd be assigned: "Those Who've Serviced Me."

Ms. Dickson, on the other hand, seemed genuinely distressed by his news. She even recommended a place in Ixtapa that had good food and overlooked the beach, they had these places all over Mexico, she told him, you could depend on the food. Senor Armadillo's. "You'll love Ixtapa. You don't need to speak Spanish and there are plenty of bank machines."

Colin had no desire to see any of his seniors other than Anna. His only regret about leaving Valley View was that he would not be visiting her, might never, would probably never, see her again. Anything could happen in three or four months. She might pass away. The woman was seventy-four or -five, after all.

He phoned her room, explained briefly that he was leaving and wished to say goodbye in person. She said she'd meet him in fifteen minutes in the lobby. Why fifteen minutes? Colin wondered, putting down the phone. It could only take her one minute to walk from her room to the lobby. Add five minutes to get ready, assuming she was in her housecoat or had to use the toilet.

Colin waited in the cafeteria. He hadn't wanted to stay around the office, Ms. Dickson commiserating with him. He had a bowl of yogurt with banana slices, and he fretted, wishing he was downtown buying his airline ticket.

Fifteen minutes. He left the cafeteria but Anna wasn't in the lobby. He sat by the window drumming his fingers on the arms of the chair. Five minutes later, there she was walking toward him, carrying what looked like a photo album. He wondered at it, having last seen her walking away half a century earlier. She was dressed up. Not in high heels like in the movie, but still they weren't flat shoes. She had on a freshly pressed black skirt, stockings and a white silk blouse. If one didn't look above the v of the blouse, didn't look at her hands, she could actually be mistaken for a middle-aged woman. But he did look at the face, the smiles creasing it now, the indigo or black eyes set in their nests of wrinkles. He noticed there was a faint trace of dark blue on her eyelids, her lashes blackened. He felt uncomfortable. She was an old woman. She crossed her legs, placed the album on her knee. He pictured himself asking her to show him how she ran the eyeliner pencil up the back of her leg. Instead, he said, "I saw 'Eaton Place.'"

He expected some commentary on it, self-congratulation or movie gossip. But Anna just smiled faintly, The big eyes on him, did something with the side of her mouth but she didn't speak.

"So, I'm, uh, like I said, going to Mexico. I've, well, I've really enjoyed knowing you. Enjoyed our talks. When I return, I look forward to us continuing…"

"Take me with you."

"What?"

She leaned over the scrapbook, her face six inches from his. Was anyone watching? Colin wondered.

"I said, 'Take me with you.' Take me out of here. Only you can do it."

"Why, whatever are you talking about?" he tried to laugh. "I can't. Why I can't do something like that, what a crazy notion."

"*Why* can't you do it?"

"It is against regulations, for one thing. Against the law. Your family…"

"My family? Haven't you heard a word I've said to you? My family! You mean my daughter who hates me, and I don't care much for her either? Rules, regulations. Who gives a fuck about them? Listen, honey. I'm dying in here. Don't you understand that? Dying. I want to live. I only have a few years left but I want to live them. I won't be any trouble. Just get me out of here. You need not feel any responsibility. Drop me off in the goddamned desert. Better the real one, than this one. I am serious so get that incredulous look off your face. And it won't cost you a cent."

He was stunned. Not only because she was saying it but because he was listening, not rejecting it out of hand, and rejecting it immediately.

Anna opened the scrapbook, and fastened to a page in the middle was a little white envelope that she opened and from which she took a small key. "I will not be a burden. Neither will I be an expense. This is a key to a safety deposit in the Royal Bank in town. I have a few dollars in there, some jewels. Here, I give you the key to go and get the stuff."

He let her put the key in his hand. He stared at it on his palm. "But..."

"Just listen. Be silent and hear me out. Please. This is my only chance. You are my only chance. I have it all figured. Today is Monday, the bingo bus to Yuallum leaves Wednesday. Why do you think I've been going down there? Because I like bingo? My idea was to befriend somebody, an Indian fellow perhaps, bribe him to hustle me out the door and drop me off down the road. Take me to Spokane or any place. They are familiar with my ways down there. I'll just head down the hall to the washroom, same as always. Only this time, this Wednesday, day after tomorrow, it's straight for the back door and you're waiting there in your car in the parking lot. I get in and we're gone. That's it. See, you follow the bus in your car on the way down. Go through customs behind us. You are a normal, respectable young man, they won't bother you. Anyway, you'll have your Valley View identification. Just going to Yuallum to see that everything's okay with the oldsters, the senior citizens with nothing better on their minds than a game of bingo. See, there's nothing to it. Bingo! You with me?"

"Yes, okay."

Colin hearing himself saying it — his voice disconnected from his mind.

Anna looked at him curiously but only nodded. She turned to another page of her scrapbook. There was a sheet of lined notebook paper between two blank pages. "Take it."

"What is it?"

"Look at it later. It is a drawing of the restaurant, the parking lot around back, where to stop the car, all that sort of thing."

"You drew this in advance. You must have been sure of me."

"No. I hoped but I wasn't sure. You see, we have something in common."

"You and me? Why, what could...?"

"We both want to live. We're both trapped."

ACT TWO

he bingo bus pulled into the parking lot on the north side of Carl's Crockpot Cafeteria in Yuallum, Washington at two minutes past noon on Wednesday. At that moment, Colin got behind the wheel of his dark blue Volvo station wagon that was parked in the lot on the south side of the building. He put the key in the ignition, fastened the seat belt and patted his sport jacket over the inside pocket that held a white envelope with $3,400 U.S. from Anna's safety deposit box. Under the driver's seat, wrapped in a paisley scarf, one of Colin's from his university days in Saskatoon, were a few pieces of jewelry that had also been in the box at the Royal Bank. Colin's two suitcases were in the rear behind the back seat. He squeezed the steering wheel and looked to his right, looked to his left, admonished himself for acting like some amateur shoplifter. He rested the newspaper, the Courier, against the steering wheel. I'm just a guy in his car, waiting for the wife, waiting for his mother, waiting for Anna Dupree to help her escape from an old age home.

Everything was just as she'd drawn it on the map. The bus had pulled into the side of the restaurant with the windows. There weren't any windows in back where he was waiting; therefore, Anna wouldn't be in general view as she got into the Volvo. Colin had parked several yards away from the back door, kept open by the weight of a bucket with a mop in it, one of those heavy wringer contraptions — because there was too much foot traffic; people going down the hallway to the washroom could see out the door. Restaurant staff came out to dump garbage or catch a smoke.

Ten after twelve. Any minute now. He glanced over his shoulder. Where is she? He turned back to the newspaper, tried to focus. Local

Crime Problem Imported. Colin read how the mayor claimed transients from Vancouver were bringing drugs, prostitution and various other socials ills over the mountains from the big town on the coast. Why was he reading that at a time like this?

Had something gone wrong? Colin tossed the paper over the seat, drummed his fingers on the steering wheel. He'd had biscuits with what the guy behind the counter — was it Carl, himself? — had called "sausage gravy." They were good. He wondered why biscuits hadn't crossed the border.

The tapping on the window startled him. Police! was the first thing in his mind.

Anna was there. Pointing to the button on the inside of the door. Her eyebrows were raised. He noticed her expression before realizing she was indicating that the damned thing was locked. He had to turn the key to raise the button. She got in as the engine kicked over. She exhaled deeply. Colin muttered "Sorry," and pulled away a little too quickly. He slowed, eased out of the parking lot, away from Carl's Crockpot Cafeteria, headed south.

Neither spoke as they rolled down the rest of the main street. Colin thought how things always looked decrepit in the States. This town typically rundown, unkempt looking. Businesses were boarded up, potholes in the streets. For the last several years it had seemed that way. He didn't go to the States that much but his trips had taken him to different cities in different parts of the country. The travel was always connected to work, conferences mainly. He liked Minneapolis and parts of Portland, but even there, the Canadian delegates were warned not to venture away from the hotel on foot. The American delegates didn't have to be warned. It hadn't been like that when he was a kid. He used to go to Bismarck with his parents, eager in the back seat because America meant shopping and excitement, everything brighter. Newer. Not any more.

His second impression of America was that people were bigger, not taller but that they took up more space. He didn't mean that one hardly saw tanned, lean or muscular types like one did all over Vancouver or Toronto, although that was true too. No, it was that average people were so large, really overweight. And more than overweight, there were so many grossly obese people. He had commented on this one time to Ian Lapham from McMaster University, when they traveled to

Louisiana State University in — what was the place? — Baton Rouge. They were at a table in a restaurant. There were two men at the counter, an empty seat between them but their sides still touched. Colin, looking at the backs of their necks, was reminded of those wrinkly dogs. Colin was advancing his theories about different diets having something to do with the fact that people were fatter in the States. "No," Ian interjected, "It is because they don't get any exercise."

Colin had replied, "So what is it in the national character that makes one group take exercise and not the other?"

"Nothing. There're afraid to go out. They don't walk. You see anybody on the street out there?"

There was no one on the street in Baton Rouge. Or in Yuallum as they passed through. You only saw people in cars, at shopping malls, at fast food franchises.

A little voice in Colin's mind told him he shouldn't be so quick to generalize about national characteristics. He hated it, for instance, when someone just returned from a foreign vacation, said, for instance, "I'll never go to Paris again, the people are so nasty." Or "Yukk! Is it ever dirty down in Mexico."

"What in the world are you thinking about?"

Colin realized he had been so absorbed in his thoughts that he wasn't aware of Anna or even of his driving. How long had he been that way? How many minutes? They were in farm country now.

"Mexico," he answered. "Just wondering about Mexico."

"I take it you've not been to Mexico."

"No. I mean, yes, I've never been there." Or anywhere else much, he added to himself, except for the States. "How long will it take to get there?"

"Depends on where we cross the border."

For a brief second, Colin thought the longer the better, a little afraid of Mexico. Why did he think the States were safer? Maybe, he laughed to himself, I feel safer because I can pass for one of them, being thirty or more pounds overweight.

"If we don't swing east too far, or west, we're probably in line for Mexicali. That would be nice. Rather than aim for Tijuana and have to pass through all that California coastal traffic. Looking at the map, we might as well stay on this road, this Ninety-seven, right down to the border."

"You've been to Mexico often? What are the hotels like? Are the beaches nice?"

"I've been a dozen times, sweetie. But mostly in the old days. Used to go to the racetrack at Tijuana back then. There was a trolley car to Agua Caliente. In my day, the beaches were wonderful. Particularly at Acapulco. This was before the hordes arrived. The sands were golden, really. I went down there one time, if you can believe it, on Levy Arenberg's yacht. Half a dozen of us starlets for decoration. That's where I met John Wayne. Well, I actually met him in Zihuatanejo which is next door, so to speak, to Ixtapa where you're going. Although there was no Ixtapa in those days, and Zihuatanejo was a tiny and quaint little fishing village. God knows what it has become. Wayne, I just cannot call him 'Duke,' had his yacht, and the two parties sailed in tandem from Acapulco up to Zihuatanejo."

"What was he like, John Wayne?"

"You mean, did I...?"

"Oh, no. Nothing like that. I didn't mean..."

"He was nice enough. It was in the early Fifties and he was not much past his prime. Big, handsome. I like my men with a little mystery, however; and he didn't have any. Not many American actors do, or did. Not many American men do, for that matter. Quinn, Anthony Quinn wasn't bad but I never met him. That whole generation of American screen actors, they might not have had mystery but, to give them their due, they were rugged and manly. Burt Lancaster. I liked Lee Marvin. Nowadays, well, they're just too obvious. Flexing their muscles and shooting their guns. Children. Pathetic children. But back to John Wayne. He was terrific in his movies. That is overlooked. But, as for men, the Europeans were more my style. Yves Montand. Charles Boyer. You probably don't know who Conrad Veidt was. But, particularly, Jean Gabin. I always picture him in some narrow gaslight street late at night, butt secure in the corner of his mouth. I am immensely proud to have finally met the man and appeared in a film with him, my last decent role, alas. But not my last movie for I was yet to do those spaghetti westerns. 'La Cave Se Reciffe.' I doubt you've seen it."

"No."

"I didn't think so."

"There's one older actor I used to like."

"And who might that be?"

"Charles Bronson."

"Colin, you are filled with surprises. I'd never have thought it. You know, I was in a picture with him once, as well."

"Really?"

"Indeed. Only he was Buchinsky then. Charlie Buchinsky. 'Pat and Mike,' it was called. Katherine Hepburn and Spencer Tracey. I wanted a part in that so bad but I couldn't even get an audition. So, despite my agent's protests, I worked as an extra. First as a golfer, then as a tennis player. See, she was a star female athlete. Tracey was some kind of sport promoter. I just wanted to watch a great artist like that up close."

"Yes, they say Katherine Hepburn was great."

"I couldn't have cared less about Hepburn, the prune. It was Tracey I wanted to watch."

"Isn't that rather harsh?"

"Perhaps. But so be it. I am at that age where I say exactly what I feel. I believe, actually, that I've always been at that age. I had a terrible time on that picture. If it wasn't one sex bothering me, it was the other, or some third sex. I had some scenes playing tennis with Hepburn. I'm in a little pleated skirt and it was flipping up and down and the crew kept making friendly but risque comments. La Hepburn got her nose out of joint, the nose she always looked down, because, you see, the attention was being diverted from her.

"And then there was the world's champion bull dyke. She made that Romanian tennis player — what's her name? — look like Jean Harlow. She watched me bend over the cup after a putt — silly game — came over to me and growled, 'Honey, I'd go down on you like the marines went down on Tripoli.' Yee Gods!

"I hope you're not embarrassed."

"No."

"Good. You're getting better. But you needn't scrunch up over there against the door. The Mexican sun will take care of your body but I shall supply salty conversation and anecdotes from a ridiculous past to lighten your mind. Don't worry, the laying on of hands, these hands anyway, need not be part of the treatment."

She stopped talking and Colin glanced at her. She was looking out the window. "Alas," she said, as if to the bare fields.

100

"What about Charles Bronson?" Colin asked, after a couple of minutes during which he'd felt uncomfortable. It was so unusual, silence between them. Or, rather, so unusual for Anna not to be talking.

"Oh, Charlie." She seemed to revive, said brightly, "He was a gangster in a broad shouldered, pin-striped suit. Wide cheekbones, he had, and eyes like slits. Kate flipped him with some judo move."

"I mean personally. I heard he wasn't a very friendly person."

"Where did you hear that? Don't tell me you buy supermarket tabloids and keep them in you desk drawer at Valley View. Hidden amongst the patient profiles. I hope you removed them all before you left. Really, I am aghast. Or do you read them after that secretary of yours is finished with them? She's the type."

"No, I don't read supermarket tabloids. I just heard it somewhere. I don't know. On television or something."

"Yes, yes. We are bombarded by trivialities. It is all pervasive, thanks to this totalitarian mass media. People are made to actually care whether or not their favourite soap opera star is cheating on his or her husband or wife. Maybe it is a better world to which I'm bound. Anyway, despite what you may have heard, I found Charlie to be a sweet fellow. Quiet, unaffected. He had an absolutely dreadful childhood. His daddy hired him out to farmers. He was a serf, basically. We swapped stories of bitter upbringing. I hope yours was not so."

"No, it was pretty average."

"Tell me about it. Please do, don't be shy. We have a lot of miles to put in, assuming you're not dumping me by the side of the road today or tomorrow. Didn't you say you grew up on a farm?"

"No, but my dad did. Mom too. My dad told me that as a kid he made a decision to get off the farm as soon as he possibly could."

"Smart daddy you have. And so he did, evidently?"

"Yes, immediately after high school graduation. He worked the summer in a lodge at a lake, and started university in Saskatoon that Fall."

"What did he do for a living?"

"He taught school, high school. Later he became the principal. He still is."

"Still is? He's not retired?"

"No, he's only in his middle fifties."

"My God! Tell me, did you go to the same school at which he was the principal?"

"Yes, and did the kids ever get on me about that."

"I bet. And your mother?"

"They met in university. He was a graduate student and she was in second year."

"So that makes him, what? Three years older?"

"Four, actually."

"My, lord. I suppose, I'm old enough to be your grandmother. I thought I could pass as your mother! Where has my mind been! Fortunately, you look older. When you graduated high school I was already getting into movies at half price. Or, at least, I would have been had there been anything worth seeing. You're still on good terms with them, I'm sure. Do you stay in close touch?"

"Yes. But how come you're sure?"

"I suppose because you seem the type. I mean, you don't strike me as the petty rebellious sort, and I get the feeling they're fine folks so there would be nothing to rebel against, anyway."

"There're like friends as well as parents."

"You are very fortunate. I hope you realize how fortunate. I guess they are pretty upset at you having to take a leave of absence due to ill health."

"I didn't tell them everything. I told them I was leaving Valley View for a time. I don't want them to worry. So what I said was I would be on a sort of sabbatical for study."

They rolled south on 97, across bleak November. It was better when they left the forests and small farms behind and hit the rolling plains that were always bare, and always the wind blew, especially along the broad corridor of the Columbia River which they saw for the first time from the top of Mary Hill. They crossed there on the concrete bridge and got gas at Biggs on the Oregon side.

While Colin tended to the automobile, Anna walked around to the side of the station, shoulders hunched against the chill, and stared back across the canyon. The hills were the colour of dust and bare except for a stone building that looked like an abandoned prison.

She glanced over at Colin who was cleaning the windshield with the squeegee, methodically wiping the rubber runner with a paper towel after every stroke. She watched him lift the wiper arm to get at the bottom of the window under there, frowning as he did so. She shivered, turned away smiling. There was something somehow endearing, his physical awkwardness, something endearing about his pudgy cheeks, pink with cold and exertion. God, she thought, was she feeling motherly? Would that she could have felt that way about her own child.

Anna looked down at the river, roiling white at the middle. She'd seen the sign for Hood River to the west, thought of Capra's 'Meet John Doe,' Walter Brennan saying to Cooper, "Come on, Long John. Let's us head out to the Hood River country." That Capra, he was a master, say what one will to the contrary. All the idiot critics parroting one another, pronouncing his films sentimental Americana. Totally missing the darkness of them, the texture, the levels. Singing the praise of Orson Welles, that pompous egomaniacal show-off. She'd been too young to try out for Capra's best films. But might have landed something in 'A Hole in the Head,' had it not been for her accent.

Before getting into the car to move it away from the pumps, being considerate, not leaving it there while he went in to pay, Colin looked over to where Anna was staring off. Staring where? Across the river and into the past? She looked small and old, all huddled up that way — not frail exactly, more like an antique doll. Exactly, he thought, a plaything from another era. Why was she smiling? Probably at some fusty memory.

Anna walked over to the station or, rather, the snack store. A fat man sat behind the counter, belly and hips, a series of blobs in polyester pants. On top of his head was a baseball cap that was too small for him. He took Colin's money with slug fingers. At the other end of the counter sat a glass case with a heat lamp. On the floor of the case were hot dogs coated with crumbs of some kind. A Mexican-looking woman opened the door to the case and took two of the hot dogs. They reminded Colin of real dogs, puppies, in a cage. She was wearing gray sweat pants that had been through the washer and drier so many times they were studded with lint balls. She turned, caught Colin looking in the vicinity of her rear end, and gave him a malevolent look. He turned away, embarrassed, then was annoyed at her presumption.

Colin saw Anna come in the store. She went over to the cooler and took out a six pack of beer, went to the counter and paid for it.

She shrugged when Colin looked displeased.

"I suppose you are young enough to have no memories of the old kind of petrol stations. Places where there was always a greasy cash register on a greasy desk, mysterious hoses and tools scattered all about. When I was a child in England, they still had glass petrol bowls on the pumps."

In the car, as Colin negotiated the service road, Anna popped the top on a can of Schmidt's with a red fingernail and held the beer out to him. Colin shook his head and Anna took a drink. "Lord! My first taste of alcohol in three and a half years."

"And how do you like it?"

"It's watery, chemical-tasting. I will get something better later. Probably not until Mexico."

Colin worried that maybe she'd turn out to be an alcoholic. Just what he needed to relieve himself of stress and tension, a drunken old woman to look after.

Ten miles, all the way to Wasco, Anna never said a word and, consequently, Colin was nervous. "What's going on in your mind?"

She sipped, swallowed. "I was trying to decide what this bleak landscape reminds me of. Or, rather, where have I seen its equal in bleakness."

"And have you come to any conclusions?"

"Yes. The Belgian countryside at the same time of year."

"What where you doing in the Belgian countryside?"

"Moliere."

"Come again?"

"I must tell you, Colin, I hate that expression."

Oh, no, he thought; the beer makes her bitchy and she has five more to go. "Sorry."

Why should he be sorry?

"Moliere, the, I mean, a, playwright. A few years after the time with those buskers, I told you about, I hooked up with a decidedly third-rate theatrical troupe — the only rate that would have me — and we toured northern France and into Belgium, doing Moliere. We had a certain cachet, coming from Paris. 'L'Ecole des Femmes.' 'Malade Imaginnaire,' 'Les Femmes Savante,' and, of course, 'Tartuffe.' Do you like the theatre, Colin?"

"I don't know."

"Do you attend the theatre?"

"Not much, really."

"Not much? When was the last time you went to see a play?"

Colin couldn't at first remember ever attending the theatre. Then he smiled, having something to give her. "I went to see a play a few, well, four or five, years ago."

"And what did you see?"

"Les Miz." He was hoping she'd be impressed, him abbreviating it.

"I beg your pardon? Or, should I say, come again?"

"Les Miserables."

Anna groaned.

"Well, did you see Les Miz?" he asked, irritated

"No, I did not."

He adjusted his hands on the steering wheel, smiled, feeling vindicated.

"I didn't have to," Anna said.

They rode on in silence. Passed through a little town that consisted of a cluster of wooden buildings huddled against the wind. They were all faded to gray and seemed to list. Kent, it was called. There was one business or there had been one business, a store that had weeds growing in front of the door. A sign in the window, the letters barely legible: 'Closed.'

Anna tossed her second empty can into the back, popped another, said nothing.

"What about you?" Colin said. "You asked me about my childhood, what about yours?"

"Ah, I was abandoned while still in swaddling clothes, you see. A party of gypsies found me as I was floating down a stream on top of a lily pad."

"You're kidding!"

"Indeed, I am. Except for the part about being abandoned, though I was out of swaddling clothes by then. Ours was a typical, lower-middle-class English family of the time, in Bristol. Daddy had been in show business, the music hall. Quit to marry and raise a family. What he got was a shrewish wife and a bratty daughter. At first, I thought it was because of me being such a handful that Daddy took French leave. Later, I realized with part of my mind, that it was Mother who had precipitated his flight. Lit out for greener pastures, did

Daddy. I wonder if he found them. We never heard a word. I suppose one reason I got into show business was to become famous so that he might look me up. I was seven the last time I saw him. It was the middle of the Depression. Mother was a drudge when she wasn't a drunk. Used to lock me in the flat during outings to her local. The first weeks, or months, I don't know, I'd whimper mostly. Read my storybooks and whimper, draw pictures and whimper. Later I began acting out the parts in my story books. I played the little girls, the little boys, the mothers and the fathers. I played the doggies and the duckies. When I had exhausted the books, or grown bored with them, I invented my own stories to act out. After we got a radio, I repeated the words and sang the songs. I hated my mother for having locked me up but, later, I thanked her, in my mind anyway. She imprisoned my body but liberated my imagination. I forgive her. Even for coming home drunk and slapping me, even for bringing home men with foul breath who'd paw her on the chesterfield. She'd take them into her bedroom for a little slap and tickle, and emerge embarrassed, all fake demure, acting horrified should the fellow attempt to cop another feel, as if wondering what on earth he thought he was up to. More than one tried to cop a feel off me, too. Sometimes she didn't see or pretended not to see. Once she told me to sit on the chesterfield next to Mr. so-and-so while she went to make mix fresh drinks. 'Show Mr. Hargreaves the pictures you drew.' Well over I go, sit down and show the man my pictures. 'That's lovely, my dear but what about the book on the table. I'd like to see the pictures in that one.' So, being a good little girl, and fearing my mother's open hand across my face, I jumped up to pick the book from the table, and Mr. Hargreaves, the instant my back was to him, reached for my rear end, cupped one cheek in what seemed to me a massive hand, and kneaded it like was dough. 'Oh, I like that,' he said, and I can still hear him. 'I like that very much.'"

"That's terrible. What did you do?"

"Nothing."

"Yes, I understand. Had you screamed and told, he would have denied everything. And you mother, having been drinking, perhaps wouldn't have believed you and you might even have gotten slapped again."

"Yes and no. All that you say would, no doubt, have happened. But I did and said nothing mainly because, although I sensed what he was doing was very wrong, it was also, nevertheless, pleasurable. A warm sensation spreading through my buttocks to my front and the tops of my thighs."

Colin started to reply, stopped. Anna saw his eyebrows dip as he frowned. "But you were, how old? Surely you couldn't have felt…"

"Pleasure? Surely I did. I was seven or eight years old. This is not unusual, love. Don't you realize this is what makes these incidents so complex? If something like that happened and there was no pleasant sensation, it probably wouldn't stay with one forever. One would remember it, if at all, as the action of just another annoying creep. But it is the pleasure that makes it all so bloody complicated. That's where the guilt enters, you see. You know that it is wrong and, therefore, because it feels good, you feel guilty. A little girl in such a situation recalls the foul breath, the clammy hands; perhaps he had hairs growing out of his nostrils; perhaps he was horribly ugly and decidedly obnoxious, yet he'd done this thing that made you feel good.

"Something like that can really derail a girl or a boy. As you know, it would be easy for guilt to dominate the whole psycho-sexual picture, if that's the thing to call it. Should such an incident be allowed to dominate the imagination, a person could get sidetracked into some quite perverse behaviour. Perverts and puritans, if one asks me, are simply two sides of the same coin. I am neither. Thank heavens I was able to get beyond the incident and a few others of the same kind. At least beyond the guilt and the ugliness. But, having been made aware of the potential of the human body for pleasure, I was determined to explore further. And haven't I just."

"What happened to you?"

"You mean in regards to my further exploration? My, my. Such prurient interest from such a proper appearing young man."

"No, I mean, your mother, your home."

"I shan't bore you with the Dickensian details. But Mummy, being incapable of caring for a child, had me put, or the authorities had me put, into an orphanage. If you have ever read English novels, you will have some notion of what that is like, only the story is invariably told by men. Seven years I spent at the orphanage and then I ran away. So you see, Valley View was not my first experience of institutionalization. And this is not my first escape. God, these last few hours, I must have been in a daze. Numbed by what has happened.

Am I free? Yes? Then you, Colin, are my saviour. My knight in a not so shining station wagon."

"I got this because I wanted extra room in case, well, I thought of getting a dog."

"No need to explain. If you had a Daimler, an Hispana-Suiza or a Morgan held together with a leather strap, I'd think no more highly of you."

"A leather strap?"

"It may be November out there but let me tell you, young man, it is springtime in my heart."

"Yes, we have done it, haven't we? We've really done it."

"And we really deserve a proper drink. That beer makes me feel bloated. I need to pee. Excuse my language. It is growing dark. Let's drive all night. Oh, by the way, I assume you remembered to get my money and the jewelry?"

Colin patted his sport coat over the inside pocket. "The money's here in an envelope."

She mentioned it so casually. What if he'd forgotten or told her he'd forgotten? Maybe he should pretend not to have the jewelry. No, that would be cruel. "And the other things are under your seat."

"Splendid."

She didn't reach under the seat; didn't ask for the money. The only money she had in the world. What would she do when that ran out? "Did you make any arrangements about your, uh, ol…your pension?" Afraid to say 'old age.'

"No. What could I do, leave a forwarding address? Lista de Correos, third palapa down from Fernando's Hideaway?"

"Well, I assume, you could collect it all, all the accumulated cheques when you go back."

"Go back! Are you joking? I'm gone and gone for good."

"But what will you do when…?"

"I haven't the foggiest. Become a palm reader in Patzcuaro. Who knows, who cares? For now, I'm free."

The headlights caught a sign indicating a pullout and Colin veered off the road. There was a garbage can bolted to a post, a copse of trees beyond. Colin stopped and Anna got out. "Did she really not care?" he wondered, staring into the blackness. Or was she pretending not to care? Was Anna really so happy-go-lucky or was she desperate, bravely putting on an act?

She opened the door. "Brrr! It is freezing out there. You didn't try to peek, did you?"

"It's so dark, I couldn't see a thing."

"Shame on you for trying, naughty boy. Okay let's go. Shall we look for a motel? I see we're only ten or so miles from a place called Redmond. I wonder if you wouldn't mind stopping at one of those charming service station convenience stores. I noticed they sell wine too. A little sip of wine would be just the ticket, wouldn't it? Our celebratory drink, eh?"

They found a store on the outskirts of Redmond, and Anna went in, came back with half a gallon of Famiglia Cribari Zinfandel.

"I thought you said just a sip?"

"This was the only red that wasn't in the cooler chest. I wouldn't chance the white. You needn't be so conservative, you know."

"And you needn't tell me what I should be."

"You're right. It's a deal."

A couple of minutes later, Anna said, "Well, I see there are two motels up ahead, one on either side of the road. I wouldn't want to tell you what to do but, in case, you haven't thought of it yourself, it might be a capital notion to choose one or the other. I leave the decision entirely up to you."

"Thanks a lot."

"You're welcome."

"Why are you crossing the road?" Anna asked. "What's wrong with that one?"

He gave her an exasperated look.

"Just kidding, love. Just kidding. This one looks fine. A single long block of doors and windows. Simply marvelous. The other one had detached little rooms, somebody's idea of English cottages. Much more charm, of course. But you have chosen this, so here we are."

Is she teasing me or what? Colin wondered, pulling alongside the glass door with the 'office' sign. They both opened their doors and got out. Colin looked across the roof. "I can register for both of us."

Anna had no smart comeback, silenced by the apprehension on his face. Reading it: What would the desk clerk think, me and this old woman?

His eyes afraid, actually afraid, yet he was so resolute and she could see the jaw muscles work under his pudgy cheeks.

"Please use my money," Anna said.

Anna surprised he didn't object or make a pretense of objecting.

He returned after a few minutes, shifted the car to a parking slot by the door to the room. Signs at each place: 'Do Not Back In.' Colin had two suitcases, offered to help Anna with her stuff. A big handbag, sort of a leather pouch with straps, that's all she had. Opening the door to the room, he felt sorry for her, sorry also that he'd been brusque. Poor old woman running away, not knowing where she's going or what she's going to do. All her money in a business-size envelope, all she owns in a shoulder bag. Even her precious scrapbook left behind.

Stepping into the room, Colin said, "They didn't have two singles. I hope this is all right, saves money."

"Yes, it would be silly and wasteful to get two rooms. We can put a sheet up between the beds, if you wish. Like Gable and Colbert in 'It Happened One Night.'"

She could tell he didn't know what she was talking about.

"I trust you, Colin. I know you won't take advantage of me in the middle of the night."

She looked into the bathroom. "Of course, if you're worried about me, you could sleep in the bathtub."

Anna grabbed the two plastic-wrapped glasses from the top of the toilet tank.

Colin hadn't responded to any of her chatter. He opened his suitcases on the bed farthest from the bathroom, took out a zippered leather case with toiletries, then slacks and shirts and put them on hangers on a metal rack. Anna waited until he was finished to hand him his glass of wine. Everything with him so precise and orderly.

"Cheers," he mumbled, taking the glass but not sipping until he had rooted around his toiletry kit, found a tube of pills and swallowed one with the wine. Anna sat on the bed and kicked off her shoes, making a show of tugging her hem down as far as possible. Colin pulled the chair out from under the writing table and moved it to the other end, away from the foot of the bed.

"Well, young man, do you find yourself often in motels with women?"

"No, how about you?"

"Silly boy. With women, never. Never with men either. At least not in recent decades. But don't think I haven't had opportunities. Oh, no. Mustn't think that. But I chose chastity and I'm sticking to it."

Colin looked at her blankly. Sipped his wine. Life, thought Anna, had not made much of a mark upon his face.

She swung her feet off the bed and as she moved in his direction, Colin flinched. "Now, now. I'm merely reaching for the jug of wine to refill my glass, your glass too. No need to be frightened."

She took her drink into the bathroom and closed the door. Colin heard the toilet flush, water running. She'll probably be in there an hour, taking all the time that women take. Putting on their faces. Daubing stuff here, pencilling there, rubbing stuff in then smudging it. He knew little about the whole procedure, just that it took them so long. And Anna, having been on stage and in films must, therefore, be narcissistic and she'll probably take longer than the rest. From now on I should probably make sure I go in to pee whenever she makes a move toward the bathroom. "What could all those women's jars and vials and bottles be for?" he wondered. To be fair, Anna had only, or he had only seen, that little pouch hardly larger than an opened wallet, clear plastic with a pink spine onto which a zipper was sewn, just a few things inside, lipstick, little pencils. Of course, she couldn't have taken too much stuff with her when she left this morning. Was it only this morning? So Anna will probably stop at a drugstore somewhere and stock up. Wrinkle cream. She should get wrinkle cream; rub it on and wrinkles, lines, crows feet, furrows, and seams disappear forever! That's all she has to do and, presto, the girl in 'Eaton Place.' Colin laughed to himself thinking Anna would need so much wrinkle cream, they'd have to rent a U-Haul trailer to haul it all. Jesus, what if it could be like that? Some magic cream. What if she came out of there looking like the girl in 'Eaton Place,' like her own younger — her young — self? What would he do then? With that girl? Her twisting her hip, showing him the seam — her walking away in that tight skirt.

But that girl didn't come out of the washroom. It was Anna, the seventy-something year old Anna. And it hadn't taken her very long. More than five minutes, less than ten. He could feel the two drinks of wine. Well that was okay. It relaxed him and it had been a day of upheaval, to say the least.

"You look much nicer without the frown," Anna said. She was

wrapped in a white bath towel. "Although the place across the street had more charm it probably didn't have towels this big. As you can see, this one covers me from shin to shoulder. Lucky for you the towels aren't smaller. I had no room to pack a robe or discreet nighty."

He'd never seen her bare shoulders. They were boney but not as he would have expected, the skin not dried and hanging loose. Her neck didn't, as with so many of the other seniors at Valley View, resemble crepe paper.

I have a robe," he said. "You could always borrow it if you need to."

"Yes, yes. There was a time when if it had been absolutely imperative that I appear in anything other than my birthday suit, they, my gentlemen, would have suggested a wash cloth or, at most, a hand towel. I sleep in the nude; how about you?"

"No. No, I don't."

"Watch this."

"I'll turn my back."

No need. I shall get under the covers and you will never see an additional epidermal inch."

She pulled back the light green-light blue coverlet, tugged at the mustard-coloured blanket and the white sheet, got under with her back to him and tossed away the towel. Only her head showed.

"Voila!"

Anna lay on her back and stared at the ceiling. Colin looked over — her mouth was open slightly, hair splayed across the pillow. She could have been dead. Colin thought of her dying. Well she was, or he believed she was, seventy-four or -five. There is the stress of sudden change. Mexico might be hard on her. What would he do if she died? Who should he call? Her daughter? What was the daughter's phone number, her last name? Should he ask Anna? How would he put it? Uh, 'scuse me, Anna? I just thought, you know, in case, well, to save trouble if you should, you know, pass away…What kind of bureaucracy would he have to deal with, her dying in Mexico?

He turned on the bathroom light and switched off the other one. Shut the door when he went in. Tried to hit the enamel edges of the bowl, in case she was still awake. He was glad he didn't have to do the other. He wouldn't want her to hear him. Then he'd have to stay in there with the window open for awhile, toss some of his English

Leather around.

He turned out the bathroom light before opening the door. Anna didn't appear to have moved, though he could barely make out her face.

But she had one eye open and she turned her head in the dark and watched him tiptoe over to his bed in his white t-shirt and checkered boxer shorts. She heard the bed creak, let a few seconds pass. "Colin?"

"Oh, you're awake."

"Yes, but before I do go to sleep, I want to thank you again for what you have done, how you have helped me."

"That's okay, Anna. I just hope everything works out for you."

"I hope you understand what it means to me. You have saved my life, what's left of it."

"I'm glad to help. Good night, Anna."

"Good night, Colin."

She listened as he got settled, sensed his back was to her. Another minute passed.

"Colin?"

"Yes?" he answered, but faintly.

"Are you awake, love?"

"Barely."

"You and Dr. Drushka. You went out together, didn't you?"

He made some kind of noise, muffled by the pillow. And more clearly said, "How did you know?"

"I could tell."

"Good night."

"Colin?"

"What *is* it?"

"She didn't show you a good time in bed, did she?"

"What a thing to ask? I don't want to sound harsh but what we did is really none of your business."

He turned again but more emphatically this time. She'd lost track of whether his back was to her or not.

"Oh, tut tut! Humour me in deference to my age. I know it wasn't any good. I'm right, aren't I?"

She waited. Nothing. Half a minute passed.

"Okay," Colin said. "Okay, you're right. Now please let me get some sleep."

*W*hen Colin woke he was on his side looking at light green/light blue drapes. He knew exactly where he was but wasn't sure he was pleased about being there. Was this a serious mistake? He had a doctor's encouragement to take a leave of absence from Valley View. It was the Anna part that had him worried. He was used to planning his entry into any and every situation. What are the benefits or advantages latent in any course of action? These he weighed against drawbacks or disadvantages. That approach, what he called his methodology, might be deemed conservative or even overly cautious by some, but it had always served him well. And, anyway, he asked himself, where would all those who decried his way of operating be if things worked out poorly? Would they be around to pick him up when he fell?

Not likely. Actually, Colin didn't mind admitting to himself that he'd never had far to fall. Yet, here I am, he sighed, in a situation I definitely did not approach cautiously. I took a plunge, a leap into the unknown. What good can come of all this? Fun and interesting experience? How can those help me in my life and career? Am I doing all this in order to have a store of cocktail party anecdotes?

But, the disadvantages — the bad that could come of this escapade! This was the first time Colin had really even thought of those. How could he have been so stupid as to not realize that Corrington and the board would never give him his job back at Valley View when it was discovered he'd run off with a resident?

I could always claim that Anna learned of my plans and followed me, forced herself on me. But, then, I'd be compromised, having to lie. Not to mention the inevitable question as to my character. I mean, how can they trust me among the senior citizens if I haven't the strength of character to resist the schemes of an addle-brained old woman? Still, there'd be some way to get my position back or at least a similar one, somewhere. So what's to worry about, really? This nutty old woman? What if she does die? In a way that would solve everything. They couldn't prove, back at Valley View, that she'd been with me. Anna Dupree? I remember her, yes. Took off with me to Mexico? What! That, that's absurd.

I should be more concerned with how I manage to put up with her until something does happen to her. Or until I'm feeling better, have a clean bill of health and am ready to go back to work. Then what do I do with her? Just say, bye-bye; it was nice knowing you?

Colin turned to see if Anna was still sleeping.

She wasn't in the bed. The bathroom door was open and she wasn't in there. Her shoulder bag wasn't in the hotel room either. He grabbed his sport coat off the back of the chair and felt the inside pocket. She hadn't taken her envelope, and his wallet was where he'd left it on top of the television. For a moment he felt relieved, thinking it was rational that if she were going to take off, she'd take her money. Then it occurred to him that he was only assuming she was rational. If she went off and got into trouble, say she was attacked and beaten — these things happen all the time, especially in the United States — he'd be the number one suspect.

He pulled on his trousers, wondering how he could have been so stupid to as to have become involved in this. Buttoning his shirt he suddenly felt guilty for worrying about himself more than about Anna, about what might happen to her, had, perhaps, already happened to her.

When he had his shoes on, Colin opened the door — didn't see her in the parking lot or on the pavement beyond. He started to go out, met the cold wind and stepped back into the room for his sport coat. Closing the door, he felt a gurgling and a sort of vibration in his stomach.

Reaching the pavement, Colin looked both ways. To the right, the way they'd driven in last night, there wasn't much — some houses, the gas station way down there. There was one tree with bare branches under a washed-out sky, a sky like dirty dishwater. The other way was the same sky, some businesses down there. No figures in these bleak landscapes.

He began walking toward the buildings. The first shop he came to housed an auto upholstery business but it wasn't open. Colin wondered what the time was. A few stores were unoccupied, broken windows, graffiti on the walls. A thrift store, faded clothes, paperback books, a sequined woman's handbag in the window. He reached the corner. There was a church across the street. He was looking at the church, the sign out front announcing that the basement drop-in centre was open all day. Maybe she was over there.

"Colin!"

It startled him. He turned around and there was Anna, fifty feet down the side street waving to him. Bag on her shoulder, a shawl, scarf wound round her neck and trailing down her back. Big smile. He smiled too, so glad to see her. Amazed how it made him feel good to see her.

"Oh, Colin. Did you come looking for me? I've been up for hours and I simply had to go out. I assumed you were going to sleep all day."

"I didn't know where, I mean, I was kind of, you know, worried about you."

"How sweet. I should have left you a note, and I will in the future. I was just about to go in here. Feel like breakfast? There was nothing open when I left the motel so I walked around the dreary residential streets. Took the key with me so as not to wake you if you were still in dreamland when I came back."

There was a cash register stand to the left of the door and a horseshoe counter in back of that, booths to the right. The place was crowded and it seemed as everyone was smoking. "It looks like central Europe in here," Anna said. "Except for the baseball caps."

There was a large, red-haired woman behind the register.

"Do you have a non-smoking section?"

"Yeah," said the woman, pointed to the back of the restaurant where everyone was smoking. "But looks like it's all full up."

They sat on stools at the bend of the horseshoe. It only took a quick look around the restaurant to assure Colin he hadn't been guilty of generalizing yesterday, what he'd been thinking about overweight Americans. He was sitting next to one and Anna next to another one. Both men stole sidelong glances at them as they raised coffee cups to their lips.

The one next to Anna, who wore a red baseball cap and could have been thirty, could have been fifty, was so intent on checking her out that she couldn't resist turning toward him and presenting a dazzling smile. The man was so surprised he knocked the rim of his cup against his teeth. "Shit!" he exclaimed.

Anna said, "Many a slip twixt."

He was about to add something, probably not very nice, judging from his expression, when the waitress appeared to head him off.

"Yeah?"

Colin looked at Anna who told him to go ahead and order.

"Scrambled eggs, hash browns, toast and bacon."

"What kind of hash?"

"Hash browns."

"Oh, you mean home fries."

"I suppose."

"Kinda toast?"

"Brown, please."

"You mean, wheat toast?"

"Yes, and could you bring me HP sauce instead of ketchup?"

"Bring you *what*?"

"It is sort of brown, a brown sauce."

"Oh," she said. "You mean steak sauce. You put it on potatoes?"

Colin shrugged.

"And you?"

To Anna it sounded like 'En yew?'

"Well I'm not terribly hungry."

The waitress tapped her pencil on the edge of the pad, her lips pressed together as she looked at Anna. Her nails were long, painted white.

The guy with the red baseball cap got up and went away and was immediately replaced by a guy with an orange baseball cap.

"Do you have scones?"

"Have what?"

"Never mind."

"Just what's on the menu."

"A bran muffin, then and coffee."

"Where you from?" That from the man on the right. He was wearing a brown suit, a yellow tie with brown horses. He had a gray crewcut and smelled of Old Spice. Anna felt like asking him why he wasn't wearing a cap, didn't he make the team? Instead, she answered, "Canada."

"You can't fool me," said the other man, the one with the orange cap. "That's no Canadian accent. You're from Australia, aren't I right?"

"No you're not."

"C'mon now. Australia or that other one down there, New Zealand. Which?"

"I was born and raised in England. Resident of Canada."

"You still have a communist government up there?" said the man with the orange cap, leaning across Colin.

"Oh, yes, indeed," said Anna.

The waitress brought their orders. The two men watched them eat for a few minutes.

"What ever happened to that Trudeau fellow? The ruler you used to have?"

"He died," said Colin.

"He was a real communist," said the crew cut man.

"He was a homo, too."

"No, Lloyd. He had all those girlfriends."

"Well then how come his wife left him, run off with the Beatles or the Led Zepellins or somebody?"

"Beats me."

"Cause he was a homo, Herbert. Is why."

"Now gentleman please don't fight over our political figures from the past."

"All right, ma'am." Herbert smiled. He had a few gold-capped teeth. "I reckon you be glad to be in God's country, aren't I right?"

"I'll let you know if I ever get there."

"What was that? It's your accent."

"Nothing."

Herbert reached inside his jacket, brought out a business card and handed it to her. Anna held it close to her eyes, then at arms' length. "I'm terribly sorry but I don't have my glasses with me. What is it you do? Sell used cars?"

"That's rich, Herbert." The other man guffawed. "That surely is rich. Sell used cars. Hah, hah!"

Herbert's gold teeth disappeared for a second, Anna thinking they were like nuggets in a creek, hidden when some dirty water float-ed by. But his smile began a tentative comeback. "No, m'am. I'm in the real estate business. And I can find you a real good deal on a little piece of freedom. Yes, a little piece of the good old U.S.A."

"A little freedom sounds wonderful indeed, sir. That is just what my son and I are after. Why, do you know, the government is trying to make my boy here register his firearm?"

Both men looked at Colin sympathetically.

"You a hunter, son?" asked the man with the cap.

Colin nodded, "Grizzlies, polar bears, that sort of thing."

Herbert said, "Well, boy. The next thing you know, they'll be taking your gun away from you. It is all planned. You don't have a gun, they can take you over, too. It ain't going to happen here, no sir. You let me find you a little piece of property down here."

"Sounds idyllic," Anna said. "My son and me and our firearms in our own pied a terre near the Wal Mart."

"If you want. Or one near the golf course."

"Ah, yes. Well excuse me but we must be going. You are ready, Colin?"

"Yes, mother."

"As they rose, Herbert said, "Why don't you give me your address and I can mail you some listings."

"We'll be in touch with you Herbert. Ta ta."

They got up and while they were paying the bill, Herbert looked at his friend. "Hell, you make of that?"

"I think the old bitch was funning you, Herbert."

"Don't believe it."

"Maybe not but I tell you one thing," the man said, looking over as Anna and Colin went out. "That boy there, he never hunted no grizzly bear. Polar bear, neither."

They went to a supermarket on the southern outskirts of Bend, the idea being to put in a long day on the road, no stops except for gas and to pee. There was a man who appeared to be in his thirties out front of the supermarket with a sign: "Need Work — Will Do Anything Legal."

For lunch, Anna fixed sandwiches on her lap on yesterday's edition of the *Courier*, slicing tomatoes with a little paring knife bought in Bend. Colin liked bagels with mustard. He nibbled at them all day long.

Anna got into the Famiglia Cribari zinfandel after lunch, sipping from the plastic motel cup. A few miles before Klamath Lake there was a field filled with huge dinosaur replicas, the largest one set by a wooden gate, 'Thunderbeast Park' painted on the gate.

"Look!" Anna said "What's that?"

"A Buluchitherium."

"Yes, that's what *I* thought. No, seriously, how in heaven's name do you know that?"

"I used to study dinosaurs when I was a kid."

He may be a man now, Anna thought, but he was a kid just a few years ago. A few years ago, she was already an old lady.

"They should have a statue of me over there."

"You were talking, yesterday — the orphanage. About being in there."

She poured herself more wine.

"Yes, that was in a long gone time when giant creatures roamed the earth but the worst beasts of all were inside, behind the red brick and dirty windows. How fondly do I recall Saturday nights. Saturday night was bath night. There were always twenty-some girls in our wing and one bathtub. We lined up, eldest first to use the tub."

"You mean they made you stand in line the whole time? While each girl filled the tub and took a bath, then drained the water, the whole procedure? And then the tub had to be cleaned so it must have taken hours and hours."

"About forty-five minutes for the lot of us."

"Impossible."

"But true. Because, you see, there were none of those niceties you just mentioned. No filling or draining, much less scrubbing the tub. We used the same bath water."

"But it would be cold and filled with everyone's dirt, and…"

"One closed one's eyes. But the worst part was the nightie We each used the same nightie."

"You took a bath wearing a nightie?"

"Indeed. The same one. Modesty, and all that. When it was one's turn, one took off one's clothes, put on the damp nightie and got into the tub of cold, clammy and greasy water. Or it was that way by the time I got into it."

"That's awful."

"It certainly was. We shared everything. Not only did twenty-some girls, the exact number changed from year to year, share the bath water, we shared the same dildo."

"What?"

"A dildo."

"But, did you use it, I mean did you know what it was when you first got there? Didn't you say you were eight years old?"

"I was just eight and I had not the foggiest notion that first sad long night, lying there in the dark, tears spilling out of my tightly closed eyes, when the girl in the next bed relayed the thing, saying, 'Pass it on when you're done.' To myself, I wondered, 'Done what?' What was it I was expected to do with this piece of hardwood, shaped sort of like a torch, a flashlight, that is, and approximately ten inches long. I passed it on and made inquiries the next day."

"Weren't you shocked?"

"Not until I learned what one was supposed to do with the thing. You do *what* with it? I'd never heard of such a thing, dreamed of such a thing. Of course, it pleased me no end when I learned to use it. When I mastered the technique, as it were."

"Pardon me for mentioning this but how was the dildo kept

clean? I mean, as it made the rounds."

"Just wipe it off and pass it on."

"Wasn't that unsanitary?"

"Yes, but it was probably safer than taking a bath."

They were passing a lake that was on the west side of the road, their right side. There was very little traffic, most vehicles were over on Interstate Five. Colin asked Anna what happened in the summer at the orphanage. Were the girls sent anywhere, were there classes? What?

"A few of the girls might have a relative who would take them in. Some even had one parent. A few girls went to temporary foster homes. Otherwise, one stayed at the orphanage. That was my lot in the beginning. For the first few years, I wasn't old enough to be pressed into slavery at a foster home. That was indeed what being adopted for the summer amounted to: slavery. It was one of the ways the orphanage made money. The foster parents paid so much for the use of the girl. Fed us as little as possible, all the better to increase their profit, don't you know. But that came later, beginning when I was eleven. The years until then I was, as I say, too young to work outside the walls but too old to elicit sympathy. Occasionally, one of the youngest girls would find a permanent foster family.

"Yes, summer at the orphanage. There was less class work and more work-work. Of book learning, there was precious little; a few kings and queens, enough mathematics for the green grocer's. You might think we'd be taught to cook but I suppose they figured no one cared about that sort of thing. They taught us to sew. We learned by doing, by sewing for the profit of the orphanage. They took in mending and washing. Oh, it was a jolly bit of fun, it was. But the best, the absolutely most wonderful day was the one Sunday each month when we went out on the town."

"Only one day a month? Then you must have been thrilled at getting out."

"Hated it, absolutely hated it."

"But why? Weren't you happy to see what was beyond the walls?"

"Not on your life. We had to march along behind one of our mistresses — they were all very jolly hockey-sticks. March to church and then a lockstep turn about the park, everyone staring at us, knowing where we were from. Staring openly, mind, like we were the sad circus parade. Some with pity but most with contempt. The town girls laughing, sticking out their tongues, the boys making obscene gestures. How I dreaded those Sundays. I was so ashamed and humiliated."

"What were the summer foster homes like? They made you work, eh?"

"From sun up to sun down. I passed three summers, including the one when I ran away, in foster homes — ages thirteen, fourteen, fifteen. It was only later that I discovered there was such a thing as the school-leaving law. I was thirteen then. I could have walked out of there. One family had a bakeshop, and it was there I was put to work. At first, I thought it was simply wonderful, getting to eat burnt scones, running my finger around the sides of copper pots of sticky batter. Soon, as you can imagine, I grew surfeited with that. I swept, scrubbed, swept, and came home — I use that word for lack of a more appropriate one — covered in flour. Ten hours a day for room and niggardly board. They weren't mean to me, those people, just hard working, tired, dull and pusillanimous. Typical of so many British of the time.

"The next summer's people were not typical in that they were doing rather well. They owned a public house with a stable out back, just like in the Earlies."

"The what?"

"The olden times. Pubs, as you may know and, if so, forgive me for being tendentious, grew out of the British trades and craft tradition. Saddler's Arms, Chandler's Arms, that sort of thing, and they catered to their kind. One put up there, one and one's horse. So the place to which I was indentured was an actual remnant of that past. I cleaned the pub and cleaned the stables, cleaned up after the men and after the horses. The stable floor was a sight preferable to the floor of the gentlemen's."

"How did the owners treat you?"

"Mister was fine. I think he fancied me and might have done something about it were it not for the missus, a shrew from central casting, sort of a dumpy sexless version of Agnes Moorehead. And it doesn't matter if you don't know who she was."

"But, nevertheless, you were probably glad she was around. I mean, otherwise, the man might have been after you."

"Not at all. I wish she had not been always around. The publican was a fine looking creature. Solidly built with thick, dark wavy hair.

He was always smiling and pulling beer, sharing jokes with his mates. Quite a man until the wife appeared and he changed into something else entirely. Quel transformation! It was part of the local mythology. Everyone wondered what hold she had on him. Was it some sort of blackmail? Something she alone knew about his past? The 'something' obviously was powerful for it kept such a handsome man tied to her, that humourless harridan. Of course, another school of thought maintained some extraordinary sexual equation existed. She was *dark* after all — black hair, wasn't conscientious about shaving under her arms, by the way — dark eyes. It all smacked of something gypsy-like, a Carpathian, Transylvanian air to it. Everyone knew those sorts had secrets, esoteric practices; the woman could do things others could not do, and usually did them under a full moon while wolves howled. Heh, heh, heh. Only the shadows know what they did."

"Anna, you certainly have a lively imagination."

"I know, I should get hold of myself, so to speak. Channel my thoughts into shuffleboard, content myself with a cruise to Alaska, associate with other old biddies instead of running off with a handsome man forty-some — Oh, my God: I said it — could it be forty-seven years my junior?"

"It is not as if you're really running off with me."

"Oh, it is not? Well what, pray tell, is this we're doing, love?"

"Well not in that way. I wish you wouldn't talk like that. I know you're only joking but, still, it doesn't sound right."

"Yes, I am joking. Of course. You could not do much worse."

"So you were fifteen when you ran away from the orphanage."

"That's right, divert the old bag, keep her talking about the past, the natural realm of the aged. If a girl was going to flee she had to do it from a summer foster home. Going over the gray stone wall of the Home was, well, I don't suppose it was impossible, but it certainly seemed that way. I used to lay there at night thinking of how to get out, lay there thinking whilst waiting my turn with Clark Gable. That's what we called it. I don't suppose you saw him and Garbo in 'Susan Lenox'? Well my mind would go over every little detail of escape, just as it — my mind — did in Valley View. When I wasn't thinking of escaping, I thought of having escaped. Living in London, being on stage, in films. Me, up there with the real Gable, replacing Garbo or Jean Harlow. Men. I thought about men. I fantasized. Did I ever. My mind ran riot. My countryman, Sir Richard Francis Burton…"

"I thought he was Welsh."

"Good heavens, not that one. Sir Richard, the explorer. He said the English have the best women in the world but least know what to do with them. Perhaps he meant specifically orphanage girls, doss house girls and boarding school girls because our fantasy life is so rich. By the time a man gets to one of us, most of his work is already accomplished. We have primed the pump, so to speak, all he has to do is work the handle. Unfortunately, the real Englishmen, if there were any, must have died out around Sir Richard's time. There certainly weren't many in my day. Upper class twits, big-talkers from the working class but worst of all, the pathetic, lower middle class. A nation of shopkeepers, indeed. Which brings me finally to the summer of 1945."

They crossed over into California as Anna told of being indentured to an upholsterer and his family. "They lived in a narrow row house with dull wallpaper. There was no place to hide from the odour of overboiled vegetables or from the husband, for that matter. He was middle-aged, middle-sized and I cannot for the life of me remember his face. As a man, he was really a blank. I do recall his hands, soft little fingers always directed toward a part of my person, any part, whenever his wife and children were looking elsewhere. The wife was saved from being mousey by her air of perpetual put-upon — as if she were heroically bearing misfortune, that malicious trick of fate responsible for her poor marriage and dreary existence. They reminded me of T.S. Eliot characters. The two children, boys, were hideously repressed. That they grew up to be wife beaters or child molesters or wankers around the public urinals, or all three in one, I have no doubt.

"I was up early to make their breakfasts, the boys just a few years younger than me and already filled with ideas but, like their father, not the audacity to act upon them. They probably enjoyed it more that way, sneaky little sods, sniggering because they thought it was dirty. After feeding everyone, I washed up and cleaned the house. The wife worked at some shop or other. When I was done all that, I had to go to the upholstery shop. I kept that clean, took care of the customers. At least, I did when they came to pick something up. When they arrived with a chair or footstool, I had, of course, to summon Mr. Penfield.

"He was always allowing his hand to brush against my bum or

my bosom, as if by accident. Never going any farther but it was certainly a nuisance. And he certainly must have told his cronies that the situation was otherwise, must have alluded to having his way with the young shop girl because on more than one occasion, I'd catch one of them tipping him the wink after surreptitiously appraising my budding young form. I don't blame them, picture me with my cute, rounded bottom and pointy breasts that were up around my neck. Now whether he had his petty little boast or not, I don't know for sure, but perhaps it was recompense for my remaining mum about his wandering hands, that he would slip me coins every so often. These I kept in a little pouch that was on my person at all times. Usually in my knickers if you must know and, at times, particularly when seated, the pouch of coins created the most pleasant *frisson*. You'd think that, given my overactive adolescent mind, the two would remain forever connected, as it were, money at the seat of pleasure, but that was not, is not, the case. I always gave it away."

Alarmed that Anna was set to go off on one of her prurient tangents, Colin hastened to ask how she'd broken free. "Did the man's behaviour get so annoying that you were forced to go out on your own?"

"Not at all. My departure was precipitated by two things. It was the beginning of August and I knew that only a few days remained until I would be shipped back to the orphanage, and that I had another entire year to put in, or so I thought, before being released on my own. An entire year. Then — Shazzam! — lightning struck, a bolt of realization. I had just to walk away, and I would be free. But, also, I realized that there was not much time to turn the idea over in my mind. To hesitate meant another year of confinement.

"Thus it was that two days later I walked away. I made breakfast for the Penfields, cleaned the house, stuffed my few articles of threadbare clothing into a paper bag, being seen on the street with my cardboard suitcase definitely wouldn't do , and I walked out of that life and into another one. By evening I was in London, Victoria Station."

"You were sixteen years old?"

"Not quite."

"You couldn't have had much money."

Colin himself had been twenty-two years old and beginning graduate school before he left home. He had commuted to university in Saskatoon as an undergraduate. When he did go off, it was hardly as if he washed up in a big metropolis with a couple of bucks in his pocket and few prospects. Simon Fraser University! Talk about being isolated from the pulse of real life. He had two fellowships and a position as a teaching assistant. He almost felt guilt when he thought of fifteen year old Anna in London.

"Weren't you scared?"

"Yes, and thrilled at the same time."

"What did you do first? Get a room, look for a job?"

"No, lose my virginity."

"Oh, come on."

"I'm serious. He approached me in the station, told me I looked lost and offered his assistance. First, however, we must have tea; tea with gin.

"He was nice looking, an older man, probably thirty. He began by being solicitous and polite then moved on to sweet-talking me. He was getting on to the *tres gallant* stage — we were having dinner by then — and I was getting a trifle impatient. Finally, I said, "How about we just get us a room, love?" He was so surprised he sprayed me with part of his mouthful of wine and almost choked on the rest. The poor fellow imagined he was seducing me.

"Well, we did get the room and he was quite the lover or so it seemed to this nymphette-neophyte, though I won't use that word so favoured by North American males, favoured probably because it is so demeaning to women: nymphomaniac. Very romantic, until he looked at his wristwatch and — presto! — became another man entirely. Seems there was a loving wife waiting at home, and he must needs run to her while reasonable excuses were still possible.

"I slept the night in that room. Much later, I realized it would have been an unremarkable hotel but it seemed like the Mayfair to me.

"In the morning, I went downstairs thinking with a laugh that *tomorrow* I was due back at the orphanage. Emerging onto the street, I thought *today* begins my new life. I bought a newspaper. *Yesterday* the Americans bombed Hiroshima. It was the seventh of August, 1945. A new world had begun. I'm getting tired."

Colin's back was sore from driving. Sacramento wasn't far off. "We should be getting to some motels soon."

Anna didn't respond. She's back on the streets of London, Colin told himself. It must have been an exciting time. Post-war rebuilding had just begun a few months earlier when the war in Europe ended.

They had just topped a small rise and rounded a bend when they saw it atop the next hill, flashing on and off against the night sky, one word, five neon blue letters repeated over and over again:

SORRY

SORRY

SORRY

Neither spoke, just watched as it came closer, and the magical was explained but was no less marvellous for that. There sat the Plains Motel, its parking lot filled with cars and pickup trucks, and only the first of three words working on the sign out front.

As they drove past, Anna turned and looked over the seat, and watched until SORRY disappeared behind the hill.

"It is more appropriate looking back."

he next day they drove through the lush agricultural land of the Imperial Valley, the road bisecting vast farms and orchards, and didn't stop for lunch and gas until they were coming out the bottom of it, at Modesto, where the land was drier.

All businesses were on a service road below and parallel to the highway. Colin took the exit at a giant billboard that advertised snuff, a baseball player on the sign taking a mighty swing but instead of a ball coming off his Louisville Slugger, there was a large can of snuff. "It's a hit!" The catcher had lifted his mask and is watching the snuff can sail out of the park and into the wide blue yonder.

"This doesn't look so much like a service station," Colin remarked, "as it does a small city."

Anna replied that she, not being raised in North America, had a different concept of 'station.' "Like in sheep stations. What you would call a ranch, like they have around here. In New Zealand or Australia, especially, they might cover a zillion acres."

"You were in New Zealand and Australia too?"

"Yes, doing Shaw and Wilde. Talk about a tank town tour: Wangerei, Kawakawa and Rotorua; Tambo, Tumworth, Toowoomba and good old Gympie."

There must have been twenty acres of asphalt with numerous small service buildings and at least two dozen islands with several gas pumps at each. Anna thought of that island in New Zealand, off what? Rotorua? The one with all the tall stone statues, many of them phallic.

There was a section in the small city exclusively for big trucks. Dozens of tractor-trailer rigs waited in rows for fuel, like an army of idling behemoths, vertical chrome stacks directly behind the cabs, sign painters' flourishes on doors: "Shawna Lee" and "A Bit 'O Country."

There was a lucky seven on a chrome grill and, above it, "Pair O Dice." Peterbilts, White Freightliners, Reo Conventionals and a few stubby Macks. Some of the drivers milled around their beasts like mahouts: lanky guys, older men with big guts, a couple of women — one stretching her large pair of black jeans to the limit. Some of the old dudes had chrome chains linking leather wallets in back pockets to denim belt loops.

Colin took in the scene through the windshield while the young man in a company shirt, nameplate with "Arvin" on it, made desultory swipes at the glass with a dirty squeegee. Probably felt humiliated servicing a Volvo station wagon. When he finished, the kid took Colin's credit card and went to the machine bolted to an island post. Coming back they watched him catch a glimpse of the license plate, look away, do a double-take, scrunch up his eyebrows to peer closer, then look back at the credit car and the slip of paper.

"Look's like Arvin there's gotten mighty suspicious," Anna said. "He's never heard tell of no place like British Columbia. He's going to think this situation over — see his mind lumbering? Sort of like one of those dinosaurs we saw up the road apiece, only in mukluks? Now see the frown disappear? He's back to his usual blank stare as he walks toward us. Must have concluded that British Columbia is part of England. Anyway, he figures, a nice-looking young man with his granny, can't be up to any terrorist activity."

"Your southern accent could have fooled me," Colin said.

The kid handed the card to Colin. "Y'all have a nice day'n come back again real soon, heah?"

Colin told him thanks. Anna leaned over, said, "Arvin?"

"Ma'am?"

"You keep your pecker up, heah?"

An embarrassed Colin threw it into 'D,' nearly running over the steel toe of one of Arvin's boots in his haste to get away from the pumps.

"Anna you really ought to watch what you say. Somebody is going to take offense and we're going to get in trouble. Just what we need."

"Yes, daddy."

Anna looked over the seat and out the back window at Arvin standing there, peering after them, probably wondering if that old lady had really said what he thought she said.

"It is not a joke down here."

Anna sighed, then said, brightly, "I'm beginning to feel rather peckish. How about you?"

"Well I am starving, now that you mention it."

"Maybe there is a place in town."

"What better place could there be than right here? You know what they say, if truck drivers stop at a place it must serve good food."

"Oh, yes. Those famous gourmands, the lorry drivers. They eat here, darling, that's why I want to go into town."

"You can be awfully contrary at times."

"I know."

The passed through quadruple doors into a large foyer where arrows pointed to different destinations. One way lead to a store that was almost supermarket size, another went to the shower room, there was an art gallery and a chapel. Even the restaurant needed arrows, to separate truckers from everyone else.

And there were signs everywhere. No Shoes No Shirt No Service...We Reserve the Right to Refuse Service to Anyone...Report Anything Suspicious...Absolutely No Profanity.

There were tee shirts on a rack by the cash register, others hanging from the ceilings, their messages either patriotic or scatological.

Anna and Colin obeyed the sign that told them to Please Wait To Be Seated, then followed a small woman with big legs in a crisp uniform and giant, plastic-covered menus under her arm. Every step the woman took sounded like a piece of paper being torn. She lead them to a banquette table where there was a telephone surrounded by a sugar shaker, bottles of ketchup and hot sauce, bowls of creamo boats and saucers with packets of artificial sweetener.

"There're more words on this menu then most people read in a year," Colin said.

"Most people? Not the ones around here. It's more than they read in a lifetime, judging by the look of them."

"That's not nice."

"It may not be nice but it is true. The couple behind you, for instance, must weigh five hundred pounds."

"That doesn't sound like so much," Colin said, thinking he himself must weigh two hundred and twenty pounds.

"Perhaps not, but the woman weighs four hundred pounds of it. I'll wager Mother and Father met at a family reunion."

"Don't be mean."

"I am not being mean. I haven't told you about the children yet. The cross-eyed girl — or is it a boy? — just poked his or her brother in the eye with, I swear, one of Momma's tampon inserters."

Colin almost turned around to look but saw the waitress approaching. She could stand up to any of them in the size department, and was homely, too. Colin was afraid Anna would start on her but she didn't. Surprised him by holding her tongue, being almost sweet to the woman.

Later, after the waitress had set down Colin's meal, Anna said, "Lord above, would you look at that mound of food you have. Why don't you be selfless and put it on a transport plane to some third world country?"

"I don't think so."

"A slab of beef oozing grease and coated with greasy breadcrumbs, plump French fries like jaundiced slugs, a heap of gelatinous green beans straight out of the can and, because it is all so bland, they give you those jalapeno slices which should be splendid for your ulcer problem. And now you are plopping ketchup on the fries."

"You're not bothering me."

"Okay. That ketchup reminds me of what your blood probably will look like after eating all that. And I can see steam rising from the plate. The hot food and that frosty ice tea should produce an extremely interesting internal effect."

"Are you finished, Anna?"

"Just about, Colin. You know that's a real athlete's meal. Yes, a discus thrower. Or maybe a viscous thrower. I like a man with a good appetite. I sense underneath that paragon-of-virtue-and-moderation exterior there is a hedonist deep down. And now I'll stop and have my scintillating salad."

"I've hardly eaten the entire trip. I've been watching my diet, as you very well know. But now I just can't help it. I'm famished."

"Yes, darling."

While Colin sawed off hunks of steak, loaded forks full of green beans and devoured log piles of French fries, Anna selected rabbit-size leaves of lettuce, chewed fastidiously. She even sliced the cherry tomatoes. She ventured a comment or two about the road to Mexico but Colin only grunted in reply or muttered half-heartedly. He was, she knew, engaged in serious business. He swallowed a belch or two. Anna picked and nibbled. With a biscuit, Colin wiped his plate clean.

On cue the waitress was there to remove his plates and ask if he wanted dessert."

"Yes," Colin answered. "I believe so."

As if he had to think about it. Anna was about to tell him not to do it but caught herself, the words half-formed on her lips. She hadn't even nagged her own child. And what was *she* doing these days? By now she'd certainly been notified that her mother had vanished, and probably surprised the authorities by expressing neither worry nor grief. She certainly wouldn't let it interfere with vigilante duty.

"We have the pecan pie on special, with vanilla ice cream or whipped cream, your choice."

"I'll have it with ice cream."

The waitress brought it and Colin ate it, then sat back, loosened his belt a notch.

"I'm full."

"Oh, are you really?"

Anna tried to picture him without the extra pounds. Were there really good bones deep in that face? From somewhere in his stomach came a rumbling. Colin could tell Anna had heard and he was embarrassed. The second time it happened, Colin reached for his wallet, studied the cheque, studied his line-up of bills, took out a few and put them on the table, cheque on top, ice tea glass on top of that. He rose heavily, "Would you mind giving this to them? I have to use the washroom."

When he was out of sight, Anna checked the total against the money and added a couple of dollars to the tip, thinking how one can never tell who was stingy, who was a generous tipper. Colin was a nice guy, generous in other things, she supposed, but she was finding out that he was parsimonious when it came to a gratuity. Her husband, on the other hand, a tight-fisted and often mean-spirited blowhard was a big, show-off tipper. And he was the kind of person who called the server by name. "Stuart? Would you please bring my coffee before the entrée. Thank you Stuart.""Well, Kim, which of the specials do you recommend?" The bastard thinking he was suave and debonair rather than patronizing.

After a few minutes, Anna gathered up money and cheque and

walked to the cash register, making a point of not looking at the tee-shirts but no will power was necessary because the new cashier sitting under them was enough of a distraction. She looked like a wax works version of a 'Fifties' country singer. Her bouffant hair seemed to be the texture of cotton candy and Anna had to restrain herself from reaching across the counter to feel it, maybe it *was* cotton candy. And it must be the weight of those false eyelashes that gives the woman her heavy-lidded look. She took the money and the cheque without speaking. Probably afraid the mask will crumble, Anna telling herself.

The two old women looked each other in the eye. Anna had the feeling — hell, she *knew* what the woman was thinking. She was thinking — I'm her age but I look thirty years younger.

"I know what you're thinking," Anna said. And turning back, added, "But you only *think* it. And anyway you don't have a twenty-eight year old man in your motel room every night."

The cashier's mouth pursed in surprise reminding Anna of an anus ringed with frosted lipstick. By the time, the woman recovered, Anna was out the door and in the hallway. But the cashier called after her, anyway: "You ain't had no man no age in no motel room or no where else since the last time Buck Owens had a hit record."

Anna glanced along the corridor toward the Men's and, not seeing Colin, took a quick turn through the store which dealt mostly in bolt-on truck accessories and varnished wall plaques bearing religious homilies and witticisms about body functions. Still no Colin, so she looked into the art gallery with its bronze sculptures of cowboys on bucking broncos and "original" oil paintings of leathery old-timers squinting into the sun and of young buckaroos in their first pair of chaps. As well, there were noble and dignified Indians who seemed about to utter something immortal about the wind blowing and the grass waving. All these lower-middle-class white people, Anna told herself, buying pictures of red Indians they'd never invite into their homes.

Where in hell was the boy and what could be taking him so long? Maybe he went down the hall to have a shower. Or maybe he made a friend in the washroom. No, he wasn't that way.

She went to the Women's and, coming out, told herself, "He probably left a split second after I went it. Now he's looking for me. Isn't that the way it always happens? But she didn't see Colin anywhere and it occurred to her that maybe he was waiting in the car. Anna looked but couldn't see it, and suddenly had a flash of anxiety, her heart quickening before her eyes located the blue Volvo station wagon. Nobody inside. She had to place a hand over her chest and take a deep breath. Women aren't supposed to be as susceptible to heart attacks as men. At least that's what they say. But *they* recast their medical truths daily. Christ, is that the way it ends? Heart attack in Modesto while looking for a Volvo?

Anna went outside and drifted over to where the big trucks were parked with their diesel motors running. Catching her reflection in a chrome stack, she reminded herself of a Modigliani dame in a fun-house mirror; when she moved a certain way her head expanded, reached a hand toward the stack and grew giant creature fingers, stood back for a better look: black skirt, white legs; from this far she could be any age.

"Hello, sweetheart. Looking for a lift?"

He was fifty, fat and friendly. Wearing a snap button western shirt and green work pants. As she backed away, he used the chrome grab bar to hoist himself up to the cab. "Take you far as Des Moines."

Anna smiled, "Better watch out, young man. I might call your bluff."

He laughed heartily, gave her a wave. "Maybe down the road somewheres, darlin."

And the big rig bucked forward. She was not deaf to the irony in the man's voice but hell it still made her feel good. Made her feel like a woman.

Anna walked out to the service road and looked around. There was another road beyond the little service city and a hundred yards along was an abandoned Mobil station, a decrepit motel, a few buildings with no discernible purpose. She was intrigued by the rundown motel. Anna looked back in the direction of the Volvo, at the restaurant entrance and, not glimpsing Colin, began to walk.

She kept her head down after the first car passed and showered her with grit. The asphalt edge of the road was all ragged like an aerial view of a coastline — bays full of pebbles and bits of trash. Her toes kicked up the bleached dirt. Walking down the road. Back home at the end of the Forties. On the road with the Charlie Kumz show. He'd been big during the War. The afternoon the bus broke down, big shot

Charlie trudging along like everyone else. Walking down the road a few years later and a few states east of here. From the hotel to the dance hall, '52 or '53, Cowboy Copas-Hawkshaw Hawkins — and that other one? Had a moderate country hit out of a song that Bing Crosby covered and made a small fortune. "Pistol Packin Mama." Pete Drexler, that's who it was. Her outfit in the laundry bag. Yes, imagine me trying to get very far walking down the road wearing that outfit. Sexy little cowgirl skirt, boots and those firm rubbery thighs and shapely calves, I had then. Where did they go? Who are these scrawny impostors now holding me up? Stars of Country Music with the Cowgirl Review. Yihaai! And ride em, pardner. Had to work behind wire-mesh screens in some of those honky-tonks. Music halls in Bristol, roadhouses in Lynchburg, Virginia — decrepit theatres in Namur, Belgium and Dunedin, New Zealand, and the floor of the Metro in Paris. Talk about paying dues. Reviewing my life, still walking. Why are all those things so clear in mind, yet the thousands of days and nights of marriage, an amorphous mass out of which an absurd image occasionally appears?

Anna lifted her gaze from the roadside gravel and out of the past, to the old motel on the other side of the two-lane. She was surprised to see a ten-foot high cyclone fence around the place which consisted of three low buildings, two perpendicular to the road, the other beyond these and parallel, each with six doors and six windows. Several were broken, stucco had crumbled from the walls and exposed the lathing but the place was, evidently, still in business because a few people were seated outside by the doors on aluminum folding chairs. Old people, just sitting. One man's mouth hung open, lower jaw down so far, Anna thought it might be stuck. But the rest of him showed no movement, either. Maybe the old fellow had suddenly gone rigid sometime in the recent past, stoop-shouldered, leaning slightly forward, mouth ajar, eyes unblinking, right hand draped over the crook of his wooden can, other hand on a bony knee that protruded from a pair of voluminous Bermuda shorts.

Anna thought she detected some slight movement in a few of the others. And the more rapid movement of a figure in green moving at the back of the buildings. In a moment she saw that the latter was a large black man wearing green work clothes and carrying a bucket. Two of the heads in the chairs turned her way. Anna pressed herself against the fence, her hands gripping the diamonds of wire — like parrot claws, she thought. A very large woman appeared at the open door of one of the rooms. She turned and looked Anna's way, shielding her eyes. Her feet were like unbaked loaves of bread. Along her legs, at the backs of her knees, the middle of her calves and all around her ankles, were eruptions of veins like clusters of grapes. She wore a cheap and filthy cotton summer dress. She ventured a few steps forward.

"Hi!" Anna called. "Hello there! What is this place?"

One of the chair-sitters rose and started walking her way. He didn't need a cane. He was wearing a jacket from a brown pinstriped suit, the pants from a dark blue pinstripe suit, and a wide blue and yellow tie. He detoured around a pit in the concrete. This one is even sprightly, Anna thought. Of course, everything is relative.

She waved to this man and to the woman. Mr. Open Mouth remained oblivious. There was another old woman, a bag of bones, hovering in the background.

"Yes, hello. Why is the gate locked? May I come in and visit?"

The fat woman looked frantically over her shoulder and back at Anna, extended both hands in front, palms down, and made pushing movements as if she were trying to get a dog from jumping up on her. She raised a finger to her lips, jerking her head to the side. "Clarence'll hear. We'll be in the deep smelly stuff then."

She had a high, nasally voice.

"Who's Clarence?"

"Shhh!"

She was at the fence now. They looked closely at each other.

"What is this place?" Anna asked again.

"Oh, it is a bad place."

"Why is it bad?"

"We's trapped here."

"You mean it's a jail?"

"Sort of. Jail'd be better. Leastaways we'd get decent food stead of the slop they give us."

"Afternoon, ma'am."

It was the old man in pinstripes. He nodded. His eyelids fluttered, they were the colour of ashes. Probably would bow, Anna thought, if he was able. "What brings you to see us, this fine afternoon, ma'am?"

"Cut the high falutin do-do, Thomas Howard," the fat woman said. And to Anna: "He thinks he's still the master of the big house stead of a prisoner in this here stink hole."

Thomas Howard smiled indulgently. "I know exactly where and what I am, Reatha. But let us not pick at each other. We get so few visitors, I'd like to hear the young lady speak."

"You are a charmer, Mr. Howard," Anna smiled at him. "I bet your were a devil with the ladies in your day."

He nodded at the compliment. The skin was stretched tight across his head and face, so tight that when he smiled, and a gracious smile it was, Anna couldn't hold back the image of a grinning skull — but one with still some wisps of white hair, fine as a baby's and combed straight forward on his crown. "Not Mr. Howard, but Mr. Lanier. Just like the awful poet of nineteenth century Georgia, who was, by the bye, a much better musician and writer of songs. My relative. My own grandfather fled west, to California. To flee his brother Sidney's verse, I'd wager. But you may call me Thomas Howard, Miss…"

"Dupree. Anna Dupree."

The old man extended his hand and smiled with embarrassment as he recognized the futility of the gesture. Anna poked the fingers of both hands through the diamond outlines of wire, and Thomas Howard touched her finger tips with his own. His hands are elegant, Anna thought, and the colour of old ivory.

Seeing this, Reatha came to the fence with her big hands raised, and reached forward. There was a desperate pleading look in her hazel eyes. Her fingers looked swollen, the nails bitten down. When Anna touched, finger tips to finger tips, Reatha began to cry. Tears came out and streaked her cheeks like bugs escaping from two holes. "Oh, I'm sorry. I'm sorry, we don't see anyone else. We're so alone here. All alone."

"Yes, that's correct," said Thomas Howard. "We are alone. You see, we have been left here."

"Dumped's what we was," Reatha was sobbing, sniffing now, wiping her eyes with the heels of her hands.

Looking beyond them, Anna saw that the other lady had moved a few steps closer to them. She was in an old and despicably filthy chenille bathrobe.

"Is this some sort of official facility for the elderly?"

"Some sort," Thomas Howard repeatedly, ruefully. "We were just put here. Yes, dumped. We had no control over it. Families did it to us. In my case, they had me declared incapable of caring for myself. I was forced to sign over power of attorney. Forced, I tell you. If I didn't do it, they were going to put me in the mental hospital. Can do it, too. All they require is one doctor to sign papers."

"And he was wealthy," said Reatha. "I wadn't and we both land up in the same place. You know, they got these old parents hanging around without sense enough to die, way they think of us. You hear them in another room, children you brung up, saying, 'Honey, if your momma died it would be better off for all us, including her.' And my daughter, she goes, 'I know but Shhh! She might hear you.' Hell, they should have just put a pillow over my head and smothered me in my sleep or shot me like a sorry-ass, useless old hound dog, put me out of my misery, stead of sticking me in a hot room, no air condition, big old fence all around."

"Aren't there laws controlling this kind of thing?" Anna asked, and at the sound of a distant motor, looked back up the road, saw the Volvo.

"No laws to speak of," Thomas Howard said. "What's most terrible is that there are no moral strictures. As Reatha said, I am, or I mean I was, wealthy but the more money spent on my useless self, the less others will inherit, don't you know. Hence we are here at the end of the world. Gruel for breakfast, something that's supposed to be soup for luncheon, ounce of greens with bits of pork rind for dinner. Day after day, except on Sundays on account of Saturday night, they send somebody, Clarence usually, to the Martee's hamburger place on the highway, and they give him all the rejected food from the whole week, and they give it to us on Sunday. Thank the Lord, it can't last much longer. But I truly am afraid of dying."

"Hallelujah!" said Reatha.

"But tired, oh, so tired, of living."

"Amen."

Thomas Howard regained his courtliness in a minute. "But aren't we being bores. What about you, ma'am?"

"I'm from Canada."

"Canada River country?" Reatha asked. "I was born near

Amarillo myself."

"What? Oh, no. Canada, the country."

Thomas Howard glanced at Reatha and smiled indulgently, "We can tell by her accent that it is from another country."

"How old'r you?" Reatha asked.

"Seventy-five." Anna surprised herself by telling the truth.

"Hell you're older'n me," Reatha said, genuinely surprised. "I'm sixty-eight."

"Reatha?"

"All right, Thomas Howard. I'm really seventy-one, ma'am. But he's eighty-five."

They all looked as the Volvo pulled to a stop a few yards away.

"You are indeed remarkable, ma'am," Thomas Howard said. "Still maintain a trim and lithe figure."

"Why thank you, sir." Anna smiled and curtsied, thinking she hadn't bent a knee like that since music hall days.

"You on that side of the fence," Reatha said. "Us on this side. You are real fortunate. Have money and a family that loves you."

Seeing Colin get out of the car, Reatha began to sniffle again. "And that must be your son."

"He's not my son."

The lady in the old robe was there now, squinting at Anna, tufts of gray hair that looked glued on a bird-like head that was set on a neck of veins and wrinkles. Twigs for legs that Anna avoided looking at a second time because the first sight of them had given her a chill at the back of her neck. Her own maybe getting that way.

"Mumma, is that you?"

The old woman spoke in a little voice from far away.

"Oh, Mumma, it is you. You have come back. You needn't have run off, Mumma. I dug up Daddy and brushed him clean. He's good as new. Working behind the mule right now. Come on, Mumma. We go out there see him. Surprise him real good..."

Anna had been about to say that she wasn't Mumma. But she didn't. Reatha made a circle with her index finger by the side of her head. "She near to a hunnert years old." Then looking Colin over, said, "He ain't your son?"

"No, he's my friend."

Reatha put a paw to her mouth and giggled.

"Colin, say hello to these folks."

Anna introduced them. Reatha said to Colin, "We was just telling Annie how we's on this side and she's on t'other side."

"Hey now! What's going on over there?"

"And that is Clarence," Thomas Howard said in a voice barely above a whisper.

The black man was holding a broom in his hand like a war club.

"But I *was* in an old folks' home," Anna said.

"You was? Your people come and get you?"

"No, Reatha. I escaped."

"You what?"

"He helped me. Colin used to be employed there. He got me out, freed me. He's my saviour, my white knight."

Reatha looked amazed, "I declare."

Clarence was coming up now, like the front of an old freight train. "Y'all there! You be movin on. No visitors! Get!"

Reatha stuck her fingers through the fence, wiggling them at Colin. "Oh, sir. Sir! Help me too. Get me out of here. I'll do anything. This ain't no way to live."

"Me, too, son. Take me along." Thomas Howard's eyes came alive with desperate hope. "I got a hundred dollars tucked away. Take me, take the money. I don't care what happens to me, long as it happens on the other side of this fence."

"You get away from that fence!"

"We're not breaking any laws," Colin told the black man.

"I'll be breaking your head, you talk back to me, you white trash."

"Mumma, I got lemonade on the sideboard. Me and Daddy just brought in some pole beans."

Clarence was there poking at them with the brooms. "Get on back where you belong."

"Why can't they talk to us?" Anna asked the black man. "You've no right to stop them."

"Shut your mouth, old bitch."

"Oh, you're real impressive you are, Clarence," Anna said. "Bet you can't wait to report to Massa, tell him what a good boy you been."

"I'll come over there, cut your heart out you white trash piece of shit."

"Don't talk to her like that," Colin said to the man who turned his flat eyes on him.

"I'll do you, you faggot."

"You'd best leave," Thomas Howard said to Anna. "Or he'll take it out on us later."

"All right, Thomas Howard."

"But come back for us in the night, if you can possibly arrange it."

"Yeah," said Clarence. "Let's see you come back tonight."

"Please!" cried Reatha. Clarence whacked her across her broad bottom with his broom, and she got away from the fence. Thomas Howard waved. Anna and Colin went to the car. Only the old bird-like woman remained, "Mumma don't leave. Don't leave me again, Mumma. Oh, Mumma…No!"

They headed southeast in silence, through Tehachapi and into the Mojave Desert. Anna was not considering how fortunate she was not to be sharing the lot of those old people back there; she shared their fates by the horror of growing old, of losing control. Rich or poor, victims of sluttish time, that bitch.

She stole a glimpse at Colin, slack-jawed, hunched forward, staring ahead, not blinking, the steering wheel loose in his hands that moved in unison, if ever so slightly. He looked like he was about to cry. Had those old people really affected him so much or had they disturbed all his academic, his professional, ideals? Maybe it was himself he was concerned about, his own health, his stomach problems. Anna didn't want to ask, particularly not about his ulcer; didn't want to seem the old lady fuss-budget. But she was worried. That must have been why he stayed in the washroom so long back at the diner. Or, maybe, he was shook up by the way that black man had looked at him, the hate in those convict eyes.

Coming into Barstow, typical roadside business sprawl: service stations, muffler shops, radiator repair places, big on those around here, franchise restaurants, a beauty salon — The Mojave's Best Little Hair House — another place devoted solely to false fingernails. All of this tossed along the highway like trash, everything with a patina of yellow desert dust.

"Anna?"

"Yes, Colin?"

"I think, I'd like to stop for a drink."

He raised the little finger of his right hand from the wheel and pointed. There was a bar at the roadside — 'Packrat Pete's.'

"You *are* full of surprises. There is nothing, and I mean nothing, I would like at the present time more than a drink."

143

Pete himself was behind the bar, an actual bar, dark wood counter and real brass foot rail. They knew the wiry little man with the iron gray flat-top was Pete because of the nametag on his denim shirt with the sleeves missing. The tag was in the form of a small prospector's pan, 'Pete' in gold plastic letters inside.

There was only one other customer, a bearded man with a black tee shirt straining across his pot belly. He was seated at a table along the wall and underneath a glass case that held a pickaxe.

When they took seats at the bar, Pete spread his hands on the counter, leaned forward and with a big grin, said, "What'll it be and where you from?"

Anna asked for a double brandy-soda and Colin said he'd have the same thing. Pete didn't move, saying "Un huh. Un huh. And where you from?"

"Bring us our drinks," Anna said, smiling at him. "And we'll tell you."

Pete didn't like that much, despite the smile. When he'd turned away, Anna muttered out of Colin's side of her mouth, "Nosey little man."

"*Anna!*"

There were gold pans above the mirror in back of the bottles, framed black and white photos of men with donkeys, men with skinny little horses, picks and pans dangling from packsaddles. There were cardboard cutouts of turkeys on the wall.

"You looking at the picks," Pete said, setting down their drinks. "Use to keep em on the walls on hooks but ever now and again some boys'd get liquored up, take em down and start swinging em at each other. Had to put em in them cases."

"Good idea," Anna said. "What about the turkeys?"

Pete knotted his brows.

"Where you from, ma'am? Thanksgiving in a couple of days."

"We're from Canada," she smiled sweetly.

"Well don't you have Thanksgiving up there?"

"Indeed we do. But it is earlier."

"You people sure like to be different."

"Like to be more realistic too," Anna said.

"What does that mean, exactly."

Colin knew that Anna was going to say something sarcastic, so he jumped in. "What she means is that because it is colder up there, the harvest is brought in earlier."

"Uh huh," Pete looked as if he was reluctant to accept that but finally he shrugged. "We don't get much of a harvest in these parts but we sure get turkeys coming in all year around."

He laughed heartily and they smiled politely. "We're having a big party in here Thanksgiving evening. Our exotic dancers — each of them guaranteed white meat — pardon, ma'am — they have got themselves turkey feather costumes. We got vodka and cranberry juice cocktails on special. You can come dressed as a turkey, and best outfit wins a bottle of — what else? — Wild Turkey."

From the back of the bar, from the man with the huge pot belly, came a sound like a cannibal might make if he was choking on long pork, "Ga gobba. Ga gobba."

When Colin and Anna turned, the fellow raised his hands up in front of his beard, "Ga gobba. Gobba gobba gobba."

"Okay, buddy," Pete said. "You practice later, dammit. Don't disturb the customers now."

To Anna and Colin, in a lower voice, Pete said, "That's Ernie over there. He's practicing for the turkey call contest. Trying to gobble like a turkey does. You know? Ernest ain't exactly right. Don't have all his marbles, you might say."

Colin wondered where that expression came from. Perhaps some child in the nineteenth century, who had come to play with his friend and had an extreme reaction upon discovering he didn't have all his marbles. He was thinking this when Pete added, "Old Ernie there, he was all right until he went to 'Nam."

"To where?" Anna asked.

"'Nam. Vietnam."

"Oh."

"You remember Vietnam, don't you, Ma'am? That's the one where your country didn't support our country like it should of."

"Yes, maybe if we had, you wouldn't have lost."

"Hell we didn't lose. We didn't flee Vietnam. That's just the way the Jews in the media interpreted it."

"Oh, God," Anna moaned. "They always get around to the Jews."

Pete was too carried away to have heard or he pretended not to, "kowtowing to public opinion…" Anna looked away, from one pickaxe to another, heard it in fragments. "Inspired by liberal reporters …terrorists hiding out in Canada…"

It was back to Canada. Canada had a history of helping those opposed to America. First it was the draft dodgers, now it's Arabs. Canada "giving succor to the enemy."

Anna unable to restrain herself, "You're right, Pete. At least, in my case. I gave succor to the enemy, succor to a few draft dodgers, anyway. When my husband wasn't around."

That stopped him for a moment. But, despite clenched teeth, Pete managed to say, "Lady, this is the greatest country on God's earth. Some of us still believe in it and don't want to hear…"

"Oh, for God's sake. You are such a tiresome little man."

Anna downed the rest of her drink and Colin did likewise. As she spun on the stool and was sliding off, Pete reached under the bar and set a cigar box on top of the upended glasses by the little stainless steel sink. He opened the box and there was the gun, a .38 automatic, black barrel, white plastic butt. "You have a foul mouth, old woman."

Colin could not believe it, said, "Now wait a minute mister. You can't…"

Pete took hold of the pistol, didn't raise it above the bar but pointed it at them through the wood. "I can do whatever I want. It is my country, my bar and my gun."

Colin thinking, What's wrong with this man? Anna grabbed Colin's arm. "Let's leave. These are not refined surroundings."

They walked toward the door, their backs to him, got almost there when Pete called out, "Don't let me ever see you two anywhere near my place."

Anna came to a stop, turned very calmly. Colin horrified at what she might do. Anna looked Pete in the eye and in a falsetto voice, cried, "Ga-gobba gobba gobba! Gobba gobba!"

Ernie at the table adjacent to them, replied in kind, excitedly, "Ga-gobba, gobba gobba gobba! Gobba gobba!"

The last thing Anna and Colin heard as they stepped outside was Pete hollering at Ernie to shut up for chrissakes, you fucking idiot.

he next morning they drove along the east side of the Salton Sea, through Brawley and into Mexico, over to Mexicali before noon, Colin taking everything in, surprised at how good the road was — half expecting, despite himself, a hardpan trail with big hapless stake trucks lurching from rut to pothole and filled with dozens of short brown men wearing stained straw hats, other men sleeping by the side of the road with sombreros pulled over their eyes. Anna sighed, "Oh, how wonderful to be once more in a land of adults."

A couple of hours later they stopped for a snack at a settlement, or agricultural crossroads. Pickup trucks surrounded a few shops and more than a dozen vendors' stalls comprised of plastic tarps draped over two-by-fours above tables heaped with textiles, electronic gadgets and food.

Anna got out of the car, spread her arms happily, looked at the sky. Colin seeing her, cloth bag swinging from the crook of her arm, unconcerned, "Better mind your bag, Anna. You don't want it to be stolen."

"No, my dear. I wouldn't want that."

She watched as he made sure all the windows were rolled up and the doors locked. He asked whether she thought it was all right, their stuff in view.

"Colin, my boy. We have just driven top to bottom through the country with the highest crime rate in the world. Yesterday a man pulled a gun on us and you didn't seem particularly worried."

He said nothing, followed her to one of the stalls where they sat outside at a wooden table. There was a scrofulous parrot in a filthy cage on the other side of the counter. The menu had been typed, an old ribbon in the machine, on white paper that was covered with plastic. The only words he recognized were "tacos" and "quesadillas," and he had no idea what he'd get if he ordered the last one.

So he told the young girl he wanted tacos. When she spoke again, Colin looked back blankly. Anna said, "She wants to know how many you want?"

"Uh, two." He held up two fingers. In Spanish, Anna told her, "The way he eats, you better bring him five."

She giggled. Anna ordered for herself.

"You never cease to amaze me," Colin said, once the girl had skipped off. "You speak it well."

"Not at all, darling. Far from it. I know some words, not as many as I once did. But they're coming back as I apply my mind. For instance, there was a sign at a side road back there, a few kilometres or so, leading, I thought, to a town called "Basura.""

"It took a couple of minutes before I remembered it means 'Garbage.'"

"Oh, so it's the road to the garbage dump."

"That's what one would think except that this sign was just like all the others we've seen for towns. Imagine Fred and Ethel motoring down here in their RV. Ethel wanting to turn, see if there were any photo opportunities in the town of Garbage."

Anna began singing, "I'm going back to Garbage Town… Remember that? No? Actually, it was 'Lonesome Town.' I used to sing that behind old Hawkshaw What's-his-name? And wasn't I thinking about those halcyon days just yesterday. Ah, me. Las Palabras. Yes, they do come back like memories."

The parrot made a noise and Anna looked over at it, stared for a moment, said "Loro! Hola, Loro."

She said it louder, looking at the bird who looked back with one unblinking eye, and replied, "Hola, guapa. Hola, guapa."

"Must be near-sighted," Anna muttered.

The girl brought the food, and Colin wanted to say he'd only ordered two tacos but she was gone before he could make up his mind how to go about it. Tasting one, he decided two wouldn't have been nearly enough. He wondered what Anna was eating, chicken bits in some orange-white stuff that reminded him of a melted creamsicle.

A couple of minutes later when he was on his third taco, a huge Mercedes bus with tinted windows pulled up across the road, chickens and kids moving out of its path, not frantically but slow and cool.

Colin was surprised to see ordinary-looking people step off the bus, some with suitcases or boxes tied with string. Everything was a surprise to him. He was still looking at the bus when the girl, she was maybe thirteen, set down two bottles of soda water and said, to him, indicating the bus, "Muy grande, si?"

Colin right away knowing what she meant, replying, "Si, si."

The girl smiled at him. When she was gone, Anna said, "I think she quite fancies you."

"Don't be silly, she's hardly more than a child."

"They mature faster down here. She's a fetching little poppet. You probably noticed her budding breasts."

"You're disgusting."

"So you have told me."

They finished eating and went to the counter, gave the money to the girl who handed it to an older woman, her mother or aunt. While she was making change, Anna spoke to the parrot, and it replied on cue, "Hola guapa. Hola guapa."

Anna told Colin to tell the bird hello. "Say 'Hola.'"

Colin, a little bit self-conscious, everyone looking at him, the girl wide-eyed, said, "Hola!"

The bird looked at him, the unnerving eye, and spoke back. "Maricon! Maricon!"

Colin thinking he knew what the bird had said, wondered why they, all three of them, were laughing — the two Mexicans covering their mouths with their hands.

Anna assured the woman and the girl that it was not true. Colin shook his head at the bird, "No maricon."

"Maricon! Maricon!" replied the bird.

Colin shook his head, jabbed at his chest with his thumb, "No, Canadian!"

This caused the Mexicans to laugh more enthusiastically.

Anna took his hand, lead him away, Colin glancing over his shoulders at the women who were still giggling.

"Am I missing something?" he asked Anna.

"Yes, but I'll tell you about it some other time."

Colin spent his first night ever in Mexico in Hermosillo, at a hotel on the zocalo. Looking out their window, he could see the tower that flashed all day and all night, showing the time, the weather, advertisements and even electronic outlines of female breasts.

They reached Mazatlan late in the afternoon of the third day. For Colin, ever since crossing over to Mexicali, the days had been, as he told Anna, "like a dream. Like travelling through a dream."

They decided to stop for a few days.

"Afterall," Anna declared, "We're free. We've done it. We've flown the coop."

Anna hadn't been in Mazatlan, in Mexico, for over forty years. Then there had been the market area, the adjoining beach area, the winding road at the south end of town, called Olas Altas, with big hotels across from the water. Now those hotels, thriving back in the late fifties, were practically deserted. The tourists were at the Zona Dorado to the north, a long strip of new hotels and discos, everything happening in English.

That's where Colin wanted to stay — Anna preferring the old part of town. They'd had, not an argument, but a spirited difference of opinion. Anna saying, "I wouldn't know where I was, what country. It could just as well be Hawaii or Florida. It is horrible, sort of a generic tropical tourist trap."

"Well at least something's happening. It is lively. There's nothing going on in the old part and it's so shabby."

"Nothing going on? Didn't you notice the people cheek to jowl on the street? What you mean is, they're all Mexicans down here. In the Zona Dorado, the only locals are waiters and maids and taxi drivers."

They went back and forth with it, Anna prevailing by pointing out the dramatic differences in prices. Still Colin wasn't ready for a room with a shared bath in a *casa de huespuedes* so they stayed at a place on the old beach. That evening Colin was all for going to play with his peers and Anna told him to go ahead but that she was staying right where she was, there being quite an inviting looking bar off the lobby. The place was brown, long brown bar, brown carved wooden counters and shelves for the booze, brown and white marble floor, the veins of white reminding him of swirls of fat in a steak. The bartender had a boom box and kept feeding it Poco Sanchez, La Tona Negro tapes.

"Maybe I'm too tired to go up there," Colin said. "All the driving the past week."

"Yes, stay and relax, have a drink or two and call it a night."

Colin asked the guy for a Margarita. The bartender shook his head. "No hay. No Margaritas aqui. Zona Dorado, Margaritas."

He wound up with a Tecate, and spent the next two hours sitting there, looking around, listening to Anna talk with the bartender and another man down the bar. He didn't know what she was saying but after a few minutes, realized she was saying it with an English accent.

Terracotta pots held broad-leafed plants unfamiliar to Colin. The place was huge and he wondered what it must have been like in the glory days, filled with people and music. In the lobby, a swordfish collected dust over the registration desk.

After three glasses of wine, Anna was ready to leave the bar but wanted to take a stroll before turning in. Walking away from the beach, along dark streets, Colin wondered aloud if what they were doing was safe. He mumbled something about the lack of streetlights but Anna didn't reply.

There were a couple of blocks of marvellous colonial homes. Anna imagined the heavy doors opening onto tile floors and dark hardwood furniture. There would be a courtyard with a fountain, a jubacu palm in a corner, its fronds reaching to the second floor balcony, pots of agave cactus and Mexican tulip poppies.

Three more streets of middle class homes and shops took them to the zocalo, quiet now at midnight but not deserted. A little restaurant, under the bandstand at the hub, was closed — the shoeshine stands abandoned. Young couples strolled by holding hands.

They sat on a bench across the walk from a doll-like man with a large head whose feet dangled above the pavement. Anna smiled and he responded in kind. It was, Anna thought, as if an Aztec mask suddenly came to life.

The peak of the church roof could be seen above the leaves of the trees. Anna and Colin talked and the little man stared at them — not with hostility or as if he wished to attract their attention. He just watched.

After a few minutes, Colin said, "Come on, let's go back. It makes me nervous being scrutinized like this."

"As you wish but the man doesn't mean us any harm. Sitting in this zocalo is probably his entire life. He knows every inch of it, you see — every shrub and the patterns of bark on every tree, no doubt; every chip out of the green paint on the shoe shine boxes — so when something changes, whenever there are additions or subtractions, it absorbs his complete attention. We are something new in his familiar landscape.

"Hey!" she exclaimed, "look over there!"

"What?"

"There. At the edge of the square, just between those trees."

Colin looked where Anna was pointing, at first not focusing on anything, like when someone hands you binoculars. It took a moment until he saw the figure, hunched over, body contorted, moving along on bent legs — a man. He took three steps, stopped, moved his head left and right and started forward again, lunging with one leg then sliding the other forward. He carried a small sack in one hand. The trees of the zocalo punctuated his progress.

"El Hermito."

The little man had spoken without taking his gaze from them, knowing what they were seeing. "El Hermito que vive en la eglisa."

Anna looked from the skulking shadow to the gnomish man. He opened his mouth again to speak. Only his lips moved. Colin tried to figure out what the man reminded him of. A turtle, he decided; he has a face like a turtle. "What's he talking about?"

"He says that is the famous hermit who lives in the church. The hermit ventures out only at night and only as far as the market where he makes his small purchases and scurries back to his quarters."

"Oh, come on! He must really think we're naïve tourists."

"What's more, the hermit's job is to ring the bells."

"Sure just like the Hunchback of Notre Dame."

"And might he have his own Esmeralda?"

"Who?"

"That's the gypsy girl Charles Laughton was sweet on."

"Oh, I never actually saw the movie."

"You must have read the book then."

"No."

"Well then how did you know that the hunchback rang the bells at Notre Dame?"

"I don't know. It's just part of the culture."

"I see. Oh, now our friend is saying that the hermit came one day to the church to beg alms from the priest who, instead of giving charity, offered him the bell ringer's job. That was twelve years ago and he has been there ever since. And, so, at night he slips along the shadowy streets."

"Do you actually believe that?"

"Why not? Look, there he is now at the church, our hermit, vanishing behind yon buttress."

"Well that doesn't mean the story's true. He probably just..."

Anna sighed and gave him a look of only mild exasperation. She stood, bid the little old man a goodnight and strode off. Colin followed.

The next morning, they compromised on the day's agenda, Anna wanting to have breakfast in the market before going to the beach at Olas Altas — Colin's wish was to do everything up at the golden zone. So what they settled on was breakfast in the market and the rest of the day up in what Anna annoyed him by calling 'Gringoland.'

"Well we're gringoes, after all," Colin stated.

"Indeed, but there are degrees."

Anna seemed oblivious to the flies in the restaurant where they ate — Colin anxious to get out of there as soon as they had walked in the place. Anna ordering some weird dish, the poached eggs sort of floating in a tomato sauce, reminding him of soup. She loved it, sopping up the last bit of sauce with torn bits of tortilla. Colin had toast with his eggs and bacon. Anna insisted on a second cup of the strong coffee, bought a newspaper from the little boy who came right into the restaurant, stack of papers under his arm. Afterwards it was necessary for her to meander through the narrow, dirty streets to reach the road along the shore. She had to stop at every stall, look in every window — Colin noting that the prices weren't as low as he would have expected. He was curious about the video stores, surprised that they even had a film industry in Mexico.

In some places you had to practically climb up from the street to the sidewalk or jump down from the curb. Buses passing every few seconds, no way to escape the stink of exhaust but no one seeming to mind. Some of the buses had been given names by their drivers; they were old beaters but brightly painted and decorated with chrome gadgets. Several had chrome wands, turn signals, mounted on the front bumpers with little lights at their peaks. Colin waited while Anna went into a shop to buy a bathing suit, another shop to buy shoes. The crowd jostled him. He patted his back pocket a few times. Nobody hassled him though. One time he lost sight of Anna and felt a slight rush of adrenalin but then he saw her and it was alright. They finally made it to the waterfront. It hadn't been so bad really but he was no less anxious to get away from there. Anna wouldn't hear of them taking a taxi. Instead she waved down some old Volkswagen van and they got in there with eight Mexicans. One lady had, on her lap, a straw basket covered with a thick cloth. Colin looked, wondering what was in the basket. The woman lifted the cloth and he saw the tortillas, warmth rising off them. The woman smiled at him and he smiled back.

He couldn't figure out what was going on. Why the van had even stopped for them. At first he thought maybe Anna had been hitchhiking when he wasn't looking. Nobody said anything to the driver and there weren't any bus signs on the streets but he knew where to stop. Not only for the Mexicans but for them too. Anna had just handed him some coins and ten minutes later, the guy pulled over and looked back at her. Colin followed her off the bus.

It was cleaner, no doubt about that. Big hotels. Some of them with horseshoe driveways, sprinklers turned on the plants, the mist feeling good as it caught them walking by. Taxis waited at the curb, drivers leaning against them wearing those guyabara shirts outside their pants. The restaurants all had patios, and waiters hustled customers off the sidewalks. They spoke English sprinkled with some Spanish, just enough to flatter: "Amigo ... Amiga ... granola ... Senor, you want Margarita? ... Cerveza ... What is your desire? ... Diga me!"

The sidewalks were wider up here, no cracks in them, fewer Mexicans, like Anna had said. Mostly there were young Americans and Canadians, some Germans. All dressed basically in the same outfits, shorts or bathing suits, tee-shirts with lettering and logos, baseball caps, flipflops, sun cream on their noses. Many of the girls in nothing but a bikini. Older women, older men turned out the same way.

Colin had his bathing suit on under his slacks but Anna needed to change in the Ladies' at a hotel. Colin went out the back door of the place to wait for her on the edge of the sand. He took off his pants and shoes under a big palm tree with a bending smooth gray trunk. Left his shirt on, unbuttoned; shy about his body; his pudgy legs, thick stomach, white skin.

He told himself not to be so damned self-conscious. There were all these other guys going by, younger than he, college age, with beer guts — not hiding anything, even flaunting it. Big hairy bellies lopping over phosphorescent baggy swim trunks, carrying bottles of Corona in insulated holders. But, no, he didn't have the personality for that; wasn't the type to follow his stomach up the beach, yelling, "Parr-dee!" or "Rock and Roll!"

He turned when he heard a jingling sound, knowing it was Anna. She had bought half a dozen cheap bracelets. Her bathing suit reminded him of the kind women wore in 1950's photographs. The top was white and fuller than a regular two-piece bathing suit; the bottom with a little skirt like a short tennis outfit. It was cute, bouncy, even sexy, Colin thought, flipping up and down like that. The *outfit* was sexy. Or it would have been on a girl of, say, twenty-five.

The skin on Anna's legs looked dry, but it wasn't that horrible sagging flesh that old men and women so often have — skin that always reminded him of grade school art class projects — gluing paper onto other paper, not putting it down evenly so there were creases you could never smooth out. Her legs themselves were thin but not scrawny sticks. He wondered when she'd painted her fingernails and toenails. They were bright red. Probably got up in the middle of the night. Anna had new shoes made of rope and canvas with wedge heels. That was her style; he remembered seeing her in a similar pair back at Valley View. Colin had a picture of all the stuff having been taken from her room in plastic supermarket bags, stored in a closet back there. She wore sunglasses too, and, if he squinted, almost closed his eyes but not quite, he could imagine her the movie star or, at least, the actress she had once been. Yes, forty, fifty years ago. It never ceased to disconcert him, thinking that, saying it to himself: fifty years.

They spread their straw mats, Colin settling on his stomach. "Let me put some of this cream on your back," Anna said, hurriedly adding, "You can't reach every spot yourself and you are so fair. Half an hour out here and you'll burn, love."

"Okay," he said, surprising her.

Colin had his hands under his face, elbows sticking out. He was expecting Anna to make some smart comment, kidding around in her sexual way. But she was all business, and he relaxed. Anna working the stuff in with her spidery fingers. It did give him a peculiar feeling when she put the lotion on his legs, the tops of his legs. He felt her fingers working their way up from his ankles, stopping several inches from the bottoms of his boxer trunks. He wondered what people on the beach might think, seeing her doing that. Probably didn't pay the slightest bit of attention or, if they even noticed, assumed it was his old aunt Millie. Funny to think that not so long ago, he had thought of Anna as merely the most curious senior on his caseload.

It was even more peculiar to think of the fingers working on him as belonging to the temptress from 'Eaton Place.' He closed his eyes for a second. "Done," she said, giving him a gentle slap on the back. "Now me."

Colin sat up and squeezed lotion onto her back. Anna getting a pleasant cool sensation from that. Colin feeling her spine and ribs under the flat of his hand. He was surprised at how her skin was darker than his hand. He wondered about her background, her ancestors. Her father must have been of French origins, a name like Dupree. Or maybe she had really made that up, as the note in the file suggested. Colin put the stuff on her calves but when he got to the knees, hesitated. "Come on, Colin. Don't lose heart now. I don't fancy sitting up to do it myself and getting sand all over me. Just grit your teeth and think of dear old Saskatoon at Christmas time."

Her thighs felt soft. He didn't mind doing it. Thinking of an old woman walking down the street, some other old woman, of the old woman's legs under her dress, that was repulsive. He must have been thinking it for a little longer than necessary because Anna, teasingly, said, "Are you done? If not, I mean if you are enjoying yourself, keep on by all means. It is fine by me."

Turning her head, seeing his embarrassment, she added, "Just joshing, love!"

Colin lay back down and felt the sun warm on his back. Last week they were in Canada, in Kelowna, in Washington, at that cafeteria in Yuallum. The idea of it, the reality of it, still such a novelty.

"Mmmm," Anna moaned. "Life, she is good, senor. Do you know, I never ever went to the seashore as a child? Not once. In spite of growing up in Bath. I was seventeen before I stuck a toe in the ocean. I had already begun to work in theatre, music hall, actually. A few of us young ladies went to St. Anthony Head. We found a splendid cove for sunbathing. At night we drank mulled wine, four of us in one room, listened to dance music on the radio, interrupted by warnings about the growing communist menace.

Colin said nothing, just let her go on. She talked about the post-War years; theatres, being in radio plays, touring with a swing band. Her words were lazy, spoken while her face rested on her bent arm, words spilling out onto the sand. Colin thought of the line, sands of time. Where'd that come from? The Bible? Shakespeare? Or some popular song?

He had to admit that what she was saying sounded romantic. Her being just fifteen when the war ended. A precocious teenager wandering through the rubble of the late-forties in London. He realized it wasn't just the distance from then to now that made her memories sound so romantic. No, Anna's youth had been lived in a truly dramatic time. What had he been doing in his corresponding years? Which would be the late eighties, early nineties?

Summers, he would go to the family cottage at Blaine Lake. There was that great musty smell the first time, opening the place, pulling back the shutters, to reveal the screens — the screens announcing summer; his father peering close at them, like Sherlock Holmes with his magnifying glass, searching for holes, pleased when he found something to patch. But, first thing, they had to get the generator going. When he got older, Colin sat on the porch with girls at night, his parents inside reading magazines from years past or sleeping, maybe sleeping. Colin always afraid they were listening to him. Horrified that the girl would say something like, "Colin, what're you trying to *do*? Don't touch me there." And he'd know his parents would have heard. In the morning, he'd be sheepish at breakfast, them glancing at him but not saying anything about what they'd heard, what might have occurred.

But even worse than that, something that actually did happen, was the night he brought Joy Andrushak over. Everyone at school used to joke about her name. Her first name. The boys would snicker about her giving it, giving joy to whoever wanted it. He and Joy used to drink rum and cokes on the beach and this particular night were being bold, having a couple more on the porch of his parents' cottage. Colin would tiptoe into the kitchen to bring back more Coke. Joy coming over and sitting on his lap in the Adirondacks chair. Her not talking loudly but certainly moaning loudly or he thought it was loudly. Going, "Uhhh…Unnnm…Mmmmmh…Oooooh!"

Not that they did anything or rather they didn't do *it*. Just extremely heavy petting. Colin knew they would have gone farther if ever they'd gotten together at the right place. Joy was slender but with good—no, great—breasts, generous but not loose. Joy worked out and had blonde hair but what really made her so sexy were her eyes and her lips. Her upper lip never completely met her lower one, so you would always see the bottoms of a couple of teeth. She never seemed to be wide awake, her eyes always half-closed like that. The last Colin had heard, she'd been making very good money as an exotic dancer in Toronto.

He tried to picture her dancing on stage with no clothes on, or hardly any. He'd only been to a strip bar one time, in Vancouver, a fraternity party when he was at Simon Fraser. The girl there at that place, the Austin Hotel, wearing a fireman's hat and rain slicker, red lingerie under that. There was a brass pole standing in the middle of the stage. Did they still have poles in firehouse? Did the men hear the call, jump out of bed and slide down the pole? The girl at the Austin had wrapped herself around the pole, pretended to be masturbating. Colin thought of Joy. Did she do something like that? Have some gimmick? She must. Colin hadn't known what to expect at the strip bar and so was surprised to see each dancer with her own elaborate act. One took a shower. There was an actual shower on stage surrounded by a transparent plastic curtain. You saw her through this, like you were peeking into her washroom. Saw her soaping herself, writhing around. What did Joy do? He tried to picture her with the fire pole, in red high heels and frilly red panties. Her long thin muscular legs that were always honey-coloured by the second week at the lake.

If they'd had sex then she would be the best looking girl he'd ever had sex with. No doubt about it. Not that there were many. Six. No, seven. He'd forgotten to count Ludmilla. Not very many but, he told himself, numbers don't prove anything. And, anyway, he'd gone steady with Margaret for over a year, hadn't been out with anyone else during that entire time. It was good not having to worry about sex, always knowing it was there. On the other hand, there hadn't been much variety, making love with Margaret. No variety at all, really. There was one way for doing it, and that was that. He wasn't kinky or anything but still. It always had to be this certain way or she'd get nothing out of it. Even though he'd only been with seven women that was enough for him to understand there was quite a difference in attitudes and behaviour. And none of the seven were kinky either. None did, or wanted done, things that he might have only heard about. He wasn't weird or anything but just take Margaret and Ludmilla. Margaret would have been disgusted at the very suggestion of him doing or wanting to do what Ludmilla wanted — no, demanded. He tried to picture Margaret in fire engine red lingerie and fire engine red high heels, rubbing up and down on a fire pole. No way. The thought was even disgusting somehow. But he couldn't see Ludmilla that way either. Joy, yes. Joy probably would do just about anything.

Strange though, Joy didn't seem to him as sexy as Anna; of course, he meant Anna of the old movies. He knew the cameras played tricks but, still, it was more than her face or figure. It was something that some women give off. Like Anna herself had said that time. Colin had this picture of being on that London street in the 'Eaton Place' movie, coming around the corner in the fog. Anna having just walked away from that Robert Rainer. Her in the long tight skirt. Then he's seeing her face, the message in her eyes…

"Colin?"

It startled him. Her voice sounding young in his reverie. Her calling him in the street. He was aware of a little tremor up and down his back, and was embarrassed, as if Anna had looked directly into his thoughts.

"Oh, I woke you. Poor boy. You gave a start. I don't wish to be an old nag but, really, you should turn over. Another minute with your back exposed like that and you'll be in agony for days."

"Yes, yes. Sure."

Colin realized he must, indeed, have been at least half asleep. He felt groggy as he turned over. Saw Anna smile at him. He was about to say something when he noticed her eyes glance at the front of his trunks. When she looked back at his face, Anna's mouth twisted into a sarcastic smile and she arched her eyebrows. "I see I did disturb you. So sorry."

Before he could make some sort of excuse, before even she saw him blush, Anna had rolled on to her back and closed her eyes.

Colin covered his face with a towel, as if hiding his embarrassment, and soon he was asleep.

When he woke, Anna was standing and drying herself with the other towel, water glistening on her body. "Oh, don't look at my hair."

She quickly made a turban of the towel. Her turn to feel uncomfortable, thinking her soaked hair looked stringy, like that of any old lady, the old lady that she was.

"The water is lovely," she said to divert attention from her dripping self. You should go for a dip."

"I'd rather go for some lunch."

They went up to the main drag. Anna changing out of her wet bathing suit, back into the lightweight cotton dress. Colin just pulling slacks on over his trunks.

"You pick the spot," Anna said, and Colin chose a place with tables and umbrellas on the sidewalk. "Senor"— somebody's, the name of it. Colin thinking that this might be the same place, a franchise that Ms. Dickson back at Valley View had mentioned. The sign on the roof, plastic, the outline of a happy campesino with his guitar, his faithful burro in the background.

The people under the umbrellas were gringos, mostly in their twenties, but older ones too, over sixty. No one in between that Anna could see. No middle-agers, no children. Looking over the group, Anna grinned, her gaze picking up flashes of light, like phosphorescent exclamation marks, like fireflies; actually daubs of sun block on noses. She thought it funny; moved her head back and forth quickly a few times. The noses stood out in the whoosh of her gaze, and she giggled.

"Anna! What on earth are you doing?"

"Oh…nothing, dear. Nothing of any consequence."

Maybe she was developing a weird habit, Colin thought. Perhaps he was witnessing the onset of a compulsion. The beginning of some Tourette's-type behaviour. There had been that poor man at Valley View who was forever reaching up to grab something, as if his fist was closing on a fly, though it merely closed on air. The man would open his fingers and look at his palm, flick at the imaginary fly with thumb and forefinger, then he'd continue walking and repeat the procedure. He did that at least three times a minute, every minute, every hour, every day. Colin had wondered if the man had that or other compulsions or tics throughout his life. He wanted to ask but couldn't ever summon the nerve. When he went back there, if he ever did, he would ask.

"Colin?"

The man wasn't on his caseload, and Colin didn't know for sure but he assumed the man hadn't developed the habit until coming to Valley View. It wasn't as if he could have been a tv repairman or an eye surgeon. Or, perhaps he could have been, and was able to control the tic when working. Colin pictured the tic in abeyance while the man made a repair to the optic nerve, then when he was done, out of his operating garb, he'd make up for the time he'd had to control it, the tic-less time.

Colin had considered the subject worthy of a paper. Until meeting Anna, it would never have occurred to Colin that the man might simply have been bored. Terminally bored and in need of something to do.

"Colin!"

He turned at the urgent voice by his side. Anna pulled on his wrist.

"They've a table for us. Where in heaven's name did you go?"

"Oh, uh, just thinking about something, that's all."

Colin sitting down, felt a little guilty because had the situation been reversed, his having to get Anna's attention that way, the waiter staring at her all bewildered, he would have immediately concluded Anna was exhibiting signs of approaching senility.

They had a corner table, young people on one side, older ones, two men and a woman, on the other. No sooner were they seated than one of the older men said something to Anna that Colin didn't hear. She picked up the menu, ignored him. What he said to her this time, Colin did hear; it was about a time share he owned in Mazatlan. Not, Hey I have a time share down here. But, rather, offering a preliminary phrase as an excuse to brag. "Beautiful, isn't it? Glad I got a time share here."

Anna gave him a cursory nod, not wishing to be impolite but not wanting to listen to him either. Colin checked the guy out. In his early sixties, deep tan, white boxer-type swim trunks, yellow silk shirt open to his belly, gold chain like two branches of a bright river descending through coarse gray and white chest hair.

The man still talking to her or at her. Anna turned to him, "Excuse me, please." Saying it dismissively, turning immediately back to Colin, "I fancy the chile rellenos. How about you?"

Colin didn't know what he wanted but not wishing to leave dead space for the man to fill, read the translation to himself and was just saying how chile relenos sounded like just the thing, when the man spoke to Anna again. "You got class. I like that in a woman."

Colin looked over at the table where the man sat with another man and a woman. He saw the woman grimace, not because the man was being presumptuous but because to her, it was obvious, the opinion was misdirected. She and the other man, her husband probably, were paler than their friend. The woman with tight, gray curls, masculine bearing. Colin was wondering why so many women that age got those haircuts, like they had little yappy dogs curled around the tops of their heads, when Anna turned full around to face the man, who was listing the wonders of his boat. He broke into a big smile when she faced him but it only lasted an instant — "Listen, you. I have no interest in your boat, your time-share or in talking to you for one more second and, since you won't take a hint, you can bloody well piss off."

Colin was surprised at her but not as surprised as the man and his companions. "The frigging nerve!" The woman fairly spitting it out. The man with the gold chain trying to recover. "Well I like that. I like a woman with spirit. Sorry we got off on the wrong foot. Say, let me buy you a pitcher of margaritas, huh?"

Anna moved her chair so that her back was turned completely to the man. But he took hold of her arm. "Hey, honey…"

Anna tried to jerk her arm free. Colin found himself on his feet.

"Take your hand off her!" Surprising the man, feeling himself trembling. The man released Anna's arm, assumed the expression of the aggrieved party, looking for confirmation. The adjoining tables of young people not giving it to him.

"Christ!" he exclaimed to no one and everyone. "Why don't you all lighten up. I came down here to have a good time."

He stood up then. Colin thinking the man might take a swing at him. But he lowered his head to say something in Anna's ear. "Sweetheart…"

Her smelling the booze on his breath. Then the waiter and the manager were there. The manager telling the man it was best, senor, that he and his party leave the restaurant. Pronto. Ahorita, my friend. He didn't want to leave, protested. The other man, who hadn't spoken before, urged his friend away. The lady shot daggers at Anna and Colin. The man walked off, bumping people's shoulders. The bus boy followed them out, looking like he was definitely willing to pop the gringo should it become necessary.

The manager returned and apologized to them, him sincerely humiliated that such a thing should happen in an establishment over which he was supposed to have control. He hoped they could forgive him and do him the honour of eating and drinking without money being exchanged. Anna replied in Spanish and the manager fairly beamed. He took their order personally, and with a flourish and a bow.

A young lady at the adjoining table, raised her bottle of Dos Equis, pointed it toward Anna, "Way to go, sister."

When their drinks arrived, Anna touched her glass to Colin's. "My hero. Ready to defend his lady's, I mean, this lady's honour."

Colin feeling proud, amazed at what he'd done or had been ready to do.

Soon they were talking with their neighbours — two Canadian girls who'd hooked up with American guys. Both of the young women and one of the young men had something to do with computers. Anna heard them mention information technology and adaptive technology. They asked questions of Colin that Anna realized were directed to determining how much he knew about or was involved with the field. They didn't bother asking her about such things. One of the girls telling her solidarity was necessary in confronting the unfortunate reality of the other gender.

"Can't live with em; can't live without em, eh?"

This from the girl who'd saluted her with the beer. Donna from Markham, Ontario.

Before Anna could reply, Donna had gone back to computer talk. Yes, thought Anna, I'm on the scrap heap of history and, judging by their conversation, that is, perhaps, not so unfortunate.

Although the two young women and one guy worked with the technology of computers, Colin and the other young man — hairy legs, black hair spilling out of his tee shirt, a tangle of black hair on his head — used computers in their work, so they all had this great thing in common. Anna pictured them seated in front of their terminals or their laptops all day, every day.

The young women had just met the young men, and now they knew Colin and it was as if they'd been hanging out for years. It was like flashing the masonic sign or something. They were enthusiastically discussing different programs, different systems, different frontiers. Lisa, also from Markham, was telling about a new technology or system or whatever that someone had invented and she had tried and so had her younger brother and his friends, and wasn't it wonderful. The rest of them agreed that, yes, it was wonderful. Yes, Anna told herself, just jolly hockey sticks. At which point, Lisa turned to her, "What are you thinking, Anna?" — as if the young woman was doing the old woman a favour by including her in the conversation. Anna noticing the pink frosted lips at the bottom of the pale flat face, limp brown hair.

Anna was about to say: I'm thinking how bloody boring the conversation is and how boring your lives must be to work at a computer all day and play at one at night — when Colin jumped in to prevent something unfortunate from happening; Anna thinking, the boy is getting to know me.

"Anna doesn't have a computer."

"She doesn't!" Ronnie exclaimed, the not-particulary-hairy fellow, as if he couldn't conceive of such a thing. "Why not?"

"Well, you see, I had to sell mine to go on the lam."

Colin looked horrified, the hair guy stared at her and the girls giggled, as if about to remark on what a joker Anna was. But Ronnie said, "Oh, in that case you need a laptop. Some of the new notebooks are no heavier than a hardback book."

Anna looked at him, wondering if he was serious. If he isn't, if he's teasing, he has a great deadpan delivery. No, he was serious.

Colin said, "Anna used to be on stage and in the movies."

"Yeah?" Ronnie said.

Anna smiled at him.

"Professionally?" Lisa, with that patronizing tone again.

"Indeed, professionally."

Anna wanted to laugh, felt good, felt there must be some heat left in the coals of her sexuality to bring out the bitchiness in this young suburban mouse.

"Anything I might have heard of?" Lisa asked, the edge in there.

"I rather doubt it, my dear." Anna flashed her best smile. "'Tartuffe,' 'Major Barbara,' 'Our Town.'"

Anna watched the girl's confusion. 'Our Town' rang some sort of bell somewhere but she wasn't about to commit herself. Anna sighed. Where's the fun in a catfight with this new breed? Colin shot her a look, but his eyes were twinkling.

Ronnie, not a bad sort, Anna concluded, told her how motion pictures would soon be made entirely by computer and eventually solely for computers. Soon it would be possible to manipulate the images of long dead actors. There'd be new Humphrey Bogart movies.

Anna announced that she was feeling tired and must return to the hotel for her afternoon nap. Colin about to respond: What afternoon nap? But she stopped him with a glance. It wouldn't do to let the truth be known, she was not tired but excruciatingly bored. They would never believe she could possibly be bored, not in their youthful and stimulating presence. At her age, an afternoon nap was readily believable. That's what old biddies did, took naps.

The young ladies certainly didn't seem put out at her announcement. Colin walking her to the entrance was solicitous. "Don't worry about me, Colin. Worry about yourself. I think the bitchy mouse fancies you. Do you have a condom?"

"Anna!" he said with exasperation, looking over his shoulder at the table, as if they might have heard.

"Yes, they're watching. How about I give you a long, sloppy kiss? That'll set their tongues to wagging, so to speak. Again, I'm just joshing. But, seriously now, better not let those straight arrows know I really am on the lam and that you assisted me. They might summon help on the World Wide Web, www.escapedelderly, sort of thing. See how quickly I catch on to the jargon? No, listen: seriously Colin, you can do much better than that, my boy. But if you think that's your only chance to play hide the weanie, well, there you are."

*W*ith that she strode off, swinging her new string bag, tossing a wise remark to a knot of cab drivers leaning against the low wall of the adjoining hotel garden and waiting for fares. They smiled broadly, said something back. Colin watching, saw them grin at each other after she'd passed by.

Anna began to whistle a slow Cielito Linda. She was feeling low. Not depressed like she had been at Valley View. She did not despair, all was not shrouded in gloom. The sun was shining and she was free. Yes, free and seventy-five. She did not care to think of what, for lack of a better word, she called, well aware of the hyperbole, her future. It was there on the edge, in her peripheral vision, and she was determined not to face it full on. No, get away from me, you old sod; get ye gone grim reaper leering over my shoulder.

Perhaps it is just as well I am my age, she told herself while she whistled. Anna thinking how she'd always shared the sentiment of that writer who'd said — who was it? — "I thought they'd make an exception in my case." She had been in one of the man's plays. Of course, Saroyan. Bill Saroyan. "The Time of Your Life." I am getting senile. First the pussy goes, then the mind. When that play hit, I was just a girl. A wonderful play but it should have stayed in America. Might have done well in Australia. But it did not translate into England. Even I knew that and was embarrassed. But, of course, I was working; if only for two weeks. Anyway, where the dickens was I? Oh, yes, indeed: the future. The youth of today, hope of tomorrow. Between my daughter — and how is she? Do I care? No — and this younger lot back there, it don't look too bright, ducks. What a bunch of bleeding bores. Lounging about sipping drinks with umbrellas in them and talking about computers. They should be wrecking saloons at their age. Swimming out to Tres Marias. Renting a jeep and roaring off to Honduras. Starting revolutions. Staying up all night breaking windows and singing the hits of the day. What hits? That's what I did and might do yet. I have a few tricks left up my sleeve. The blue meanies, that's what I've got right now or have got me. And there's nothing for it, nothing for it at all. Except to go shopping. That's right, feeling blue young lady, old lady, any kind lady? Well go buy naughty underwear, dress up, paint your toenails. Do something constructive. Or destructive.

Eight o'clock that evening, nearly seven hours later, when Colin, more than slightly tipsy, came reeling back to the hotel, he thought his key had opened the door to the wrong room. There were five people in there, and he didn't recognize any of them. Four were Mexicans, two middle-aged couples, the other a gringa he did not, truthfully, recognize as Anna Dupree. The only thing familiar, at first, was the hairdo, that strange, wavy peek-a-boo style, only now it appeared fuller and a different colour or, rather, the same gray only darker. Later, Colin figured he must have looked like an idiot standing with his fingers on the key that was still in the lock, swaying there as if the door was keeping him up, staring from one to the next, mouth open.

"Do come in, Colin. Join the fun."

It was Anna, all right. Somebody's boom box emitting brassy Mexican pop music. Anna sitting on a chair that didn't belong to the room. Anna in a snug peach-coloured lightweight dress, stockings, wedge heels. She had made up her face. Her eyelids faintly purple, eyes black rimmed. From the doorway Anna looked at least thirty years younger than the last time he'd seen her, those seven hours earlier. As he moved into the room, she got a little older but as he sat on the edge of the bed, next to a Mexican lady, her boyfriend or husband on the other side of her, Colin kept looking at Anna, thinking, "Not *that* much older."

The introductions passed in a blur; he caught the names Marta and Enrique but only those. What was going on, who were these people? If Colin moved too quickly he got dizzy, so he sat as still as possible. Aware of trying to be still. They talked Spanish. They were very mannerly, it seemed to Colin. Happy, not aggressive. That guy today, the one with the hairy legs, had ruined the party by becoming aggressive. Colin felt a twinge of pain in his stomach, high up. But it was gone in a couple of moments. He accepted a beer that someone offered. Anna had a glass of wine in both hands, the nails perfectly shaped and painted pale pink. On the table in back of her was a bottle of wine. Not a regular bottle but a carafe with a wide mouth. 'Padre Kino' on the label. Where'd he seen or heard that name? Somewhere on the highway not too long after crossing the border. Oh, yeah, near that place Guaymus. Everything was Parde Kino there. Colin had taken four years of German. Padre Kino must have been the father of Mexican movies. A German immigrant. Anna smiled at him. One of the women, not Marta, the other one, sat with her legs crossed. Colin couldn't help glancing at her chubby thighs. The skin was nice, the colour of it, like coffee with lots of cream. She caught him looking and giggled.

Soon all the Mexicans got up and started to leave. They'd been chattering away, Colin trying to look anywhere but at the woman's legs, and the next thing he knew everyone was shaking hands and saying *hasta la luego*. He managed to get to his feet. All four Mexicans spoke to him and he muttered back at them. They shook his hand. One of the men patted him on the shoulder. Very friendly people, Colin decided. The other man, looking at Anna, pointed at the boom box, spoke to her in Spanish, and she answered, nodding her head. The boom box stayed where it was. The man grabbed the chair that didn't belong with the room and took it with him, as he and the others left.

"Now, Colin. You sit right back down there on the bed," Anna told him. "Can I get you another beer? There's some Mescal left in the bottle over there."

"Beer."

She brought a bottle to him.

"I have to use the washroom. Don't you run away."

Colin smiled, looked after her. I couldn't run, he said to himself, I probably couldn't even walk. Why did she take the Padre Kino bottle in there but not the glass? Maybe there's one in there already. She'll sip wine while doing whatever it was they do in there that takes so long. Only he remembered that Anna didn't really take that long.

Colin drank, swayed on the bed, massaged his stomach, reminded himself he must avoid the spicy food, cut down on the booze. After

all, that's why he's down here. To get better. But one has to relax.
Mind and body. They must work together for good heath.

That girl. Donna. She'd played games with him. Led him on at
that bar they went to after lunch, dancing close, encouraging him,
then acting as if he'd tried something horribly outrageous. Looking at
him, what's the word, aghast, like his actions were astoundingly inap-
propriate. Whatever gave him such notions? All that.

Colin took another pull on the bottle. Best to put it out of mind.
What was Ludmilla doing this very minute? Maybe his evenings with
her hadn't been so bad. If he hadn't been in poor health, he might
have taken a different view of those times.

The bathroom door flung open. It really had been flung open,
knob banging against the wall. Anna's eyes fixed on him. Colin thinking that he hadn't heard water running or the toilet flushing. She had
Padre Kino by the thick neck and she poured some in the glass on the
dresser. Knocked back a mouthful and came over to him. Colin felt
dizzy as she stepped up to him. Her knees against this shins. Anna put
both hands on his shoulders, Colin telling himself, she must be steady-
ing me; I'm swaying, ready to pitch forward and don't realize it. She
pushed on his shoulders and he couldn't resist because the ceiling was
swirling. Anna climbed right on to him. Colin saw long pink nails flut-
tering at his fly — her fingers looking like a young woman's fingers.
He didn't understand what she was doing at first and by the time he
realized, Anna had his cock in her hand. He started to remark upon
this, considered whether to protest, but didn't say anything. It was too
late. Anna was bent over it, and before Colin even registered the fact,
she had her mouth around it.

Colin raised his shoulders off the bed to look at what was tran-
spiring. He was confused, not thinking it wasn't right what was happening, just surprised. He was looking at it sort of objectively.

"Don't look at me, honey. Close your eyes."

Colin did as he was told, dropped his head back on the bed, a
glimpse of wavering ceiling before closing his eyes. He didn't feel so
dizzy now.

What he did feel, he never felt anything similar. He didn't have
all that much experience, sure, but he had a little. When women had
done this or girls had done this before, Colin always had the feeling
they didn't really want to do it. They seemed to just put their lips there

and the feeling was like a ring around it, them wanting as little contact with it as possible. But now it was completely enveloped. She was probing it, tickling it — the soft underside of it, near the top — with the tip of her tongue. It's Anna doing this. Colin giggled. Anna from Valley View.

The feeling stopped. Anna saying, "You think it is funny, do you, love? Well just wait until you feel this."

She raised up off her haunches, balanced on her knees and reached under to take hold of her underwear, the seam at the top of her right leg.

"Lord, forgive me for what I'm about to do."

She got into position over him, began lowering herself. His penis just fine, not too big, not too small, thick though and standing up. Thank, God, Anna telling herself, that he's not too drunk, just drunk enough to let it happen. Drunk enough not to stop me, to run hollering from the room, vomiting as he stumbles away in utter disgust. "Oh, yes, darling. You spoke? It feels good, my sweet?"

The boy groaning under her.

Lord knows I needed help from Padre Kino and it was necessary to anoint myself with a handful of sun tan lotion but here I am.

Speaking soft and low to Colin, "Getting to this position, my love, was not easy. My guile would be all for naught had not fortune smiled. And finding myself here, you can damned well bet I was going to take advantage of it. You like this? What I'm dong?"

She had been alternately rubbing her bottom against his pelvic bone and rising up on his cock, settling down on it. He moaned again, muttered. Anna asking, "Anyone ever do this to you? Wait. Okay, there. How's that?"

He muttered again, something that was incomprehensible even to himself.

"Yes, I'm sure that's true, dear. I haven't used these muscles for donkey's years, my precious. I'm so grateful that I still have them."

I'm so grateful to you, too. So grateful.

Jesus, I'm beginning to feel it myself. Hold on, this is a surprise. I would be entirely content to have it inside me. But, this, this is entirely unexpected. You don't think I might actually...Oh, I do declare. It might, I might. Yes, I just might.

"No, surprises, love. Hold on there. Hold on. We're making...Uh huh. Thank the Lord, for alcohol. No, don't go making any moves yourself. Just keep still, dammit. That's right. Yes. Oh, yes. Here we go! Get ready!"

Anna got all the way down on it, grit her teeth, feeling the bones of her bottom pressing on him. She grimaced, squeezed her pussy, grinding her clitoris on the base of his cock until she was burning down there.

Colin made a noise like he was hurt, like he had entered a darkened room and someone stepped from behind the door and punched him in the stomach.

And Anna cried out.

ACT III

She woke on her side and, raising her head a few inches, noticed mascara smudges on the pillow. Her top hip felt cool and she saw that her dress was around her waist, the hip exposed, one white garter strap dangling over the side, stockings, garter belt askew. She had no panties on. She looked at herself, thinking she might see to enhancing it with a bit of colour, dare she dye it? Colin was lying there as she'd left him, across the bed. Sleeping the sleep of the just, of the innocent. But, staring at him a moment longer, Anna allowed herself the horrible thought that it might be the sleep of the dead. Finally she saw his thick middle rising and falling. I couldn't, she told herself, be *that* good.

It was six-thirty a.m. Her little brown plastic clock that had been operating on one double-A battery for four years, sat next to a bottle of Bohemia beer on the bedside table. Not long ago the clock had been marking institutional time.

Anna observed Colin. The mouth open, sleeping penis like a pale cigar butt, and concluded she'd best get out of there for a goodly period of time. She imagined his feelings upon waking and remembering what he'd done or allowed to be done. He'd probably be, at worst, dreadfully ashamed, maybe he'd send her packing; at best, and the most she could hope for, was that he'd just be terribly embarrassed, lay down the law to her with repeated assurances that such a thing would never, must never, could never, happen again.

She slid quietly out of bed and gathered some more of the things she'd bought the day before. She had to pee very badly but would do that in the "Senoritas" off the lobby. And wash her face there as well. Didn't want to risk waking him with bathroom noises. But with lipstick, on the bathroom mirror, she wrote: "Gone out — At 10 on bench across the Avenida?"

She tiptoed out, shoes in hand.

In the zocalo, the old Aztec turtle man was at his place, and smiled, bidding her good morning, his hooded eyes giving her the once over. Guess what I've been doing, old man? She was tempted to tell him but passed on to the green metal building at the centre of the park. Only the roof was above ground. You went down a few steps into a tile-floor café. There were workers inside having breakfast. Anna took her coffee outside to a formica-topped table. Not even seven o'clock and already some of the shoeshine stands were busy — customers seated, reading newspapers, while the men worked on the shoes. Bottles, rags, brushes all arranged in their places in the box under the footrest. So wonderfully old-fashioned. Anna bought a 'Diario' from the same urchin who'd come into the restaurant the day before. He smiled in recognition, grabbing a paper from the stack under his arm, deftly folded and handed it to her in a flourish, adding a little bow. For this he was allowed to keep the change which was as he expected.

Anna read as much of the paper as she could comprehend, had another coffee, dawdled, watched the early coming and going. After an hour, she got up and joined the crowd.

There were several Indians on the church steps. In from the Sinaloa countryside. What with their serapes and sandals, Anna was reminded of the hippies she'd seen so many years ago on the Spanish Steps in Rome. There were government buildings adjacent, and secretaries visible in windows seated before a variety of typewriters, big manuals and antediluvian-looking electric ones; in the middle of the room, one woman, the queen bee, seated at a large tan-coloured computer that even Anna knew was an old-fashioned one.

Across the park on the smaller street bordering the zocalo, smart shops sold cosmetics and CDs. At a bakery near the market she bought a brioche and nibbled it as she walked, swinging her new woven bag. She felt good, even though worried about Colin's reaction. She was sore but pleasantly so; it had been a long time. Such a long, long time.

Colin was stretched out on his back on a straw mat, a tee shirt covering his face. Anna looking at him from the top of the stone steps leading to the sand. There were his topsiders, not tossed on the sand but just-so, like sentries at the head of the mat. She knew he had keys and passport and money stuffed in the toes. Again she tried to envision him thirty pounds lighter; he'd have a nice body. The morning before, on the beach at the zona dorado, a little kid hustling cheap masks, squatted down there after making his unsuccessful pitch and gave Colin, who was sleeping, the once over, saying to Anna while pointing at Colin's belly, "*Leche. Leche, si?*"

It was said with no hint of malice, but out of curiosity — skin that colour being so unusual to him. The boy had held his forearm next to Colin's wondering at the contrast.

Can't stare at the young man any longer, she told herself. Have to go down there and face the music. What kind of music will it be? She fished in her bag for a hand mirror and lipstick. He will be looking at me much more critically now. Must do all I can to temper his reaction. There is not all that much that can be done, alas. Thank God for the bone structure. Well, here goes.

She hummed, walking down the stone steps. Da da da dum.

"Well, then, enjoying our vacation, are we?"

Colin lifted the tee shirt from his face and looked at her, didn't say anything for a moment just stared, then bid her a good morning.

That's not too bad a start, Anna told herself. Desultory, but at least he didn't bite my head off.

"A lovely morning it is, indeed." She said. "Have you breakfasted yet?"

"Ugghh."

Colin draped his right arm over his face. Anna thinking the "Ugghh" was another hopeful sign.

"Un cruda, eh?"

"Huh?"

"Hungover are we?"

"Yes. My head feels like it's in a vice. My stomach. I can feel my ulcer."

"Can I get you anything? Medicine? I'd be happy to. I know — how would you like a licuado? Remember that stand we saw, all colourful, the two young men working there, making drinks with fruit and blenders? Yes? I can run, fetch you one made with milk."

"Maybe in a little while. Thanks. I couldn't keep it down now."

"Just say the word."

Anna lay down. The morning sun felt good. She began to hike her hem, thought better of it. He might look and be put disagreeably in mind of the night before. She was afraid to say anything else, afraid of pressing her luck. She hid behind her big new pair of cheap sunglasses. Folded her hands on her flat stomach and closed her eyes, thinking: I must be perfectly honest with myself. No illusions, no delusions. Just the truth. There is no way I look a day over sixty. I look therefore, fifteen years younger than I am. She savoured the idea, was about to consider whether, in all honesty, she could go for fifty-seven, when it occurred to her that if Colin looked fourteen years younger than his age, he'd look half his age — fourteen.

"Anna?"

"Yes, love. I mean, yes, Colin?"

"Last night..."

Oh, God. She bit her lip, waited.

"Last night did that, uh, you know, did it really happen?"

Anna wondered exactly how to answer. For a moment she thought of replying, 'Did what really happen?' Feign innocence. On the other hand, she might act contrite, beg forgiveness. Or turn the tables on him. You brute, coming home with liquor on your breath and molesting me. Me, an old woman. Yes, that would be funny.

"Did we, I mean..."

At least, he said "we." Not did "you" — as in: Did you take advantage of me?

"Did we, you know, do it?"

"Yes, Colin. We did."

He was silent.

"But..." Anna began, not finishing the thought because she heard these sounds coming from him, caught in his throat as if he were choking. She felt her heart race, thinking he was, indeed, choking. When Colin removed his arm from across his face, she saw that his face had gone lobster red, and tears were rolling down his face but they were tears of laughter. His stomach heaved up and down, up and down, and as it did, his hips moved in counterpoint. Colin struggled for a deep breath. Got it. And was off on another jag.

"Well, I don't think it was *that* bloody hilarious."

"No. No. It was…" Colin paused to run the back of one hand across his eyes. "Remember that story you told me about the fellow you met in Toronto who was selling the newspapers? You had that affair with him and when it was over and he was going away, he told you that you were the best, uh, you know."

"Yes, I do remember. And what, pray tell, made you think of that?"

Colin had stopped laughing. He turned his face to Anna. "You know."

Anna felt the tears well up behind her eyes. She clenched her jaw and blessed her sunglasses. She touched his lips with one finger. And when she was able, spoke. "There's plenty more where that came from, young man. You play your cards right."

He started to laugh again and Anna felt the tears ready to come now. "I think you're ready for that licuado. Wait right here."

Later that afternoon when the beach became too hot, Colin wanted to go back to the room and take a nap. In the evening, he felt good enough to go for a walk with Anna, who'd spent her day alternately nursing him and keeping away from him. She felt guilty for feeling so good, tried not to show it in front of Colin — but didn't want to appear morose either. He was a good patient; never complained, didn't require babysitting. With his resistance down, Colin could even be funny, as if he felt so bad there was no need to hold anything back.

He went to sleep at nine-thirty, and Anna nipped down to the bar for a couple of glasses of port. She could have used two or three more but returned to the room to get away from a man who was making passes at her. He was about fifty, she reckoned. Anna supposed she should be flattered but wasn't. My guy's more than twenty years younger than that, she told herself with something between a snort of irony and a giggle of mischief.

In the morning, Colin announced he was feeling much better but wasn't one hundred percent. His stomach still bothered him. He was hungry though and, not being prepared for the jitney trip to zona dorado, was willing to brave the smells of some Mexican restaurant.

"A clean one," he emphasized. A place where he wouldn't have to see flies on refried beans. They went to the biggest hotel on that part of the beach, where tables in the dining room were covered with white linen, and Colin had poached eggs with whole wheat toast. Poached eggs on top of the toast. And wasn't that a test of Anna's vocabulary.

They made small talk, tiptoed around each other until Colin asked if she wanted to start south. "I'm not interested in staying in Mazatlan any longer and, the way I'm feeling, it's a good day to be driving."

Anna was all for it so they got on the road, that winding, swooping coastal road, and by evening were in San Blas, a beautiful spot that had finally been discovered not all that many years ago. Discovered and nearly overrun despite the constant assault of mosquitoes.

Their room had screens on the windows, a ceiling fan and mosquito nets over each bed. Colin was delighted, having never seen anything like it. "I feel like I'm in a movie," he said.

They didn't use both beds. Anna parted the net on the bed Colin had chosen, thinking it was as if she was going out on stage, telling herself that in a sense she was. She had, after all, no other opportunity to perform and, hence, gave it everything she had, everything she'd learned from hundreds of other parts. And she offered up a silent prayer that Colin would not become disgusted with her. She decided to show him, over time and starting now, things that she was willing to wager, he'd never experienced, some others he'd probably never even thought of.

They reached Puerto Vallarta late the next night, coming into town along the beach road past huge hotels and condo towers. By the time they found a decent room, they were too exhausted to do anything but fall asleep. In the morning, outside, Anna could not contain her feeling of revulsion as she looked around. "But it is beautiful," Colin said. "Beautiful beaches, beautiful old colonial buildings."

"That's what makes it so horrible. All this natural beauty and lovely old architecture overwhelmed by hordes of slovenly young people. The dignity of the place, not to mention the people, compromised by having to accommodate them."

"Aren't you overstating your case?"

"Not at all. They remind me of the Hitler Youth Corps. Without Hitler. Which only makes it scarier. Some Aryan super race but dressed worse. Poor old George Orwell, that muddle-headed idealist could never have dreamed this. Him dressing as a worker, thinking he could pass in Wigan Pier. I met him once. There was talk of a film based on *Down and Out in Paris and London.* A love interest had to be inserted and guess who was to be it? This load of old nonsense had little if anything to do with his book, of course. But it never got made, thank goodness. Anyway, what say, ducks, we get Rosinante back on the road again? We could be in Ixtapa in a day and a half. I feel as if I'm trapped inside a bloody beer commercial."

They drove all day and spent the night in Colima where the road turned back toward the ocean. Colin, the next day, whistling as he drove, feeling better the farther south they got. Colin amazed by his own good spirits, even imitating the disc jockeys. The guy from the Morelia station saying the call letters, the name of the city and then the state, drawing out its name, MMMMisssssh-waaah-Khhahhhhn!" They might have a contest going because, just over the state line, they were able to pick up an Acapulco station, the fellow there outdoing his Michoacan counterpart with his stentorious "GGgggrrr-Rrrrare-row!" Anna laughing at Colin, laughing with him, thinking "my lover."

They stopped for lunch about fifty miles north of Ixtapa-Zihuatanejo. It was a somniferous beachfront town. Colin half expected to see banditos with cartridge belts over their shoulders come riding down the middle of the dusty main street. Their meals were served by an entire family: man, woman, two daughters, who stared at them with unfeigned curiosity the whole time. This made Colin a little uneasy at first but after a few minutes he was smiling at them, raising his Bohemia in their direction. As they were leaving, Colin merrily said goodbye, trying out some Spanish, giving the females a 'Buenos dias' at three in the afternoon. Them smiling shyly. When he got to the father, Colin said, "Vaya con Dios."

The man, about five feet six, bronze-faced, looked up at Colin, crossed himself, solemnly repeated the words, "Vaya con Dios.'

Getting into the Volvo, Colin asked Anna if she had noticed the expression on the man's face. Anna said, indeed, she had.

"Why do you think he looked at me like that?"

"Because some believe it is a jinx or, at least, a tempting of fate to say that. Vaya con Dios. Go with God. As if you were telling him to go with Him, post haste, as it were."

"But he said it to me."

"To throw it back at you. Balance things out, I suppose, and thereby rob the curse of its power."

"Superstitious, eh?" Colin started the Volvo and moved off down the sleepy street, headed for the highway. "They sure have weird customs, don't they? All the Catholic iconography. Dia de las muertas, with the dressed up skeletons."

Colin remembering a conversation with Ludmilla. Wondering what she was doing.

"Imagine what they think of some of ours. Christmas is coming up. Instead of their relaxed three weeks of fiesta, we build and build toward our couple of hours, and worry and shop and get in a frightful mood, and when the big day appears, it can't help but be anti-climactic. We have the birth of a saviour mixed up with a portly gentleman in a red suit who flies around at midnight in a sleigh pulled by reindeer, the favourite being the one with the red nose. And then there's an even weirder holiday, and that's Easter."

"Yes, I see your point."

"As a little girl I was sure the Easter bunny had something to do with the crucifixion and the resurrection. The way I figured it, the bunny rabbit was at the foot of the cross while events transpired and suddenly there it was at the tomb, the cave. Mary Magdalene saw the rabbit first, then she saw Our Lord Jesus."

They had taken a few beers away from the restaurant and were drinking them in the car; Anna remembering how nervous Colin had been when she'd bought that six pack in Oregon.

The ocean was on their right. Breakers, sun glittering off the water like crystals floating on the surface. Anna scuttled over to sit against Colin. Reaching into her string bag for suntan oil, squirting some on her hand and going under her dress. Colin glancing at her, turning his head from the road to her, and back. She took his right hand off the steering wheel and put it where she had put the lotion. Colin playing with her, giggling, his hand bent under, crab-like. Anna pushed his hand flat on the seat, palm down, and began riding up and down on his wrist. Rubbing herself against the knobby bone on the outside of his wrist. Taking about three minutes to have an orgasm, going rigid as she did so, then collapsing like a rag doll.

All the while, Colin stole glances at her, thinking how he'd never met a female remotely as sexually oriented as Anna. He wondered what she could have been like when she was his age. It suddenly occurring to him that the age difference didn't matter. For the first time he thought of it without reservation. In fact, Colin told himself, it is a good thing she isn't my age or twenty, even thirty years older than me. She would wear me out.

As it was, Anna recovered after a few deep breaths, was unzippng Colin's fly, taking out his cock, already hard. She stroked it before going down on it. After thirty seconds, she took her mouth away. "Better pull over and stop the car, my love. This is how Ramon Novarro died."

*H*alf an hour later, they had passed the Club Med property and were entering Ixtapa, one of the country's government-backed resorts. On the inland side of the road were condos and new stucco subdivisions. Further along was a shopping centre. On the beach side, big clean hotel towers sat far back from the road. Lots of activity out front, each hotel with a porte cochere, doormen, valets, waiters hurrying in and out carrying drinks on trays. Even from an automobile, you could get a glimpse of the driveway and through wide-open lobby doors to the pool and bright ocean beyond.

Dr. Hickey's building wasn't nearly as bad as Anna had feared. Not one of those cigarette lighter towers but rather a compact little building containing four apartments, two up, two down. Theirs was a top one. It was strange opening the door and having that first look, everything new, knowing that it would become familiar in a short time. Pale gray wall-to-wall carpet with some throw rugs, probably bought from vendors on the beach. Off-white walls throughout, a couple of ubiquitous masks — modern kitchen, clean, no surprises. Sliding glass doors gave on to a terrace at the back or, east side, of the apartment. Anna and Colin went out there and looked, gazed upon their neighbour, a golf course. Right beyond the yard of the apartment building was one of the greens, the flag with the Mexican colours sticking out of the hole. Sand traps on three sides. About fifty yards away from the green was a kidney-shaped pond and another similar one only ten yards from that. Between the ponds was something that was thick and a chalky gray-white colour, about twelve feet long. Anna and Colin stared at it without speaking, wondering was it, could it possibly be, both figuring it out at the same time — "An alligator."

They waited for the monster to move, and five minutes later, it glided smoothly away, a stunning sight, all of that bulk moving so quickly. It stopped at the edge of the water — motionless. Colin and

Anna laughed, wondering out loud why it had moved, what was the purpose. "Alligator reasoning," Anna said. They tried to come up with jokes about alligators and golfers. Giggling like kids.

After taking turns in the shower, unpacking, hanging things up, Anna fixed drinks and they toasted each other out there on the terrace. The monster hadn't moved.

Anna leaned on the railing and realized she felt a bit numb, or stunned, by her good fortune. So she wasn't to play out her days in an old age home. Hold on. Why not? She brought herself up short, realizing: there's still plenty of opportunity for that. Who knows what will happen? What happens when he gets tired of me? The money will run out. I'll have to go to some home but this time a place for indigents. And I'll be older. Even older. Yes. I'll be incontinent. We'll all be incontinent in there. Nurses will have to change our diapers. I can just see them, pretending not to be disgusted, offended. All business-like as they pull on the latex gloves and grimace. From ashes to ashes. Diapers to diapers. Well, let me pray that I will be thoroughly senile when the time comes and never twig to what's going on. But with my luck, my mind will be razor sharp, as ever. I'll be an incontinent old sex pervert, attacking old men, causing heart attacks, broken bones as I jump them and they topple over in their walkers. Scourge of extended care units. They'll lock me in a cage with my trusty old Coke bottle. Ah, death deliver me. But not just yet.

"You're so quiet," Colin said.

"And is that so unusual?"

"It sure is."

She punched him on the shoulder.

"What were you thinking about?"

"Not very pretty thoughts, I'm afraid. Alligators and crocodiles. When I was down in South America one time, in the fifties — did I tell you? Six months, I was there."

"Really? You might have mentioned it one time."

"Mmmm. I was on tour. Played all the towns. I believe it was near Manaus, the town that rubber built. They had a grand opera house crawling with rats and roaches. Beautiful square in front, all black and white marble. Manaus is on the Amazon, as you know. In Brazil, as you also know. It was there that an old man told me about these beasts. The man took a fancy to me. Anyway, they will grab a swimmer — they've been know to grab a person right off the shore — give a violent shake or two, break the bones to stop the panicked struggling, then dive and drown the victim. They don't eat a lad or lassie all at once, you understand. In fact, they may not even have the tiniest bite."

"You mean, they kill for the hell of it?"

"No, they are good scouts, and think ahead. Evidently they have caves in the banks for the express purpose of storing an unfortunate fellow or gal. Allow one to rot until one's nice and decomposed and tasty. They swim back for a little thigh one day, your head, or what's left of it, the next."

"Thanks for telling me. I don't believe I'll be playing any golf in Ixtapa."

"I suppose the bright side of being an alligator's dinner is that one does not know it."

"Well that's something, I suppose."

Anna turned from the railing and put one foot between Colin's feet, straddling his leg.

"Anna!"

She started rubbing herself against his thigh. Colin looked away, to the next porch, there was no one there. Nevertheless. "What're you doing?"

"What do you think? Talking about being someone's dinner makes me feel sexy."

"You're shameless."

"I know. So what? And you haven't done that to me yet."

She took his hand and lead him to the bedroom, lay out on the bed. She told herself she may appear a lascivious old slut but she was actually timid and scared. Afraid he would be revolted. If he will do this, she thought, well, let the alligators take me.

An hour or so later, still in bed, Colin appeared to be dozing with his drink in his hand, drink hand on his stomach But he moved his head, looked at her. "Anna?"

"Yes, my sweet?"

"I've been wondering about something."

"And what may that be?"

"Who's Ramon Novarro?"

It didn't take long for Anna to become bored with Ixtapa. About two hours from the time she got out of bed the next morning and had her constitutional. It wasn't as crass and lower-middle class as the Zona Dorado in Mazatlan; it was, however, more beautiful and more bland. Late that first morning she went over to Zihautanejo, a fifteen minute ride on a cranky old Bluebird school bus painted baby blue and filled with Mexicans returning from work at the resorts. Colin stayed behind, not feeling his best. Having a little stomach discomfort, was how he put it. The idea was that he'd come over later. They'd looked at the map and picked a spot to meet — the public market, perhaps, at one.

She got off the bus at the basketball courts near the town beach. This was not the cleanest stretch of sand she'd ever seen. Even without the sprinkling of garbage and vague odour of sewer water, it looked dirty, the sand dark gray. She didn't see any other tourists sunning themselves and reasoned that's probably why the beach wasn't kept clean. There were tourists across the street, in floppy hats with cameras and pink legs, shopping at the arcades. She went over there and looked at everything.

Odd, she thought. Nothing was familiar to her. It was as if she had never been in this town. She vaguely recalled rowing to shore from the yacht. Stepping out of the boat and discovering a quaint fishing village. And nearly fifty years later, this is what became of it. Well, what the hell, there's the answer, you old biddy.

Anna liked it better the farther she walked, liked it better once she'd gotten beyond all the places with racks of tee-shirts, boxes of sunglasses with phosphorescent rims, nylon hammocks and plastic sandals. She had breakfast at a little place on a narrow lane that reminded her of Paris, the labyrinthine, medieval streets of the Left Bank. Well, okay, I'm stretching it, she told herself. There was a frizzy-haired, middle-aged white woman who smiled when Anna happened to look in her direction. Anna smiled back and the woman picked up her coffee cup, came over to the table. "Do you mind?" she asked, her hand on the back of the other chair.

"Not at all."

"You look different," the woman said, sitting.

"Different than what, than whom?"

"Oh, like, you know, the usual gringa."

"Well, I certainly hope so."

The woman laughed. She was wearing a gauzy full blouse with gold metallic threads shot through. That over a cotton halter top. Her substantial bosom sagged, nipples very much in evidence.

"Zihua is being overrun. It used to be pretty groovy."

"I take it you live here."

"Yeah. I have for nearly forty years. Back then you could rent a place on the beach for five dollars a month. No shit. Eat well for that much a week. This your first time here?"

"It might as well be. I was here in the fifties."

Anna got the feeling, the woman didn't like her trail blazer status being usurped.

"Nineteen sixty-seven, I showed up. With my old man. And after I was here a couple years my parents sent me a thousand dollars hoping I'd take a bath and fly home. They intended it to be a kind of carrot. There's more of this sort of thing to be had up here in the good old U.S.A., Marin County."

"And what did you do, my dear?"

"I used the money to buy two houses that year. Lived in one, rented out the other to a commune. Then I bought another house the next year. Later, a building in town with shops. A couple of others. I'm having a place built now, on a hill overlooking La Ropa Beach. It would be perfect for you. I'm choosy about who I have in my places."

I bet, Anna thought to herself, then apprised this hippie, turned real estate-tycoon, that she was already set up in an apartment.

The woman whose name was Helen showed her disappointment but only for a moment, pursing her lips and screwing up her mouth so that thin lines converged there like water swirling down the drain. The lines went back to partial hiding. There would be other opportunities. "What about your old man?" she asked.

"I'm meeting him at the market. And your fellow?"

"The one I hung out with back in the Sixties? That's ancient history. He lasted a year or so then took off to be a roadie with 'Chicago,' you know? The band? There have been a string of men since then. Bet on it. They're such babies, really, but you have to have them. Or some of us do. It's always good to find one who's handy, I mean around the house. A Mr. Fix-It type. I'm meeting the father of my son tonight at Jambalaya. He's flying in from John Wayne. The Orange County airport. Haven't seen him for three years. He's into software. I hope he isn't going to hassle me. We've always had issues. But I have to see him. There's some trouble with out fourteen year old who's in prep school in New Jersey."

Helen offered to show Anna around downtown Zihua and Anna went along, an hour before she was to meet Colin. The younger woman introduced her to an old man who was a silver worker and to a middle-aged man who used to dive off the cliffs at Acapulco when he was a kid. This man was sexy, Anna thought, pock-marked with a wide mouth and hair like a juvenile delinquent would have had the first time she visited Zihuatanejo. They encountered him outside his restaurant as he was preparing for the lunch crowd. Later, Helen told her that the man had been able to open the place with the tips he'd made at Acapulco. He gave Anna a devilish smile with just the hint of a leer. She knew the look had been used so often, sparing no woman of any age, that it had become second nature to him. But, still.

A couple of blocks later, they ran into the famous American painter Larry Pond who, Helen said, had been coming to Zihua for years and years. He had a home near the one she was building, between the beaches at Madera and La Ropa, closer to the latter. Pond was nearly Anna's age but he looked at her dismissively, as if for no other reason than she was an old lady. Or, perhaps, dismissively because he figured she was of no importance. Pond was a small man with an air of old-time Manhattan about him, that furtive, always on the nickel attitude. He seemed dirty, though he didn't smell, didn't have dandruff — clothes appeared clean enough. While he and Helen were having their teasing, ironic conversation, Anna was thinking the guy probably didn't wash his private parts or his rear end. Why in hell would I think that? She asked herself. Adding to herself that he probably stuck the one into whatever was convenient and wasn't choosy about having things stuck into the other. A little voice told her she was being unfair and she told the little voice, so be it.

"Whadja say?"

Pond was addressing her. Christ, Anna thought, I *am* getting senile. "Oh, I said, I'd love to see it. Your show. At the…"

"Yeah, right."

As they walked away from Pond, Helen said, "You know his paintings are worth a fortune. I should have gotten hold of one years ago but I was too stupid."

"Do you like them?" Anna tried to get a clear image of one. Seeing vaguely a sort of collage but not of different materials. A painting that was supposed to call a collage to mind. His stuff was part of the mass media culture. Maybe there was a horse in there, a flag; she had the idea that it was an American flag. She didn't dislike what she remembered of his painting, didn't like it either. It was just there.

"No, to tell you the truth, I don't like them." Helen said, "But, hey, what the hell does that have to do with it? If I had one of them, I'd turn it over and buy a hotel or something."

The tour ended at a big shop stocked with masks and jewelry, carvings, paper-maché figures, silver bowls, hangings and coffee table books about Mexican craft and folk lore. There were also the ubiquitous Frida Kahlo posters. It took a full minute for Anna to realize the store belonged to Helen. She felt in a way like she was back in the Okanagan and, having been shown around the vineyard, introduced to the vintner and the grape pickers, was suddenly whisked to the gift shop where she was supposed to buy some of the product or maybe some crystal wine glasses, at least an Ogopogo ashtray.

Anna gave the place a polite once over, Helen dogging her heels but with nothing so crass as an old time floorwalker's spiel. It was a line of patter for a New Age that she laid down, stressing the spirituality of The People, the crafts people who made the stuff, that transcended their poverty; as if Anna wouldn't really be helping her, Helen, by fishing the credit card from her string bag — as if she had a credit card in her string bag or anywhere else — rather, she'd be somehow helping the spiritually-advanced natives in their perpetual struggle against the brutality of an unjust Mexican government and its cohorts, the Yankee oppressors. Buy two bracelets and save the rainforest.

Anna bent for an obligatory look at an expensive silver and jade brooch, straightened up, smiled. "You know, I'd love to stay longer. There is so much of interest but I just can't decide."

"We'll hold anything for you. Just put a little down. You change your mind, you can apply it to another purchase."

"Those paper maché peasants are simply divine but, you see, I have to meet my fella at the market. Yes, time does fly."

"Hey, no problem."

There was the spiral of lines again.

"Why don't you and your dude come out to La Perla tonight? It's on the beach. Meet the crowd. After I finish with Dietrich, I'll be out there. About nine? If I'm not there just introduce yourself to the rest of the gang. Believe me, you'll know them when you see them. They're really an off-the-wall bunch."

Anna replied that she would like that very much, and got out of there.

*S*he reached the market just as Colin was untangling himself from the front seat of a purple-coloured Volkswagen beetle taxi. He looked all around him, disoriented. Anna again thinking his awkwardness was endearing. She called to him from across the street, waving. He waved back. An old woman on a folding chair amidst her pyramids of fruit and vegetables looked from Anna to Colin and back, just her eyes moving. She was calm, stoic, resigned, had seen it all from her market perch. Anna wondered about the woman's childhood, early womanhood. Had she been a beauty with her dark skin and big brown eyes? I was a movie star in my day, my pretty. Well, at least, an actress. And you? — You mean me? I was here before such vanities. I'll be here long after any memory of you has disintegrated, like old film stock. I am ageless and forever. The eternal market woman.

And there's Colin with a big smile. Just a minute, love. I've been seized by an idea and will greet you warmly in a moment. Until then be content with my huge smile. The eternal market woman — what a theme. What an idea for a one-woman show. Of course, I couldn't play a Mexican market woman. It would never work, no matter how much make-up I trowelled on. So I must be something else. French or English. Or Welsh. It would translate to any culture. I've seen it all from my folding chair here at the great bustling market place of life...

"Colin!" Anna called, stepping onto the curb. "Why, you don't look ill."

"Hi, I'm feeling better now. Weird, I was having a hard time getting going. I felt weak and a little nauseous but I'm not bad now."

"Did you take your antacid tablets?"

"Yes."

"Splendid. Dr. Dupree recommends you take it easy today. Rest up for our date for drinks tonight. Yes, I've been giving the town a

slant. Attending to our social calendar. And have secured us an invi-
tation for nine-ish."

"I'm amazed. You don't exactly have trouble meeting people, do you?"

"Odd, isn't it? Though I've never been the social butterfly, I have,
my entire life been approached by strangers wherever I have been,
whatever I may be doing. This has been both a blessing and a curse,
believe me. There was one horrible period, a few years there, the years
of fleeting semi-fame, when I was recognized on the street, in Europe,
anyway. Accosted by, dare I say the word? — fans. Many of this breed
were lecherous men and there were a few lecherous women. Some
people merely looked from the middle distance. And some of the
women who recognized me, I knew what they were thinking: she's
nothing special...the scrawny little thing...What's she got that I
haven't got? ...Yeah, I wonder what she had to do to get the part. You
know what Shelley Winters said when she won her Academy Award?
Well never mind...

"The only time any of that was ever fun was in South America.
They still showed the old black and white films, even in the big cities.
I do not mean at repertory cinemas or art houses, either. No. In Lima
and Montevideo, the main feature might be twenty-five years old.
Crackling 16 mm. Things with hairs in the gate and big chunks missing where bugs had been at work. I tell you, it is a disconcerting thing
to have a stranger respectfully pronounce your name while whipping
off his hat and bowing in the centre of the square in Santiago while
above and beyond, an active volcano mocks this human comedy."

"But all kinds of people approach you. I mean, even now."

"Even now that my looks have vanished and I'm an ancient
nobody?"

"I didn't mean that, I meant..."

"Of course, you didn't my sweet."

"It has nothing to do with movies or the stage. You're like a magnet."

"So long's I attract you is all that matters."

"All kinds of people," Colin said, ignoring her remark. "Rich,
poor, all ages, all types. It is as if they think you're one of them, as unlikely as that might appear. How do I say it, you have a sort of chameleon
quality. I guess that's not surprising, you having been an actress."

"I must protest, my dear. At least in regards the second part. As
for the first, I think it is that people believe that I am one of them yet,

simultaneously, not one of them. I've not analyzed it, and don't wish to. This quality, this thing, has provided me with wonderful moments. I shall do nothing to jinx it, whatever it may be. As for being an actress: Bah! People would sense the phoniness of it, were I playing a part. As for this seeming aptitude for blending into my surroundings — to appear to take on the local colour — it is not only unconscious, it is what has held me back from being a great or even a very good actress."

"How so? I mean, I bet you could be convincing as any sort of woman."

"Thank you. Look at that ginger. When was the last time you saw fresh sticks of cinnamon? But I could never totally assume the role, become the part. I have always held back."

"You? Hold back! I don't believe it. Held back what?"

"My personality. You see, from an early age, I knew who I was. Even when I first went on stage that was the problem — *I* was the problem. I did not want to be completely absorbed by the role. I wanted to live, on stage, on screen but, more importantly, I wanted to live off stage, off screen. And that is what separated me from most of the rest of them. They had no personalities of their own. No life when they were not working. Oh, yes, they had their usually miserable existences, of course, which mostly consisted of anguished waiting for the next part. But I was no hero. The rest of them, in a way, were heroes. Outsiders may think actors vain and self-conscious monsters. And how true that often is, yet, how perfectly understandable. And so touching, really. Understand, the actor has abdicated. Having cut loose their true selves, actors are adrift, and those poses and gestures others think pretentious and affected are their only way of keeping their heads above water. Seeing them you may tend to think them terribly self-assured with their flourishes and 'Dah-ling!'s' but it is just so much frantic doggy paddling in the oh-so-turbulent seas of this life.

"To me it was a job. A supremely interesting job but still it was: learn the lines, recite them and go home. Well I didn't always go straight home. Wherever that happened to be. But, nevertheless: 'Live first' was my motto. What am I saying? 'Live first' is still my motto."

After an hour's perambulating, Colin declared that he felt like getting something to eat. They had ceviche and beer at a stand near the basketball court, watched kids shooting baskets, others ones kicking a soccer ball along the shore where the sand was flattened down; and by the fishing boats older men fingered their nets like rosary beads. "I'm really thirsty," Colin said, "The beer didn't help. Must be the seafood, it's really salty. I don't want to have another beer and feel bloated. Do you think I should chance a glass of water?"

"You must be daft. We can go across the street and get bottled water."

They did, and Colin had drunk half a litre before they found a spot on the beach to lie down, both with their legs and chests in the sun, heads in the shade of an old coconut palm with a trunk like elephant skin.

"I was thinking this morning about what I'm going to do," Colin said. "You know, later, when I'm better. Go back to Valley View? Or try to. I don't know. That seems so remote. Maybe I'll get my doctorate and teach."

"You have plenty of possibilities. It is good that you feel well enough to think about those things. On the other hand, maybe the best plan is to continue what you're doing, taking the sun, getting some loving."

There was that bashful smile that Anna had come to like so much. His cheeks always seemed sort of dusty until you looked close at the millions of black dots. He was so religious about shaving. If he didn't shave for just one week, Colin would probably have a thick beard. She wondered what he'd look like with a beard. Wondered what he'd feel like. But she wouldn't mention it to him, she laughed to herself, for purely salacious reasons.

"Perhaps some exercise would be in order," Anna said. "Other than the kind you've been getting."

"Hmmm, maybe in a few days." He smiled, "I mean for the new kind."

Anna looked away, two little girls playing in the surf. Their mother sat close by minding them. Her pink dress was tight across her middle, brown legs stretched out before her, feet turned outward; the soles of her feet as white as Anna's own. One little girl, three or four, was naked, the other a couple years older wore a dress that the ocean had stuck to her body. They dashed in and out of the surf, jumped up and down, laughing, teeth brilliant against their dark skin. Anna wondered what life held for them. Anything but child bearing and drudgery? But, then again, why assume that is their mother's lot? After all, here the woman was in the middle of the afternoon sitting on the beach. How many mothers in the rest of the world were free to do that? So maybe those little girls will not have seven kids each by the time they are beaten-down thirty-year olds. Maybe they will be miraculously absorbed into the new world that was aborning, a world Anna could hardly envision except that it would have much to do with technologies she could not comprehend and be held together by state or corporate control. Well, I am certainly glad that I will not live to see this new order of things. But, on the other hand, it beats the alternative. And, God, if that is not old lady thinking, I don't know what is.

She put these matters aside and saw that Colin was sleeping. She stood and went down to the water, lifted her skirt and walked into the surf, aware that the little girls were watching her. Smiled at them and they giggled, glanced at their mother. Anna walked along the shore, kicking at the shallow water. She looked up at the perfect blue sky and heard her thoughts, herself thinking, "Lord, if I believed, I would thank You. Make no mistake about it."

Colin was still asleep when she got back several minutes later so she covered his chest with his tee shirt, his legs with her towel and went for another walk, this time through the thick sand, feeling her calf muscles working, tightening up, deciding she'd make a habit of it. Not only would it be good for her, Colin might be encouraged to follow her example.

Half an hour later, she prodded him with her toe, seeing the red-painted nail disappear into his side. Colin moved his head, opened and closed his mouth like he was finishing a last mouthful but he didn't open his eyes. Anna placed her foot on his chest and pushed down. He looked at her, squinting. She moved her foot down to his stomach and then a little more until she had to hop to keep her balance. "I'd best stop or you'll be damaged goods."

"I wouldn't want that to happen."

"Nor I. How do you feel?"

"Groggy but also, uh…that word, I hate it but…"

"Me too."

"You, too, you hate the word I'm thinking of?"

"Not only that but I'm feeling the same way."

"Well…"

"Well," said Anna. "Maybe we should go to the movies."

"The movies? Why…"

"Come on."

The theatre was at the far end of the main street, away from the beach. It was all Mexicans up there. Next to the theatre was a bank, out front of which stood two teenaged soldiers with blunt Indian features — each leaned on his rifle as if it were a crutch.

Anna was pleased to be inside such an old fashioned place. It reminded her of the movie palaces of her London youth. Was that really me or am I being afforded a glimpse into some stranger's life? I seem to remember a girl who's rather familiar, sitting in the dark, captivated by the shadows and movement and the motes of dust in the projector's shaft of light. Thrilled but studious at the same time, I was. I loved Louise Fazenda, the American comedienne who was in Max Sennett comedies and in 'Cuban Love Song.' She married Hal Wallis, the poor woman. Now what was the first film I ever saw in London? It was by Michael Powell. The Colonel Blimp one? No, it had to have been 'I Know Where I'm Going.'

That afternoon they were seeing something called 'La Batalla Desconocida,' the forgotten battle. Except for two bad men, it was an entirely Mexican cast. The story was set before the Revolution. Simple and honest peasants toiling on lands owned by a dastardly gringo who didn't even live in Mexico yet nevertheless controlled the lives of hundreds from his opulent digs in Los Estados Unidos. He had Mexican henchmen to carry out his orders. But there was one peasant smarter than the rest and more handsome too; also, Anna noticed, lighter skinned. He had begun to stir up trouble among the campesinos. Word of his activities got back to the evil gringo who dispatched a villain to take care of the fellow. The would-be killer passed himself off as the landowner's overseer, down to check out operations but, of course, the hero wasn't fooled. The gringo made matters worse for himself by trying to cozy up to the hero's woman, she of the luxurious black hair and off-the-shoulder blouse and ice cream shoulders. The hero beat the would be assassin in a fair fight but later the killer shot him in the back. The paragon uttered stirring words of revolution as he died in the arms of the beautiful woman.

It wasn't bad, Anna thought, and the gringo hit man was familiar. Not from other movies but familiar as if she knew him or had seen him somewhere in real life. In the cast his name was Diego Castillo but he was obviously not a Latin. She transposed the name into English but it meant nothing to her.

During the second act, which had begun slowly, consisting mainly of shots of Castillo galloping across the plains headed for Durango, interspersed with scenes of discontent fomenting in the fields, Anna put her hand on Colin's lap, slowly unzipped his fly, took out his cock and began to stroke it slowly, never taking her gaze from the screen. At least not until Colin started to squirm. She looked in back of her, the doors closed, nobody standing in the corners. Then she slid down, pulled at Colin's leg, got between and put her mouth around it.

When he came Colin almost smashed Anna's head against the seat behind her, his knees launching forward and banging into the seats. Him making a sound like he was being smothered.

Anna got off her knees, looked over the seats like she was peeking above a trench in a first world war film and decided nobody had her in their sights. By the time she sat down, Castillo was climbing from a horse on a dusty Durango street wearing black and an aura of doom.

They had a late dinner and took a taxi out to La Perla. It was a seafood restaurant, the tables outside under a vast palapa, and separated from the water by fifty feet of sand. Helen was there with her gang, ten or more of them, dinner over, bottles and glasses obscuring most of the linen tablecloth. She waved Anna forward, told her she was glad she'd come. "Oh, your husband couldn't make it. I'm sorry. This must be your son."

Before Ann could make a comeback, Colin stuck out his hand. "No, I'm Anna's friend, Colin Childs. And you are?"

Helen introduced them, a blur of names. They were middle-aged, gringos all. It was immediately apparent that they presumed to be in the know about all things local. Looking down on other tourists, smirking when those others at nearby tables, ordered meals or drinks in awkward Spanish. It wasn't long — perhaps ten minutes — before Anna felt oppressed by their air of smug complacency.

Most of them had what Anna thought of as hippie traces. Some of this was in their dress, some in their conversation. Only one seemed to be different, a guy in his late fifties — they were all in their fifties, as far as she could tell — a guy from New York named Tommy. He told Anna his job was selling souvenirs.

"At parades, big events, whatever. I'm there with my pennants, trinkets. All kinds of crap. I make out like a bandit, got a nice rent-controlled apartment in the city, and I spend four months a year down here. I got it made, sister."

"Yeah, until you get something else at El Coyote."

That from a woman with short thick gray hair, dried up skin. A desiccated one-time flower child. "If you're not worried about your health, you should think about those poor little girls."

The woman's hectoring diverted Tommy's attention, and Anna had to listen to Dietrich, Helen's ex-husband offer an example of the trouble he was having with their son, the one in private school in New Jersey. The boy's name was Winter. "I have a younger son name Spring," Helen said.

"*We*," said Dietrich, "have a son named Spring."

Helen ignored him. "I named them after the seasons when they were born." She smiled proudly at Anna.

Anna smiled back as if acknowledging that she had indeed done something particularly brilliant.

Dietrich continued the story. "Winter came home for Thanksgiving holidays and he was totally upset. At first, I couldn't get from him what the problem was. Then it finally came out that he had issues with the other kids, they were hassling him about his name. He said, 'Dietrich, I don't want to be Winter anymore.'"

"'What do you want to be?' I asked him."

"'I want to be Michael.'"

Anna giggled and Helen shot her a look before turning on Dietrich, telling him he should have patiently explained to Winter that his name had spiritual significance. "But the trouble with you is you have no patience. You probably didn't tell him how his name connected him with the earth, with the eternal passage of he seasons."

"Well, I did do that, actually."

"And how much more interesting a name it is than Michael, a name from the bible. And didn't he wield a sword or something? I mean, the bible is all about people who had no feeling for the earth.

And there's this patriarchal figure who just wants to conquer the earth, part the seas and that kind of shit."

The woman with the short thick gray hair jumped into it at that point, beginning a catalogue of 'environmental damage' in the bible. Others interjected their assent to the litany, reminding Anna of members of parliament with their "Here, here's!"

Poor Winter who just wanted to be Michael was quickly forgotten. From the ecologically unsound bible they got on to endangered species. One man in a Rolling Stones tee shirt — Anna wondered how a grown man could walk around with a tongue on his chest — voiced the desire to go to the Galapagos Islands. Someone else said it might be a good business proposition to organize an eco-tour to the Galapagos.

Colin and Anna looked at each other. Anna thinking how these were like the silent exchanges of lovers. How magical that you could look down a dinner table, across a crowded room, catch your lover's eye, both knowing exactly what the other is thinking. Anna had been in love a hundred times. But, maybe, she thought, staring at the African beads in one woman's hair that means I've never been in love. Let me love this young man here. This boy. What a unique position I am in. I can be his lover, mother and, yes, his goddamn grandmother. I'll play any role I have to. Assume any position, so to speak.

She looked back at Colin and rolled her eyes. Colin raised his eyebrows, and Anna stood, announcing that it was past her bedtime. The gang at the table, some of them, offered polite good nights but they sensed Colin and Anna were not their sort. Anna hearing the man with the tongue on his tee shirt asking Colin, "What is it you said you do up in British Columbia?"

"I used to deal with the problems of the elderly but now I'm in logging."

Walking up the lane to the shore road where the taxis waited, Anna said, "What a load of bloody bores."

"Yeah, baby boomer bores."

*B*ack at the apartment, Anna went into the bathroom and got prepared for bed. Applied lipstick, eye shadow, the works, having understood from the beginning that Colin liked that sort of thing. She didn't mind, even enjoyed the play aspect. She would have donned a skimpy maid's outfit and fishnet stockings, anything corny like that, if he so desired. Colin liked to undress her or partially undress her. The make-up, the lingerie — of which in Mexico there was no lack in the shops — like a disguise but the darkness was the best illusionist of all.

Colin was even becoming something of a decent lover. He had been much too eager at first: in and out, in and out. Anna teaching him to hold back, to move slowly at times or not to move at all. He, as always, much better the second time.

When Anna came out of the bathroom and strutted over to the bed, Colin reached for a pillow. Anna knowing this meant she was in for a pounding, he was going to put her on her stomach over the pillow and get in from behind. Gratefully, it would be a brief pounding. This time Colin put a second pillow underneath, Anna thinking, 'Uh Uhh.' She stuck it up even higher so he would get it over with even quicker.

When he was finished, Colin got off and said he was sorry for not being more considerate.

"Don't apologize, honey." Anna thinking that at her age being fucked with enthusiasm was plenty good enough. At her age being fucked with*out* enthusiasm wouldn't be bad either. Anyway chances are, she'd have an orgasm the second time.

She considered herself lucky when it came to orgasms. She'd always had them, except with Andy Anderson.

In the beginning, Colin had mentioned condoms.

She'd replied, "You certainly don't have to worry about me becoming pregnant."

"No. That's not what I mean. I mean, well, you know."

"Oh. Yes, well, you won't be catching anything from me, love."

"But…"

"But if I catch something from you? Well, after all, I am…There's no need me mentioning my age. One realizes that diseases and any number of afflictions are closing in, pushing and jostling to be at the head of the line. Anything I might catch would have to wait its turn."

Anna, wearing her flimsy dressing gown, went to the kitchen to fix them drinks. Wouldn't do to let Colin see her skin in the harsh kitchen light. Still in her shoes, one stocking down at her ankles, the other held up by one frilly strap, breasts like wine skins, not even filling the cup of the brassiere — an old grotesque, lipstick smeared across her chin — sluttish time in Mexican trollop shoes.

She switched off the lights, Colin was at the window, hands on his hips, bending his trunk from side to side while leaning backwards.

"Doing our calisthenics, are we?"

"I just had a pain or more like a tight knot. High up in my stomach. I don't know. It's not a gas pain."

"Probably what my dear old mum, the hag, used to call a 'stitch.'"

She handed him his drink.

"Look out there, love. See? Our friend Mr. Alligator."

There in the dark, the shadows of trees against the sky, the sand traps like dull gray slashes in the night, the beast an almost luminous bulk.

"I've heard they live to be over a hundred years old."

Yes, Anna thought, that thing out there will be scaring the dickens out of duffers long after I'm fertilizer for the greens, my bones grit for the sand trap, spirit long gone down the memory hole.

They got back into bed. Colin saying his pain had gone away. For a few minutes, they sipped their drinks in near silence. Then Colin put his glass on the table, kissed her chest and began working his way downward. She'd encouraged him to do this at these times. He wasn't a great conversationalist, and this filled the minutes while he was waiting to be ready. Anyway, he seemed to really like doing it. I know I like having it done, Anna thought, and it prepares me. When Colin was ready, he'd move up on to her and whenever he seemed to be getting too carried away, Anna clamped her hands on his chubby buttocks to slow him down. She squeezed his cock with her muscles, and thought of times in the past. It excited her remembering, particularly occasions she'd done it when there was a chance of being discovered. There had been so many times, so many men. And now I'm a lover reborn, up from the ashes.

Anna woke hearing the toilet flush, the room lighted by the bathroom door, then the light being switched off. She fell back into sleep and was awakened who knows how much later by a heavy, thudding sound. Opening her eyes, she saw Colin; he looked to be in a crouch, both hands gripping one side of the doorway between the living room and the kitchen. She must have closed her eyes again because the next thing she knew he was standing upright; it looked as if he was hugging the side of the doorway, the door jamb. Then she watched dumbly as he fell. Colin had given a little yelp and crumbled. That's the word she thought of, a 'yelp.' Like a dog would do.

He had probably stayed awake and had more to drink. Anna, groggy with sleep, yet aware of her attempts to reason. He must feel terrible, poor boy, sick to his stomach, everything whirling about him.

Slowly coming awake, Anna began to worry about him lying there on the floor, but, in his condition, drunk like that, bed or floor, it probably didn't matter.

Lying on her side, head on the pillow that had been under her stomach, she looked at his form sprawled asymmetrically beyond the living room, in the middle of the kitchen, the door of the refrigerator open.

"Oh, God!" she heard herself cry. "Oh, God, no!"

Anna was so frantic rushing to him that she stumbled taking the first step out of bed and fell to the floor herself, landing on one knee. She limped over to Colin, each step feeling like someone smashing a lead pipe against her kneecap. She stared over the bulk of his hip, in horror at the blood on the white linoleum tiles. Kneeling she saw blood smeared over Colin's lips; it covered his chin and cheeks, as well. Anna thinking it was like her lipstick on him after sloppy kissing. There was blood underneath him too. Bleeding from there. She pushed at his shoulders. He murmured. His eyes half-opened and he whimpered.

"I'm going for an ambulance, love. You'll be fine. Yes, you will."

Aware that she had almost said, "Now, you wait right here."

Anna grabbed a sheet from the bed, covered him, and was horrified to have done it, to see the sheet over his body. She put on the green satin dressing gown with the black lace trim that she had bought in Zihuantanejo, bent to kiss him on the lips.

There was no telephone, of course. And their downstairs neighbours wouldn't have one. It was too complicated and costly a thing to get a phone installed in this part of Mexico. Anna rushed down to the street, no shoes, in stockings. What to do? Take a chance and pound at the door of the Mexican family down the street? But if they weren't at home, or didn't have a phone, she would have wasted precious time.

She hurried toward the boulevard and the big hotels. Her knee hurting, a searing pain each time that leg landed. Her feet sore on the asphalt. It couldn't have taken more than six or seven minutes but it seemed like an eternity before she was rushing into the lobby. The horrified expressions on the faces of the bellman and the girl behind the desk. Was the guy about to laugh at her? If he was, Anna's cries of "Emergencia! Emergencia!" put a stop to the idea.

"Quiero un ambulancia, por favor!"

The girl's hand was already on the receiver, the other hand punching in the number, while she stared at Anna, at the blood on her mouth.

She spoke into the phone and asked Anna where the ambulance was to go. Anna realized she didn't know address of the apartment. There was no street sign. She pointed beyond the doors. "Alli, alla!"

Not knowing the word for golf course, telling her. "Golf. Cerca de golf." Near to the golf. She had left the light on, told the girl the upstairs apartment, segundo piso, with the lights on. She could have told her to have the ambulance come to the hotel but she wanted to be with Colin.

"Diez minutos," the girl told Anna, holding up all ten fingers, then speaking rapidly to the bellman, telling him to drive the lady where she wanted to go, and quickly.

The boy, no more than seventeen or eighteen, looked at her as she hurried out, saying nothing, glancing at the black bra visible through her careless dressing gown, as they got into the purple Beetle. Anna wondering if it could possibly be the same one Colin had ridden to the market earlier that day.

Pulling up before the condo, Anna gasped her thanks, the kid saying a cool, "Da nada, senorita."

Colin hadn't moved. Anna shook him, massaged his chest, his feet, his temples. "Don't fade, Colin. Look at me. Stay with me. I love you. I'll take care of you always. You are my everything."

She moved away from him only long enough to grab a dress from the closet, yanking at it, the hanger flying off the bar and onto the carpet. She put the dress on standing over him, picked up the pair of pink panties off the floor and pulled them on, she was aware of his semen running down her leg. While she was straightening the dress, Anna placed her foot on his chest, massaging it, but stopped when it reminded her of earlier, just this afternoon. Could it be?

She was pulling on her shoes when the ambulance attendants arrived. They were very efficient, asking her questions in Spanish and in English. They got Colin onto the stretcher and down the stairs. Her thinking the groans were his — about to tell them to be careful — until she realized they were struggling with his weight.

He regained consciousness in the ambulance, blood flowing from the plastic sack into his arm. Colin opened his eyes.

"Anna…Anna," he murmured her name over and over. Her kneeling on the floor, kissing his forehead, stroking his bloody cheek.

He died at four in the morning, of a massive hemorrhage. The doctor, in flawless, nearly unaccented English, explained to Anna about peritonitis, how the ulcer had perforated the stomach wall. She just stared at the man. He looked like a young Caesar Romero. She nodded as he talked. Anna wasn't surprised that Colin had died. She'd been preparing herself. As soon as she'd seen the blood on the kitchen floor, she knew there couldn't be much hope. She had already done her crying on the bench in the hallway. The other people, Mexicans, had looked at her with pity. She tried to imagine how it would have been in a hospital somewhere else — Canada, the United States. The rest of them in the waiting room embarrassed or even angry at her and her weeping.

The doctor took Anna into a room to look at her knee. Made her get up on the leather-covered mat. His long, brown fingers holding her knee. He gave her a needle. "There will be much to do tomorrow. Forms, papers to sign. Your consulate, in Acapulco, will have to be contacted, of course. You will need to be in full control of your faculties, senorita, to face such an ordeal. So now you must sleep."

Such a nice man. Such competent hands. Manicured nails. What was that movie about Cortez. That Romero was in? 'Captain of Castile.' In his conquistador's armour. Colin in the suit of armour, the metal visor covering his face. No way to break through the armour and get Colin out. Colin no more; Colin gone forever. I'll never have a man inside me again.

EPILOGUE

The immaculate, black, four-door 1954 Cadillac turned off the plaza, making heads swivel as it made its way along Avenida de los Martyreros. Straw hats and short-sleeve shirts, a burro, shop signs, women's legs all appeared and were gone in an instant in the gleaming fenders and the chrome bullet-bumpers that seemed to burst out of the massive grille. A montage of the street, a montage of the streets of Mexico. A montage such as might have been the centrepiece of a great movie from the era when great movies were made. And, inside the Cadillac, in the back seat next to his producer, was a man who continued to make movies that way, movies with all the experimentation of the earliest days of cinema, but movies with the humanism of the same period and to which he applied — but never obtrusively —the latest technology.

That montage in the bumpers and the fenders of the Cadillac; why, he had used that forty years earlier, filming the very same automobile in his noir-ish, indigenous gangster epic 'Ladrones Muertes.' That was the film that made him famous. 'Dead Thieves.' That had made him the darling of European cinema, just as, half a dozen earlier pictures had made him, indisputably, the number one moviemaker in Latin America. But what did he do? Forsake his native country? Spend the forty years in a European or Hollywood decline, churning out mannered cinema, loved by aesthetes but ignored by the people? Not on your life. He did a Bunuel in reverse. Returned to his mother country after two Spanish pictures. He was a hero. He was El Maestro. He was Rodrigo Luzardo Amundez. El Luzardo — not 'The Lizard,' as they wanted so much to believe in the English-speaking film world. And he certainly looked the part as his tall, lean frame emerged from the Cadillac in front of La Jambalaya. His name fitted him even more appropriately, 'Luz' meaning light. He was a magician of light.

Luzardo was six feet-one inch tall and, though born in one of the worst barrios of Mexico City, with skin as dark as the darkest Aztec, he was thin and as fine-featured as a Spanish aristocrat. Luzardo wore a white linen suit. He dyed his hair jet black, dyed his eyebrows, his pencil-line moustache, dyed them nearly every day of his life — a vanity that was easily overlooked. El Luzardo was now into his early seventies and, after all, a genius.

He was followed out of the back of the Cadillac by his producer, Jaime Munoz, a shorter and lighter-skinned, stout man — Luzardo's partner from the very beginning, and the one who kept things running smoothly or as smoothly as possible in such a crazy, nervewracking business with all its envy, intrigue and financial shenanigans.

From the passenger side of the front seat came Julietta Rivera, in her thirties. The woman would have been a ravishing beauty were it not for a harelip. A decade earlier, she had been discovered by Luzardo and Munoz in a carnival and they used her in 'Debago de los Farolles,' after which she was given the permanent position of locations manager. Julietta, since a very small child, had traveled every road in Mexico, from Tiajuana to Tuxtla Guiterrez.

The new film of Luzardo-Munoz had gone through pre-production: 'Alma de Fuega,' it was called, 'Soul of Fire,' a mostly true account of a woman who provided the heart and soul of the great but aborted rebellion of campesinos in Guerrero in the early days of the century. The story was little known apart from legends of the people.

It was the fervour and love of justice of this woman that had inspired so many of the great heroes of the period, Emiliano Zapata in particular. But Luzardo, the master, always looked for what was not readily apparent to others. A story about a woman who provoked a rebellion was fine if, perhaps, hackneyed. There were scores of people calling themselves filmmakers who would take the raw material and bring forth a predictable picture about the dramatic days of struggle, not resisting the temptation, here, there and everywhere, to be by turns didactic and sentimental. He, Luzardo, the master, would centre his picture on the days, the years, *after* the rebellion. What happened to this woman?

She had, in fact, lived on well into the 1950's, winding up as an entertainer, known as Elena d'Alma, in low-down nightclubs and cantinas with pretensions in Acapulco and Mexico City. She did not sing pop tunes but songs of the streets and of the people. So the film finds her, an old woman. There she is on the street, still performing. She is at work in a club and in between sets tells the story of the days leading up to the rebellion. The levels of time are juxtaposed, orchestrated with flashbacks. He could do that sort of thing, had done it so often, without losing the sense of continuity — do it and keep the narrative speeding forward. But there was another angle. One of the gifts that heaven so often dropped in the lap of the master: Elena d'Alma was a gringa.

Her real name was Helene Burns. *Burns.* Her father had been a mine owner and his holdings included silver works in Mexico. Highly respected, even revered in his native state of Pennsylvania, he had made his fortunes on the backs of peasants, black, white and brown. When she was five years old, Elena's parents were killed in a mine explosion. Was it accident or sabotage? The little girl was raised by a Mexican peasant family.

So that was the story. And what a story.

Now anyone who wasn't in the know, would have been astounded to see the driver, the chauffeur, after locking the Cadillac and recruiting a gamino to stand guard and wipe down the gleaming machine with a clean chamois rag, step onto the terrace of the restaurant, approach the table of the great film people and sit down with them, joining their conversation as if he were an equal.

He was a muscular man in his mid-thirties with eyes that rarely blinked, a nose that had been broken more than a couple of times, and the scars that fanned out from either corner of his mouth could not but remind one of cat's whiskers — hence, the man's nickname 'El Gato.' Juan had been found in a heap of garbage in an alley in the Moctezuma section of Mexico City. He was spotted by Munoz as they cruised the city for extras and locations a dozen years earlier. Juan had been a member of Los Pueblos, the toughest gang in the Federal District. But he was always a reluctant member, his heart never much in the gang's activities which were, mainly, drugs, prostitution, extortion and, given their neighborhood, hot auto parts. But he was born to it — Los Pueblos being an hereditary affair. There seemed to be no way out. But the very thing Juan kept hidden was what provided his escape, although a vicious beating was part of the farewell. Juan was a homosexual, enthusiastically so, as it later turned out.

So Juan was one of the four of the inner sanctum, serving as bit-part actor, driver, script adviser, sometime casting agent — but if Juan had to be given a title that would best describe his invaluable contribution, it would be Consultant for Verisimilitude. Luzardo set his movies on the streets, those of dirt or paved with gold, those of good intentions or broken dreams, but always en la calle.

Almost everything was in place for the new film. Julietta had spent the past month searching out her locations. Acapulco no longer bore traces of the fifties, so Zihuatanejo would have to stand in. Although the Master trusted Julietta implicitly, it was still necessary for him to see for himself the sites she had chosen; he had to have them firmly in place in his mind as he began imagining his scenes, writing them, blocking them.

There had been no trouble securing the financing, so Munoz was at liberty to devote most of his time to the myriad details rather than trusting them to line producers. They had cast the film too or all but one part. They'd needed to look no farther than their repertory company for the Mexican players, and the girl who'd play Elena as a young woman was discovered, not in Hollywood, but as part of a stage production in Chicago. A company called Steppenwolf. Munoz, having been tipped, went up to scout and, liking what he saw, summoned Escalero to Chicago. El Gato nodded his approval. The actress's niece would be in a few shots, close-ups as flames envelop the silver mine of Elena's father, then as she is taken in by the Mexican family and plays with Mexican children.

That left but one part to fill. The most important: the gringa. Elena as an old woman. Luzardo and Munoz had been deluged with emails, faxes and special delivery packages from Hollywood and New York. Should they ever have visited their offices, they would have found on their desk, veritable Popocatepytals of eight-by-ten inch glossies. It seemed as if every actress in America who had a pedicured toe over the line of forty, had sent along pic and res. It amounted to a frightening gallery of mediocrities and non-entities; harridans and hags, everyone of whom had teeth like the grille of the Cadillac.

When the Most Famous Agent in Tinseltown, Binky Arbetz,

attempted to pressure Munoz into signing his top client, a curtain-chewing, talentless two-time Academy Award winner, the producer replied that he and Luzardo would be shooting rock videos in the San Fernando Valley before that happened. Binky replied, "Hey, like, no problema, amigo."— as part of the package, he'd get them one of those too. Munoz hung up the phone.

They had a laugh about that, traded anecdotes about the hacks of Hollywood. But Munoz, swallowing a mouthful of Chile en Nogada, waved his fork in the air. "Yes, it is funny or it was funny. But it is now beginning to appear as if we must laugh to keep from crying. We are paying for every day we put off beginning the shoot."

"But it has always been something similar," said Julietta. "At the last moment, a miracle."

"Hah! It has never been this bad. So when the men with the bankrolls and the men waving the insurance policies track me down — tonight? — tomorrow morning? — I'll tell that to them, 'Not to worry, senores, a miracle is bound to happen.'"

"Perhaps," Luzardo began. "We finally must make calls to England, elsewhere. I do not understand the difficulty," he snorted down his long nose. "All we are looking for is a gringa who looks seventy or seventy-five, who can act and sing and speaks Spanish."

Anna turned the corner onto Independencia. She had just left the hospital and she was beat, used up, disgusted. Her kneecap felt like it was going to split apart and she ached everywhere else. Her string bag dragged behind her on the street like a dead dog on a leash. She felt every day of her seventy-five years. She was so grateful the doctor had given her that shot. She'd slept until noon. Upon opening her eyes, there was that wonderful moment — wonderful looking back on it — when she'd not known where she was and was oblivious to what had happened just a few hours earlier; that brief moment Anna so wanted to retrieve once she became fully awake.

She could not imagine having gotten through the following four or five hours without the doctor's help. She was numb, half asleep, as he gave her papers, punched in phone numbers, told her what to say and do. The worst of it was going to the room where she sat in a chair before a large window with a white curtain. Someone on the other side of the glass drew back the curtain and there was Colin on the gurney, just his head sticking out of the white sheet. He wore death's grin. The rest of him was like a mountain range covered by snow. The body which only hours before had been on top of her, joined to her.

She had spoken with the Consul in Acapulco, then with people at the Canadian Embassy in Mexico City. Fortunately, they would contact the parents. Still there was more to do tomorrow. Now she just walked, not knowing where she was going, not caring. At some time, she would have to get on the jitney or take a taxi back to Ixtapa, face the apartment, clean blood from the kitchen floor. Pack up Colin's belongings and send them to Saskatoon.

She glimpsed herself in the window of a bakery. Stopped, looked. Face and scraggly hair floating above disembodied white cakes. Little men and women stuck in icing. Anna almost laughed, bitterly but almost laughed nevertheless. What would she do? For the first time that day she considered her situation. I'll give up. Collapse. Walk into the sea. Who cares? No one. Not a solitary soul. Certainly not my daughter, and I don't blame her. I am not going back to Valley View, all humble and contrite, begging forgiveness. No, better the sea swallows me. It'll have to, the sharks will head the other way when they get a glimpse of this old sea hag. Even the golf course alligator wouldn't want any. He'd flit like a gecko should I stroll over near his green.

Oh, Lord. I simply cannot go another step.

Anna lowered herself to the curbstone and stretched her sore leg out into the street; rested her head on her other knee, and didn't give a thought to where her hem had got to. She rubbed the back of her neck. Looked up at the sky and back down into the gutter.

Julietta was saying, "Well since this does appear to be the absolute last moment, I don't suppose it could do any harm to make some calls to Canada."

"One moment," interjected El Gato who hadn't appeared to be paying much attention to the conversation.

"Australia while we're at it," Julietta added.

"A moment, please!" El Gato requested.

"Might as well," sighed Munoz. "Mother of God, try New Zealand, even."

"Enough!" They stopped chattering, turned to El Gato.

"What is the matter with you, Juan?" asked Luzardo.

"I do not think it will be necessary to make these calls. I believe I have found our star."

"What!"

"Juan, you mean you've been holding out on us?"

"You devil, you."

"No. It is just this moment that I have found our Elena."

"Just this moment? Whatever are you talking about?"

He pointed across the street to where Anna was collapsed on the curb.

"My God!" Julietta exclaimed. "It is her! It is, it is."

"You can see right up her dress," said Munoz. "Would you believe it? Look at the panties on the old dear. Itty bitty frilly pink things."

"But wait. You have not seen the best," El Gato implored them. "Wait until she raises her head. It is as if she is looking for God down there in the gutter. The poor woman appears to be grief-stricken, hoping He might show Himself and deign to supply the answer to her problem."

"She looks," said Munoz, "like she has more than one."

"I don't know if He will solve her problems," announced the director. "But it appears He has solved our own. That is Elena d'Alma, as I live and breathe. That is her as I have been seeing her in my mind and in my dreams. That look of experience yet of tenderness, of having suffered but still carrying on. What do you say, Juan?"

"There can be no doubt about it, boss."

"I hate to add even the smallest note of discord," Munoz interjected. "But there is the slight matter of — oh, I realize it is of infinitesimal importance so, please, forgive me mentioning such a practical trifle — but there is the matter of acting ability to consider. Have you romantics thought of that? I think not. And, dare I mention singing? Oh, and let us not forget that our star must do these things in the language of Cervantes?"

"I can tell she speaks Spanish, and can sing too."

"Oh, you can, Juan. Without hearing her and from forty feet

away? Perhaps the view up her dress has addled your thinking, yes? But if you insist that she can speak the language, fine. I am certainly relieved that small matter is settled. Now, the acting? The singing?"

Luzardo smiled at his old friend and partner.

"I have a feeling that we do not have to worry about that. This one looks like a trouper. Juan, please go across the street and invite her over for lunch. This is our Elena, our Alma de Fuega. Our star."